The Scoundrel Falls Hard

No one believed she loved him. No one believed he loved her.

Well, he would have to show them. He would prove it.

He seized one of her hands with his bound ones. With a tug, she tumbled forward, caught off guard.

"Wh-what are you doing?" she sputtered, her eyes flaring wide.

"What else? We're in love," he rasped against her lips. "You said so yourself."

And now he would see that everyone here believed that.

If possible, her eyes flared even wider. He didn't have to duck his head very much. She was quite the woman indeed. Tall and full-bodied. He should not notice, but he felt every inch of her pressed against him.

He couldn't take his eyes off her. Perhaps it was because she could be the last woman on earth that he would ever hold. Or kiss.

The last woman he would ever taste and he wanted to devour her.

By Sophie Jordan

The Duke Hunt Series
THE SCOUNDREL FALLS HARD
THE RAKE GETS RAVISHED
THE DUKE GOES DOWN

The Rogue Files Series
THE DUKE EFFECT
THE VIRGIN AND THE ROGUE
THE DUKE'S STOLEN BRIDE
THIS SCOT OF MINE
THE DUKE BUYS A BRIDE
THE SCANDAL OF IT ALL
WHILE THE DUKE WAS SLEEPING

The Devil's Rock Series
BEAUTIFUL SINNER • BEAUTIFUL LAWMAN
FURY ON FIRE • HELL BREAKS LOOSE
ALL CHAINED UP

Historical Romances
ALL THE WAYS TO RUIN A ROGUE
A GOOD DEBUTANTE'S GUIDE TO RUIN
HOW TO LOSE A BRIDE IN ONE NIGHT
LESSONS FROM A SCANDALOUS BRIDE
WICKED IN YOUR ARMS
WICKED NIGHTS WITH A LOVER
IN SCANDAL THEY WED • SINS OF A WICKED DUKE
SURRENDER TO ME • ONE NIGHT WITH YOU
TOO WICKED TO TAME
ONCE UPON A WEDDING NIGHT

SOPHIE JORDAN

The Scoundrel Falls Hard

THE DUKE HUNT

AVONBOOKS

An Imprint of HarperCollinsPublishers

Excerpt from *The Duke Goes Down* copyright © 2021 by Sharie Kohler.

Excerpt from *The Rake Gets Ravished* copyright © 2022 by Sharie Kohler.

THE SCOUNDREL FALLS HARD. Copyright © 2022 by Sharie Kohler. All rights reserved. Printed in the United States of America. No part of this book may be used or reproduced in any manner whatsoever without written permission except in the case of brief quotations embodied in critical articles and reviews. For information, address HarperCollins Publishers, 195 Broadway, New York, NY 10007.

First Avon Books mass market printing: August 2022

Print Edition ISBN: 978-0-06-303571-3
Digital Edition ISBN: 978-0-06-303572-0

Cover design by Nadine Badalaty
Cover art by Alan Ayers
Back cover image © design box/iStock/Getty Images (border)

Avon, Avon & logo, and Avon Books & logo are registered trademarks of HarperCollins Publishers in the United States of America and other countries.

HarperCollins is a registered trademark of HarperCollins Publishers in the United States of America and other countries.

FIRST EDITION

22 23 24 25 26   BVGM   10 9 8 7 6 5 4 3 2 1

*For my cousin, Laurie Duke. You've been in my life
from the very beginning. I loved you then
and I'll love you always.*

The Scoundrel Falls Hard

Chapter One ❧

*T*here was an angry mob outside and what they wanted was *inside* Gwen Cully's shop.

She tugged off her thick work gloves and tossed them aside. Her leather apron slapped at her legs as she walked to her window and curiously peered out, appreciating the fresh breeze on her heated face even as she gasped at the wild sight before her.

There were no less than thirty villagers charging down the lane—her friends and neighbors with faces mottled red with ire. She had no notion of what had precipitated their wrath. She had never witnessed the like in all her eight and twenty years. Not in the entirety of her life in Shropshire.

They were not frothing at the mouth. They did not wave pitchforks, but several of them held sticks in a militant fashion. Mr. Fyfe, the village wainwright, waved a fire iron that she herself had crafted years ago for him. At the time she had not imagined it to be used as a weapon.

The horde growled like a beast coming closer.

Their shouts were indistinct, one great amalgamation of voices growing in volume as they advanced down the street of the village.

What they wanted was inside her shop and what they wanted was a man.

A specific man.

She whipped back around and squinted into the murky confines of her shop, her gaze searching, seeking him, the intruder, the interloper . . . their prey. Moments ago, he had exploded inside her smithy and flew across the space in a blurred streak.

Hands on her hips, she peered into the shadows before moving cautiously past her burning forge. She found herself wishing for additional light. Less lighting was needed for her work, so she could better see the glow of heated metal, and yet she wished for the full light of day now as she came to a stop and glared down at the figure concealing himself in the corner behind a worktable. Although *conceal* was not really the proper word. Indeed not. The man was too big to be concealed anywhere.

Even crouched as he was, she could see at once he was a veritable giant. Impressive shoulders and biceps filled out his jacket. His thick thighs strained against his trousers. Her stare fixed there on those muscled tree trunks. It was with some difficulty that she moved her attention away, sliding her gaze lower, assessing the boots that hugged a pair of well-muscled calves.

She blinked and swallowed and reminded herself that she was irritated and not . . . enthralled.

With a form like that, she would have assumed him to be a man accustomed to work and vigorous labor. And yet his garments told another story.

He was dressed as a gentleman of means, but she had never encountered a gentleman who knew a thing about hard work. His jacket was made of the finest merino wool and his boots expensive Hessian leather. Gentleman or no, he had done something wrong. Something grave indeed for the villagers to be after him.

"You are trespassing," she accused in a stern voice, her gaze resting on his face and not that riveting body.

Although his face was equally distracting.

He stared up at her with wolf dark eyes framed by lashes much too long and thick for a man. The face possessing those dramatic eyes was too rugged to be called pretty, but still quite arresting. On anyone else his nose would be too large, but it fit his granite-carved features perfectly.

She swallowed. Altogether he was the kind of man she admired. At least physically. Big and well formed with hands larger than hers. Able to carry her from a burning building if the need ever arose. And carrying a woman like Gwen was no easy feat. In fact, no man had carried her since her papa. And not since the age of five.

Even flattened in displeasure, his wide mouth was surprisingly lush. "Please."

The single word uttered in his deep voice did something, twisted something inside her. Pity gave way and crumbled loose within her before she could stop it.

She fought for detachment and demanded, "What did you do?"

"Do?"

"Yes. What did you do?" She motioned to the window. "Believe it or not, the good people of this town do not usually lose their heads and chase a man down the streets without just cause. They are, for the most part, sane. You must have done something. What did you do?"

"You don't recognize me?"

She blinked and looked him over again as though she could have perhaps forgotten him. Impossible, but she reassessed him nonetheless since he seemed to think she should know him. "Should I?"

It was his turn then to survey her. He looked her considerable form up and down, missing nothing of her near six feet.

She held her ground, unblinking, unflinching, reminding herself to breathe and feel nothing under his perusal. She had long ago accepted herself as she was. She would wilt under no one's inspection.

He glanced away and swept his gaze over their surroundings before again fastening his gaze back on her. "Who are you? What is this place?"

Who was she? *Who was he?*

"You mean the place you have taken refuge?" She snorted and crossed her arms. "It's a smithy. I'm the blacksmith." She inwardly winced. Not *the* blacksmith. Unfortunately not anymore. Not in this town. Rather, she was *a* blacksmith.

Once the only smithy for miles and miles around, her family's long-standing business ever since her grandfather, ever since her father and uncle, had now fallen to her.

Gwen was the third generation Cully to manage her family's forge. The third generation wielding hammer to anvil. The third generation . . . and she was alone.

Her grandparents and father and uncle were no more. They had schooled her in all there was to smithing and she did it herself. There was not a sibling to share the load. Not an uncle, aunt, cousin. No one.

The smithy was hers alone.

She was no longer the *only* blacksmith working in the village. Now there was another. *Another* blacksmith who did not bear the name Cully, and he had set up shop and was taking her business.

She inhaled against the sharp sting of that hardship—and she was no stranger to hardship. She knew loss, but this was particularly bitter to consume.

Over the last few months, she had gone from having more business than she could manage to a decided decline in customers. When she confronted her longtime clientele and asked why she had lost their patronage, they all had the same explanation. She took too long. She was slow. Unreliable.

The truth stung.

The last few years she had been generally slow to complete all her work in a timely fashion, to be certain. With her uncle ailing and bedridden, she alone had been responsible for his care. Her attention had been divided and the shop had suffered for it. At first it had not mattered though, as she had been the only smith in town.

Until now.

Meyer had recently arrived with his two strapping sons. They'd opened a shop one lane over and had steadily been taking all her business, the three of them working so much more quickly than she could.

It did not matter that her uncle had passed away over a month ago, expiring from a long, wasting, cancerous sickness and she was now able to devote more time—*all* her time—to her work. The damage was done. A goodly amount of her customers had already left her for Meyer and his sons.

Faith in her had been shaken. She liked to think it had nothing to do with her gender. She had lived in Shropshire all her life. Worked here all her life. These people knew her. They were her neighbors. Her friends. She did not wish to think they were more at ease with a newcomer simply because he was born a man. That seemed vastly unfair and a cutting betrayal.

The din outside increased. She glanced over her shoulder as though she could see out her window from where she stood. "They're coming closer," she remarked almost casually, as though she were accustomed to men bursting into her smithy every day.

He nodded once in the direction of the sound. "Aye. They mean to hang me."

"Hang you?" What nefarious deed had this man done? Who was he? "Why?" Certainly he exaggerated. Her village was full of law-abiding citizens.

Without waiting for his response, she marched back to the open window and looked out again to verify that they were indeed near. The bloodthirsty sight of them did not bode well. Settling back on her heels, she tsked. "I fear you may be right. I don't know what you've done, but they are out for blood."

No answer met this declaration, and she moved from the window, lifting a rod from her nearby tool stand. She flexed her palm around the steel.

A strange man had taken refuge inside her shop.

He was likely dangerous, and certainly desperate. That mob was for him. They were after *him*. She was not so foolish as to dismiss him. Indeed not. She would not underestimate him. He could very well attempt to use her as a hostage to protect himself.

Armed now, she kept a careful distance. "Come out from there, you," she demanded in her gruffest voice.

As big as he was, he had moved like lightning only moments before, charging through the front door of her shop to the corner where he now hid. She did not permit herself to forget that. He was spry on his feet. She flexed her grip on the rod, waiting and wondering what this man had done, but determined that he should not catch her unawares.

He rose and her breath caught. He was more than big. He was big *and* tall.

He unfolded himself from his hiding spot, revealing himself to be well over six feet. *Taller than me.*

He nodded at the poker in her hand. "Do you mean to use that on me?"

"If necessary."

"I mean you no harm." He held up both hands and bounced them on the air as though attempting to appease an unpredictable animal. "I simply need a place to hide until they pass along."

Gwen angled herself slightly toward the window again, prepared to call out if he made a threatening move toward her. "You cannot expect me to shelter you without knowing what you did." Assuming, of course, he would be honest with her.

He shook his head and sounded tired as he spoke. "Just a small matter of—"

"I think he went this way!" The shout was close. Right outside her shop.

She inched closer and peered out the window again to spot the mob converging on the wainwright shop across the lane. For whatever reason, they thought he took shelter there. Fortunate for him.

"They're at the wainwright shop across the way," she informed him.

The stranger exhaled, his stoic facade cracking slightly. His relief was palpable.

"You were saying?" she prompted. "What did you do?"

"It is just a small matter of fraud. Nothing that warrants . . ." He waved a hand. *"This."*

"What is a *small* matter of fraud precisely?" She pointed her rod at him. "If I were you I would stop prevaricating. Time is not on your side. One word from me . . ." She permitted her voice to fade away, letting the implication hang.

He nodded grudgingly and expelled a breath. "My father has been pretending to be the Duke of Penning. And he is not." Another heavy exhale. "His ruse was discovered as the real duke has now arrived."

The *real* duke?

"Wait a moment. The Duke of Penning who has been cavorting all over the countryside these last many months . . . is *not* the true Duke of Penning?"

She had met the duke at the Blankenships' ball and once about town. She had heard of the son's arrival, but not seen him.

The Duke of Penning had commissioned her to do a number of improvements at the hall when he first arrived. That was before Meyer moved here, of course. She had only completed one of the smaller projects when she had spotted Penning's fancy carriage out front of Meyer's shop a fortnight ago. Apparently, like everyone else, he preferred working with the new smith over her. It had stung even though she did not blame the duke—or who she thought was the duke. He wanted a smith who could work in a timely fashion and produce results.

He nodded with a grim expression. "That is correct. He is not."

Gwen started feverishly clicking all the pieces together in her mind. "He was your father? That means . . ." She broke off to laugh. "Oh, my! This is rich! You are the illustrious son that arrived a short while ago who has the village buzzing! You are the Duke of Penning's most *eligible* heir! Only you are not. Not at all." She motioned him up and down. "You are simply some bloke pretending to be a swell, taking all his riches for yourself."

He continued to stare at her grimly, accepting her words, not bothering to defend or excuse his perfidious actions.

She had seen the duke out and about—or at least the man pretending to be the duke. He had sent his housekeeper when he commissioned work from her, but she had made his acquaintance. A middle-aged fellow, jovial and friendly. He had been in Shropshire for quite some time, reveling in his role apparently, stolen as it was. Everyone liked him. The Blankenships hosted a ball in his honor, after all. This shocking revelation had to sting all those that had pandered to the man.

His expression turned almost rueful—and yet not. There was an air to the man before her. A level of dignity and acceptance for what he was. Or perhaps it was resignation. "I'm aware of what I have done."

What he had *done* the villagers of Shropshire would not like. Not at all. They had been making fools of themselves over the new duke and his heir. Bowing and scraping and tossing their daughters at the both of them, hoping to win a slice of a dukedom for themselves.

"So you are a thief. You are a swindler," she pronounced. That was the plain and simple of it. She looked him over—every immense, impressive inch of him. He was a beautiful man. Of course there had to be something wrong with him. "A grand pretender. You steal lives and claim them as your own."

Something passed over his features. He did not like hearing that. And yet she spoke only the truth. She had no patience for a man like him. She led an honest life. He could take his illicit ways elsewhere. She had work to do and no time for this nonsense.

"I suppose. Yes," he grudgingly admitted even though the corners of his mouth tightened.

"Where is your dear papa?" Her lip curled in distaste. "Why is he not hiding in my smithy alongside you?"

"He managed to avoid . . . detection."

She digested that, and then translated. "He escaped? And left you here?"

His father had left him.

She digested that a bit more. His father had *abandoned* him to face a mob. For some reason, she avoided laughing at this. It felt a little sad.

His father was just as guilty. *More.* He had been in Shropshire longer, pretending to be someone he was not and reaping all the rewards of that wrongdoing months before his son even arrived.

He nodded once, tersely. Clearly she did not need to point out to him that his father had deserted him. He was aware.

Deciding he was not dangerous, Gwen lowered her rod. "They will not hang you." The people of her village were reasonable.

"I would not be so certain of that," he said grimly.

"I know these people."

"Be that as it may, I would not like to test the limits of their tolerance today."

She set the rod back in her tool stand. "I suppose you may remain here until they disperse." She did not condone violence. Whilst she did not think the good people of Shropshire would hang him, she could not deny they might give him the thrashing of his life.

His features eased and some of the tension seemed to dissipate from those great big shoulders of his. She tried not to stare overly long at those endless shoulders . . . at any part of his body really, but it was difficult. His physique was remarkable, and she could not help thinking how easily a body like that could labor in a smithy. *Her* smithy. He would be quite useful.

If she'd had an apprentice like him her business would not be under threat by the arrival of a competitor in the village. She quickly steered her thoughts away from the notion of *if*. *If* was not real. *If* did not help her now. She must cope with the reality of her life.

"I appreciate that." He nodded once, his throat working as he swallowed. "More than I can say."

Suddenly another voice intruded on them. So close. "Oy! Here he is! In the smithy! He's right here!"

Gwen swung around and spotted young Ben Hawkes, the tanner's son, looming in the window of her shop. He waved a spindly arm wildly, motioning others over to him. Apparently they had moved on from the wainwright shop.

The swindler occupying space inside her shop made a strangled sound and looked around wildly for an escape.

"Oh, bloody h—" The words died in her throat.

She did not have time to say or do anything else before her place was invaded. A dozen men charged in and made a direct line for the intruder. He didn't have time to evade them—not that there was anywhere for him to go. They had him cornered. He seemed to realize this. Turning, he faced them as stoically as a soldier confronted with the enemy.

They seized him roughly and began dragging

him back toward the door. His face remained fixed, like something etched in stone. There were no tears, no panicked pleas, no blubbering as one might expect. Her worktable was toppled over in the process, tools scattering to the packed-dirt floor.

She called out in irritation and moved to heft her table back up to its legs.

Her closest neighbor, Mr. Fredericks, whom she had known her entire life, looked back at her contritely. "Sorry about that, Gwen."

Then they were all gone, pouring outside in a great racket, hauling the hapless swindler with them.

She moved to the window to observe, frowning at the sight before her. She wanted to walk away, to turn her back on it all. It had nothing to do with her. She had better things to attend to, work waiting for her that she needed to do well and swiftly so the word got out that she was reliable once again. Uncle was gone now and her time was her own, but her customers were still not returning even though she had all the time in the world to devote to her business.

One stranger's fate was no concern of hers.

With that reminder, she turned away, but then stopped with a hard breath. The din outside was impossible to ignore.

Bloody hell.

With a groan, she whirled back around and departed her smithy to witness the chaos unfolding outside. As much as she wished she could scrub this from her mind, it was too late. She had seen him. She was part of this now. His stoic expression was imprinted in her mind. He might be guilty of fraud and all manner of thievery, but she was invested in the drama of it now. There was no unseeing it—or him.

She had to know what happened next.

Chapter Two ❦

The moment Gwen stepped outside, the fall air pleasantly cooled her overheated face. Her smithy was excessively warm from the forge. The first breath of fresh air after being cooped inside was always welcome. She lifted her face to the breeze. Even though it was late in the afternoon, it felt more like dusk with the overcast sky.

She stood on her tiptoes and peered after the crowd. She could not see him anymore. The imposter had been forced somewhere to the front of the group, out of her range of vision.

She hastened forward and fell in behind them, pressing in with the others and becoming swept up with the tide of bodies, accompanying the mob down High Street toward the village square.

The crowd seemed to have taken on a life of its own. She glanced around uneasily. It felt bigger. Well over thirty people now. The villagers grew even angrier, their faces flushed red in high temper.

She recognized most everyone. Some people she knew better than others, but a few were unfamiliar to her. The town was growing. New businesses. New families. She winced as she was suddenly confronted with direct evidence of that, for there, among the faces, was Shropshire's newest blacksmith—her gloating, swollen-faced rival, Meyer. His two thick-necked, dull-eyed sons stood beside him. As always. They were never far from his side. Constant shadows. They were close in age to Gwen, but she only ever thought of them as boys. They did not make a move or decision without their father's approval and direction. Meyer's sons were simply mind-less drudges, laboring in their father's smithy and following his bidding.

Meyer's gaze found hers. He arched a bushy gray eyebrow at her in silent question. She knew the question though. She had already given him her answer in indisputable terms, but apparently he thought she still might change her mind.

She forced her gaze off him and searched the crowd, looking for its quarry.

They reached the square and the throng of peo-ple spread out, fanning wide, revealing the swin-dler. The sleeve of his jacket had somehow been torn, and it occurred to her that she had perhaps underestimated the extent of her neighbors' bad humor.

She scanned the faces, observing the bloodlust in the eyes of so many. She had said there was nothing to fear from them, but now she was not so certain.

Mrs. Dove, the serene and jovial baker's wife, waved a glossy-skinned fist in the air and called out, "Put him in the stocks!"

Gwen winced. The stocks still stood at the center of the square, but she had not seen them used as punishment for years. Not since she was a child. Still, she recalled the incident acutely. A thief had been locked in the wooden frame, forced to stand there overnight. Villagers jeered at him and tossed rotten food. It had struck her as the height of cruelty then. Thankfully such punishments had stopped once the new magistrate came into authority.

"No stocks for him," a voice cried out. "Hang him! Hang his black soul!"

Gwen jerked at the cry. Several others took up the call, chanting, and she scanned the crowd, searching for the magistrate. He would bring sanity to this chaos.

"Where is Mr. Redmond?" she demanded of no one in particular, simply hoping someone would hear her or—even better—that the magistrate himself would step forward to put an end to this.

No one answered her and she shouldered her way ahead. Spotting Dr. Merrit, she latched on to his sleeve. "Where is the magistrate?"

Dr. Merrit glanced down at her distractedly.

He was clearly riveted by the spectacle. "Mr. Redmond? Ah, I believe he is visiting his daughter's family in London."

Brilliant. The one man who might have injected law and order into this chaos was not in residence.

She waved to where they were dragging the hapless gentleman to a nearby tree. "Dr. Merrit, do something."

He was a prominent man. A healer. Certainly he would put a stop to this.

Dr. Merrit shook his head, his lips pressed into a grim line. "He's gone too far. He made a fool of everyone." His lips thinned. "He danced with my own daughter at the Blankenships' ball and she has not stopped talking about him since. She will no longer even consider any other suitor."

Clearly, Dr. Merrit held a grudge. She tugged harder on his sleeve, insistent. "And he deserves to die for that?"

His face flushed in clear agitation. "Every mama in this town pelted their daughters at him as though he were a prince."

She stared intently at him. He was serious on this matter. He would not speak up on the man's behalf. Doubtlessly his wife was one of those mamas.

"No! Stop!" she cried out before she even quite knew what she was about.

Some people heard her. A few heads turned in her direction, curious expressions and frowns marring their faces, but she had not attracted enough notice for anything to be done, for anyone to actually stop. He was still being dragged toward the large oak tree a man was scaling. Another man waited below with a rope, ready to toss it up to him.

This could not be happening.

The people in her village were not doing this horrible, wretched thing.

And yet they were.

It was as though they shared a collective brain. They were operating under a hive mentality. No one was thinking independently.

If the old vicar were here, he would put a stop to it all. Except she knew that he, too, was out of town. She had only bumped into his daughter a week ago on the street. Imogen had told her that she was journeying with her husband and father to London to buy a few items for their new home, a lovely house they had just finished building outside of town.

Gwen expelled an anxious breath. The magistrate *and* Mr. Bates. There could not be a worse time for *both* of these honorable men to be gone. She released a hot puff of frustrated breath and shook her head in bewilderment.

Retired or not from his role as vicar, Mr. Bates was a good man who would have injected reason and compassion into the situation. His daughter, too: Imogen and her husband, Peregrine Butler. They were decent people. They would not have gotten swept up with the crowd. They would have put a stop to it. If only they were here. Why was there no one here that could stop this madness?

Only you.

You are here.

You can stop the madness.

She swallowed and tried again, using her size and elbows to push farther to the front. "No!"

No one could accuse her of reticence or timidity. She'd spent her life working in a man's domain. Her father and uncle had raised her like a son, teaching her to stand on her own two feet and command attention, to demand respect. Yes. She could do that.

She *would* do that.

She now noticed that at some point during the trek to the village square that his captors had bound his hands. He was pushed forward to stand directly beneath the tree, its branches a canopy overhead. The man climbing the tree had almost reached the branches. Leaves rustled and showered from above.

"Enough of this! You cannot hang him!" She

searched for a single face in the crowd that reflected reason, someone who was capable of good judgment. She winced at her findings. There was still far too much bloodlust in the sea of eyes and a decided lack of sanity in the expressions of these particular residents of Shropshire.

"Mind yer business, lass." Meyer's son, the eldest one—although she could not be sure given their similarities—sidled up beside her.

Both sons were of like age and appearance— each of them dull-eyed with mouths that hung open with their sawing breaths. *Especially* when they looked at Gwen. Their jaws went slack and excess saliva gleamed on their lips. They never hid the crude direction of their thoughts when they looked her over, their attention resting on the swell of her breasts. Considering their father's insistent proposition that she marry one of them and they then merge their smithies, she knew they were envisioning her indelicately. As a potential wife in their beds.

She scowled at him. That would *never* happen and she had informed Mr. Meyer succinctly of that at the time of his rather aggressive offer of marriage.

Gwen moved at least two paces away from young Meyer, putting some much-desired space between them whilst managing to get closer to the tree. "Do not do this!" She waved at the grim-faced stranger they had swept from her shop. He looked somewhat accepting of his fate. "There has to be another way!"

"He deserves to be punished!" Meyer countered almost shrilly.

"This is murder," she thundered over the clamor. "The punishment should match the crime."

Gwen noticed then that some of the ferocity had started to ebb from the crowd. Mrs. Dove, the baker's wife, gazed in distaste at the rope that suddenly dropped from the tree branch and swung in the air. "She is correct! We cannot kill him."

Mr. Dove turned and faced the crowd, waving his hands in the air as though he were confronting a wild beast. "She is right, of course. There has to be a more fitting punishment."

Hope fluttered in her chest. The tide had turned. The crowd became divided then, half still clamoring for his hanging, the other half urging restraint.

Dr. Merrit, of all people, a supposedly learned man, lent his voice. "The punishment *does* fit the crime. Impersonating a member of the aristocracy is punishable by death." He pointed a damning finger to the bound man. "If he was to face the courts, they would sentence him to execution. I say we handle this matter ourselves!"

"Indeed," Mr. Pedersen, a solicitor seconded unhelpfully. "It is a crime punishable by death."

A chorus rang out to greet this unwelcome bit of legal truth.

She groaned. This only breathed fire back into the crowd. Those who had been vacillating were suddenly shouting for his head again, reassured with this latest information that justice was on their side from both the good doctor and the esteemed solicitor.

See there!

Righto!

There you have it! 'Tis the law!

Hang him!

Even Mr. Dove, who only moments ago had urged restraint, added his voice to the choir, apparently indifferent to his wife's displeasure when she swatted at his arm.

No one was listening anymore. This new information gave everyone the last bit of justification they needed.

No one cared about her objections. She could say nothing to sway them. Not a single word to gain anyone's empathy . . . or even their attention anymore. They had moved on from her. She was dismissed.

"That man deserves to hang!" This was shouted from the young and fashionably attired Emily

Blankenship, one of the daughters of the village's wealthiest citizen. The pretty girl's eyes were remorseless burning embers as she pointed to the man who would soon be dead.

"You're just saying that because you let him kiss you behind the church and you thought he was going to propose! You *thought* you were going to be a duchess! Ha! Look at your would-be duke now!" another girl shouted.

Miss Blankenship's face turned multiple shades of red. She whirled around and propped her hands on her hips. "And you let him do *more* than kiss *you*!"

"You take that back, you tart!"

"I will not, you—you jezebel!"

The girls lunged for each other across the crowd with fury. They were stopped before they even got within one yard of each other, dragged apart in a flurry of skirts and indignant screeches by members of the community who deemed it too gauche for such esteemed young ladies to escalate to physical violence. Not too gauche though to witness a rogue execution. If she wasn't so troubled by the circumstances she could have laughed at it.

"The man has had his way with half the lasses in town," a man near her grumbled plaintively, clearly aggrieved that he himself lacked such favor among the fairer sex, and then he bellowed in a louder voice: "Let him hang!"

Ah. So now she understood everyone's very invested ire with him. He was a swindler who had taken advantage of the good women of Shropshire. That was enough for men and women alike to thirst for his blood. He was fortunate someone had not already seen to his demise.

A man looped the rope around his neck.

Desperation drummed hard and deep in her blood. She lunged ahead to reach him, unable to stop herself.

The man was a stranger. A swindler. A womanizer. But he did not deserve this. She didn't care what the law stipulated. Not that a court of law had been permitted to make a ruling on this man's fate.

She grabbed the arm of the man tightening the rope around his neck. "Don't do this. Please."

She did not know him, but he was familiar. She had seen his weasel-like face about the village before, walking the streets. She thought he worked as a rag-and-bone man, collecting people's scraps to be sold. He was not a big man. She stood a full head taller than him. At her touch on his arm, he looked her up and down with widening eyes, scowling as he did so. It was not the first time a man looked at her with aversion—as though her towering height over him was a personal affront to his sense of self.

Weasel Face shook her hand off his arm and went back to adjusting the rope.

All the while, the imposter stood tall, stalwartly staring straight ahead, his lips pressed into a grim line. That was perhaps the worst of it—the thing that could not allow her to quit, to walk away and let people have their satisfaction with him. If he was weeping or begging for his life, she would have been less moved perhaps. But he was stoic. Accepting. Almost . . . dignified.

"Remove the rope," she insisted, clamping her hand down on Weasel Face's arm once again.

The wretched man whirled on her with a curse and shoved her hard, catching her off guard and propelling her to the ground.

She shouldn't have felt such astonishment. The man was happily volunteering as executioner. Of course, he would react with violence against her if she dared to thwart him.

A sound of protest swelled over the crowd. There was that at least. They did not like her being harmed. They had not lost all conscience apparently. Even the culprit at the center of all this mayhem, the man with a noose around his neck, did not approve of her mistreatment.

His wide shoulders tensed. He growled and attempted to step forward, even as the rope cut into his throat. Weasel Face stopped him with a swift punch to his stomach.

"Oof." He bent slightly at the waist, but did not otherwise react. No crying out. No dropping to his knees. No sign of weakness.

"Ho, there!" Mr. Dove stepped forward and helped her to her feet. "Apologize to Miss Cully, you rogue!"

"Shame on you!" Mrs. Dove shook her fist.

Others joined in with similar castigations.

Weasel Face glanced around, measuring his audience and instantly determining that his man-handling of Gwen had not gone well and he himself might soon be hanging from a rope. He inclined his head in humble meekness. Insincere, of course. "Begging your pardon, Miss Cully. It won't happen again."

She knew he only apologized because it was demanded of him. His eyes shouted his resentment loud and clear.

Apology tendered, he turned his attention back to the true offender, checking the rope once more and satisfying himself that it was snugly secure about his neck. That was what he was about. Violence. Vigilante justice. *Murder.*

"Come now, Miss Cully. This is no place for you." Mrs. Dove gently took her arm and started steering her away. "Clearly you are too tenderhearted. Who would have guessed it? Big strapping thing like you." She shook her head with a tsk as though an illicit hanging were of no account . . . and as though it was perfectly acceptable to call another female big and strapping. "I will accompany you back to your smithy and prepare a nice pot of tea to calm you."

Gwen looked over her shoulder as she was being led away. Mrs. Dove was right, of course. She did not have the stomach for this. Who would have the stomach to witness a man being killed? Hanged by the neck? It was terrible.

Still. Perhaps she could have been led away then—*if* she had not locked gazes with him again.

He stood at the center of all this chaos, a vision of soldier-like resolution, and in his eyes was coolly grim acceptance—the dignity she had already observed in him that made her chest ache.

No.

No. She could not abide this. She would not permit his murder.

She tugged her arm free from Mrs. Dove's grasp and staggered forward. A quick scan of the crowd revealed that no one else was going to stop this. They were only cheering and shouting encouragement. A few watched in slack-jawed amazement. None would stop it though. No one would say the words to put an end to it.

No one but Gwen.

"Stop! Release him!"

At this point, no one paid her the slightest attention. As before all her commands and pleas fell on deaf ears. No one would listen. No one could hear: *No. Stop. Don't.*

"You cannot do this!" The blood pounded in her ears. She paused a beat. *Everything* in her paused, holding and squeezing tightly as the next words hovered on her lips . . . and then exploded free in a violent release that propelled all the air from her. "I love him!"

Chapter Three ❦

$\mathcal{F}$rom the moment Kellan woke today, it had been one unpleasant, jarring shock after another. Even so, the tall, fair-haired Viking shouting that she loved him? That was the most astonishing and incredible thing of all.

He had never even met her before. He would have remembered. She was mouthwatering. The manner of woman most men would be too afraid to approach. Only the most bold—or idiotic—would even try. His lips twisted wryly. He doubted anyone felt a bigger idiot than he currently did.

How else had he landed himself in this predicament?

By listening to Da, of course. As always.

Kellan had ignored his gut. He had wanted to leave a fortnight ago. From the start, really. This sham had felt too precarious. He'd attempted to persuade his father, but Da had been unwilling to budge, enjoying himself far too much in his role of grand duke.

The plump woman beside the Viking looked

at her in horror. "Gwen Cully! What in heaven's name are you saying?"

Gwen. That was her name.

This woman who professed to love him. She herself had said she'd never seen him before, so why was she lying?

Because it might be the one thing to save you.

He had accepted his fate the moment hard hands seized him and dragged him from the smithy. It had been pure happenstance that he took refuge there. He considered himself fit, but his legs were burning and a stitch twinged painfully in his side.

He'd been running for so long, for miles. Penning Hall was half a day's ride by horse, and he'd been on foot. Desperate. Hunted. He had avoided roads, sticking to the woods and avoiding his pursuers as he made his way to Shropshire, hoping to find some manner of salvation there.

They had been gaining on him as he darted down one street, then another and another, until he spotted the smithy looming like a church offering refuge. He couldn't resist. He couldn't go any longer.

He had escaped the hall by the skin of his teeth. Unfortunately, he'd had to leave everything behind. His belongings. His mount. He couldn't reach the stables. Unlike his father who had reached the stables at the first whiff of trouble, not losing even a moment to wake Kellan. At least that was what the housekeeper who had taken pity on him told him as she directed him down the servants' stairs and out a back door. He owed Miss Lockhart for that kindness. Otherwise angry members of the Penning staff would have dragged him from his bed.

He knew his father well enough to know that the risk to himself had been measured and then ruled far too great. Kellan was simply a casualty. Blood relation or no. Da would not risk imprisonment or his own neck to warn his only son that they had been discovered. And discovered in a spectacular fashion, no less. The new duke, the true and legitimate duke, had arrived to claim his rightful throne and oust them.

Kellan had reached the village where he had hoped he might pilfer a horse. Apparently his misdeeds had reached the ears of the villagers, however, and they joined those from Penning Hall who had given pursuit. They all wanted to see him punished for his perfidy. With his father in the wind, he would bear the brunt for both their sins.

"I love him!" Gwen Cully cried out again as though she had not been heard, as though her words had not shocked everyone. "You cannot hang him. I love him!"

Her words achieved the desired result.

Everyone stopped. Frozen, they stared. Even the wretch tightening the rope about his neck appeared flummoxed. For a moment, Kellen did not even feel the discomfort of the rope. He could only gawk at the woman uttering the most outrageous thing he had ever heard in his life.

"You love him?" Emily Blankenship squawked in outrage. "You! *You!*" She laughed then, rudely and shrilly. "That's ludicrous! You don't even own a dress."

He looked at Miss Blankenship and marveled that he had ever let himself become ensnared by her. It was true. He had kissed her in a weak moment. Although he was not quite the philanderer they made him out to be.

He had been pursued, of course. From the moment he arrived in this bloody town, the ladies had been pelting themselves at him left and right. He had no notion a noble title could make such a difference. Another reason he had tried to convince his father they ought to give up on this perilous swindle. It felt too bold. There was no staying beneath notice. Maintaining a constant vigilance against the advances of title-hunting ladies and their matchmaking mamas was exhausting.

Miss Blankenship had been one of the more clever and determined lasses to chase him. She had made it so very difficult, hunting him with such resolute steadfastness, proffering her lips at every opportune, and inopportune, moment.

"Yes, me!" Miss Cully replied with equal indignation, her pretty face flushed pink.

"I haven't seen you with him even once."

"And you have been with him every moment of every day since his arrival, have you?" Gwen Cully challenged, looking scornful and lofty and imperious, her eyebrows arching.

The woman was a blacksmith. Salt of the earth. A laborer. A commoner from common stock. And yet she looked as regal and as commanding as a Viking queen.

"You are lying," Miss Blankenship said tartly.

Miss Cully looked down her nose at her. "I love him," she proclaimed simply. Her bright gaze whipped back to him, fastening on him with a hot fervor that gave him a hard jolt.

Suddenly he felt alive.

She reminded him that he was not a man on the verge of death as he had been only moments before. As he assumed. *As he had been.*

Indeed, he was *still* alive and preferred to stay that way.

He was alive because of her. At least for the moment. He was not out of the woods yet.

She was the only person to speak out on his behalf. All the women who had so ardently pursued his favor now turned their backs on him. She alone had granted him an escape—potentially—and he was no fool. He knew how to seize an opportunity when it was tossed at him. He was quite adept at that. He'd journeyed through life doing that very thing.

"I love you, too, Gwen," he called back to her, feeling foolish and yet knowing precisely how he looked—a man standing on the gallows, proclaiming his love for all and sundry. A moving scene worthy of the stage, to be certain. Hopefully moving enough to dampen the hot temper of the mob.

He'd always been accomplished at acting, at artifice. He'd been trained since birth by his father, a man who had perfected such skills himself. Da could persuade the most hardened individual to part with the clothes off his back, and Kellan could do the same. In fact, Da claimed Kellan could sell a pitcher of seawater to a sailor.

Kellan's declaration brought the crowd to a fever pitch.

"Whaaaat?" Miss Blankenship screeched over the sudden burst of voices. Her father arrived at her side then. The most influential man in the community, aside from the duke himself. Kellan was well acquainted with him. When living at Penning Hall, he and his father had found themselves in the company of the Blankenship family often.

Mr. Blankenship draped an arm around his daughter's shoulders and turned her away. "There now, princess. Let us leave this unsavory business. It is not a sight for your tender eyes." He cast a fulminating glare Kellan's way, leaving no doubt that he supported the notion of vigilante justice.

The thug who had secured the rope around his neck finally found his voice. "What does any of this matter? He's still a bloody thief! An imposter! A lowly criminal!" He gave a hard tug on the rope. The rough material cut into Kellan's neck, choking him. He released a stinging hiss. His hands flew there, clawing to loosen the noose where it choked him. "So she loves him! So what? It doesn't matter." Through his blurring vision, Kellan watched the man wave in a gesture of disgust at Miss Cully.

Sounds faded into background noise as the beating of his heart took over in his ears, a whooshing thump, steady and rhythmic.

Amid his clouding sight, he saw her. Hell, he had been able to fixate on little else since he first burst into her shop. He blinked several times at the vision of her, charging across the distance, her fair hair a halo around her in the fading light of dusk.

"Unhand him! And get that noose off his neck!"

She reached his side just as an older burly man pushed to the front, his furry, tree trunk arms shoving people aside without a care. "She is lying! She's not in love with him. She's merely trying to save his worthless neck."

"To what purpose would she do that?" Mrs. Dove demanded.

"He's big and strong. She obviously wants him for free labor. So he can work and break his back in her smithy. Everyone knows her business is failing since I moved to town."

Gwen's face burned bright with color. "Watch your tongue, Meyer."

The mountain of a man strode forward, thrusting his sweating face close to hers. "Liar. Liar. Liar."

Kellan did not like it. Not the words. Not the physical intimidation. He had witnessed a great deal of ugliness in his life and that included abuse against women. He could not abide it. He had never been that manner of perpetrator. No, his crimes were not violent in nature.

Sometimes he and his father were flush with money, but more often than not they were not. As soon as they landed a purse, Da would spend it. New clothes. Good food and drink. And how Da loved the gaming hells.

Naturally, Kellan had spent plenty of time in the rookeries of Seven Dials and St. Giles, scraping by, eking out an existence when they were between the plush spells.

He had seen things. All sorts of things. He had never been a fan of bullies. Especially men who bullied women or children.

Restrained wrists or not, he lifted his hands and squarely shoved them into the man's chest, forcing him back several paces.

The man's face reddened as he blustered and regained his balance. "How dare you put hands on me, you bastard!"

"Mr. Meyer," Mrs. Dove objected hotly. "Please mind your language!"

The man caught himself. He glanced around, quickly assessing his audience, clearly noting all the frowns cast his way. He compressed his lips and smoothed a hand over his scalp as though it had some calming effect on him. "Begging your pardon."

Mrs. Dove nodded sternly. "Miss Cully is a longtime member of this community. She is respected here. I am certain her words are every bit sincere, Mr. Meyer."

Meyer's composure slipped ever so slightly again. "Rubbish! Everyone here knows it's nonsense, too." He waved to Kellan and Miss Cully. "These two do not love each other. I'll wager my left foot on it."

"And how can you be so sure?" another woman at the front of the crowd demanded.

"Look at her." Meyer waved to Kellan. "And

look at him. Why would a lofty nobleman, as everyone believed him to be, have given the likes of her a second look? She is scarcely a woman! She might have a yen for him, but this blackguard does not love her." He cracked a laugh and the lass beside Kellan flinched. "I doubt they've even spoken before. I've never seen them together." He turned in a circle and addressed the gawking crowd at large, flinging his arms wide. "Have any of you? Come now! Has anyone here seen them in conversation?"

Several members of the crowd murmured their assent at the fair question. No one had seen them in conversation because they had never been in conversation. They had never even met. Their paths had never crossed.

"See there!" Meyer nodded in satisfaction. "I say they are strangers. She's merely looking for a man to toil in her shop."

Her face reddened even further, impossible as that seemed. And yet she did not appear capable of summoning words. Her lips worked, but speech eluded her. The nasty fellow seemed to have taken the wind from her sails and the crowd was staring at Kellan again with renewed bloodlust.

He released a sigh. Well then. That was that. She had tried. He appreciated her altruistic efforts on his behalf. Unfortunately, they had failed.

He should have left this town and abandoned Da's foolhardy scheme sooner—even if that meant turning his back on his father. He could blame no one but himself.

"Hang him! Hang him!" The chant began again with renewed vigor.

He groaned. *These people. These wretched people.* They would be the death of him. Quite literally. Whilst his father was gone, in the wind with whatever jewelry and valuables he had managed to abscond with from Penning Hall.

Kellan knew Da well enough to know that he had not departed empty-handed. He was far too clever and enterprising for that. He had a bag ready, likely stashed under the bed where he could access it quickly.

Rough hands grabbed his arms again and started to haul him back toward the tree. *Bloody hell.* This was it then.

He had never imagined living to a ripe old age, but he had not thought he would meet his end this way. Not that he had spent a good amount of time envisioning his death. He had been too busy living in the moment.

In the moments that led to this.

"No!" His would-be rescuer cried out, lunging toward him as though she would use her not inconsiderable body to save him.

She was within reach.

It was an opportunity he could not ignore.

Instinct took over. Years of experience, of living on the streets, of getting out of scrapes, of surviving by his wits and using the tricks and skills taught to him by his father, all came to life in him.

No one believed she loved him. No one believed he loved her.

Well, he would have to show them. He would prove it.

He seized one of her hands with his bound ones. With a tug, she tumbled forward, caught off guard. He lifted his arms up in the air and looped them down around her, encircling her and forcing her flush against him.

"Wh-what are you doing?" she sputtered, her eyes flaring wide.

"What else? We're in love," he rasped against her lips. "You said so yourself."

And now he would see that everyone here believed that.

If possible, her eyes flared even wider. He didn't have to duck his head very much. She was quite the woman indeed. Tall and full-bodied. He should not notice, but he felt every inch of her pressed against him. Every line and curve, and there were so many luscious curves. *Christ.* Her breasts plumped generously into his chest.

He couldn't take his eyes off her. He kept his eyes open as he pressed his lips to hers. Perhaps it was because she could be the last woman on earth that he would ever hold. Or kiss.

The last woman he would ever taste and he wanted to devour her. He wanted to see her, to watch her as it happened. To make a memory as fleeting as it might be.

Or perhaps it was simply because she was beautiful and there was no denying he always had a weakness when it came to beautiful women.

Whatever the reason, he watched her as he lowered his head. As he claimed her mouth. Covered her lips with his, savoring her gasp, savoring and drinking it like the finest wine. His final taste of anything.

She stiffened for the barest moment, and then softened against him.

The world melted away as he slipped his tongue inside her mouth. His arms tightened around her, enjoying her ample body. The feel of her shudder. The taste of her—blackberry and bergamot. She'd indulged in tea not too long ago and jam. Blackberry apparently. Delicious.

Her tongue felt warm and slick. He stroked his way inside her mouth in savoring licks, coaxing a response. This was no longer pretend. Hell. Perhaps it never was. He was not faking it. He could not even examine what it was he felt. He could only feel. And he felt a heady warmth suffusing his body.

He deepened the kiss, forgetting the world around them.

As far as final kisses went, this one was everything and more.

He longed to put his hands on her. It was tragically unfair that he couldn't touch her. Couldn't feel the texture of her hair. The softness of her skin. The fullness of her breasts—however wrong it would be to do so in public. Who cared? A rope was waiting for him. Propriety could go to hell.

Groaning into her mouth, he tugged against the bindings at his wrists. It did no good. He never wanted it to end. Her tongue was like sugar. He could not stop licking and tasting and consuming. Nothing could induce him to break this kiss. The choice was not his, however.

The rough hands were back then, cruelly pulling him away, forcing his arms up and over her. Tearing them apart.

She cried out, reaching a hand for him, stretching out her fingers as though a single touch from her could save him when they both knew it could not.

No one could help him.

Chapter Four ᚛

Chaos erupted. It was a melee. Apparently Miss Cully's profession of love (and his in turn) had gained them some supporters. Enthusiasts of star-crossed lovers, clearly. The crowd was not *all* against him anymore. Neighbors attacked each other.

Miss Cully broke free and returned to his side—or attempted to. The wretch who looped a rope around his neck blocked her.

The noose cinched tighter around Kellan's throat, dragging him back, away from his would-be savior. There were others now, those in favor of hanging him, pulling at the end of the rope. His boots scrabbled over the ground, struggling for footing as he slid along with fire igniting his throat.

"Release him!" she pleaded.

He didn't know what he had done to earn her stalwart defense, but he admired her for it. Even as he was slowly being strangled, a smile played on his mouth. She was a comforting sight to take to his death. That combined with the memory of her lips, that kiss . . .

There were worse ways to die.

His feet came up off the ground and his body reacted, flailing, fighting. Struggling desperately, kicking, choking for air. He looked down. Spotted her beneath him. He watched her shout and rush forward. She ran at the men pulling on the end of his rope, knocking them down with the considerable force of her body. They released the rope.

He dropped back to earth, hacking, gulping in sweet air.

Wheezing, he struggled back to his feet, his gaze locking on her. She slapped at one of the men who reached for the rope again, ready to pick back up where he'd left off and continue to merrily hang Kellan. Miss Cully wasn't having it. She set upon him again. The man turned on her, shoving her . . . knocking her down.

Fury seized him.

He could do very little with his hands bound before him and with a rope about his neck, but that did not stop him from trying, from raging like a bull when the rotter so hungry to hang him dared to put hands on the Boudicca battling nobly on his behalf.

Bending, he charged and jammed his shoulder into the man's middle, even though that only cut the bloody rope deeper into the skin of his neck and made him gag. But at least the bastard fell to the ground.

Miss Cully delivered the villain a solid kick before whirling around and hastily setting her fingers on Kellan, loosening and releasing the noose
from about his neck.

He was finally free. Gasping for breath, he
rubbed at the raw and ravaged skin of his throat.
The crowd buzzed and rumbled around them, the
tinder still lit and not yet extinguished. He wasn't
dead, but the danger was nevertheless very real.

And yet . . . his attention centered fully and
forcefully on the woman saving his life—or attempting to at any rate. She was the only person
in this entire town willing to speak out for him,
to risk her own neck for him—who gave a bloody
damn. He could kiss her for that. Again.

That enthusiastic thought brought his attention to her mouth. To those wide lips, rose-petal
pink, and his gut tightened and rolled over as he
recalled their texture and taste.

He winced, imagining it was wildly inappropriate to experience such feelings at a time
like this. Or perhaps it was perfectly appropriate. Logical and rational. When one faced his
own demise, perhaps it was a desperate grasp to
feel . . . something. *Anything.*

One last chance for feeling, for sensation, for
the reminder that he was still alive, however fleetingly.

"We need to get you away from here," she said

in an earnest whisper. Her gaze flickered somewhere just beyond his shoulder then, and something akin to wariness and trepidation passed over her face.

He turned, following her gaze.

A lone horseman rode at a fast clip into the square. Individuals parted, making way for him. Kellan didn't recognize the man, but he recognized quality horseflesh . . . and quality garments. The gentleman was in possession of both.

The stranger pulled to a hard stop. Everyone else stopped, too, turning their attention from Kellan and the lady blacksmith to gawk at the newest arrival to the party.

"What goes on here?" the gentleman demanded in a voice that for all its quietness sounded booming over the fraught air.

Gwen inched closer to Kellan, her hand stealing around his arm, clinging to him, holding on to him as though he might be wrenched from her side at any moment.

"Who are you?" an unidentified voice called out from somewhere in the crowd.

The gentleman swept his frosty gaze over the crush of people. That cool stare seemed to freeze everyone in their tracks and put to silence all the murmuring.

"I am the Duke of Penning."

"Says who?" a voice shouted.

"That's right! How do we know who the real duke is? Apparently anyone can lie about such a thing." Mrs. Dove chimed in and nodded accusingly to Kellan.

Kellan winced at that. The man, whom he rather suspected was, in fact, the Duke of Penning, turned that icy stare in his direction, assessing him, rightly judging him.

Mr. Carter arrived then, stopping his mount beside the duke's magnificent destrier. On closer inspection, Kellan recognized the animal from the duke's stables. His father had attempted to ride the beast, but that had not gone well. Da was only a passable horseman, and the destrier had been too much horse for his father. But not, apparently, for the true Duke of Penning. That felt appropriate— that the true Duke of Penning had mastered the finest beast in his stables in a mere day.

Carter's throat worked as he gulped a breath—as though he himself had made the trek from Penning Hall and not the horse carrying him.

Kellan was well familiar with the valet. He had served Kellan's father most diligently during their charade as duke and heir. For Kellan, Mr. Carter himself had selected a footman to serve as his own personal valet, directing him in his newfound role to attend to Kellan. He felt rather embarrassed to be faced with the man now. The valet had been very good to him and his father.

Mr. Carter held up a hand, gaining everyone's attention. "Gentle folk, be assured, it is confirmed. This is the Duke of Penning. All proper confirmation has been made. There is no mistake." His gaze landed on Kellan then. "*This* time."

The duke edged his mount closer to Kellan. "You're the man then? The one who has been pretending to be . . . me?"

"No, Your Grace," Mr. Carter quickly inserted. "That man fled. He was an older gentleman. *This* man"—he gestured to Kellan—"pretended to be the heir."

"Ah. I see. So you were the heir to the dukedom. Er, *my* dukedom, as it is." The real Penning looked at him and nodded once, tersely. He was of similar age to Kellan. Lean and sophisticated with patrician features, he looked born to the role. Unlike Kellan, who always felt like a bit of a brute in drawing rooms, sipping from delicate teacups. He continually feared the finely made furniture would break beneath him at any moment.

Kellan knew he could choose this moment to remind everyone present that he had simply pretended to be the *heir* whilst it had been his father pretending to be the actual duke. He could argue that his crime was the lesser offense and plead for mercy. He could even go so far as to blame his father for all misdeeds. The man was not here, after all, to suffer for his perfidy or offer a defense. There were innumerable options for him.

Kellan also knew he could feign ignorance—plead that he did not know his father's claim to the dukedom was false and foul trickery. Implausible as that seemed, he had a proven history of persuading others into believing the implausible. Call it a gift.

At this moment, he could put all his skills of subterfuge to good use and insist that his father had tricked him, too—duped him into believing he was the actual duke. It could give Kellan a much-needed reprieve. A long enough pause on all this madness to at least make his escape.

Except he'd had enough.

Perhaps it had been the events of the day, culminating in finding himself hanging from a noose with his feet dangling in the air. Such an occurrence gave one a change in perspective.

He had been pretending his whole life. In this town especially.

Ever since the day he had arrived at Penning Hall to discover his father committing his grandest of swindles yet, masquerading as a bloody aristocrat, stepping forward as the mystery duke returning from afar to assume his title, he had been swept up into the drama of it all. Just as his father had swept him along in a river of lies and shams all the days of his life.

He was not deluding himself into claiming to be transformed. He had spent a lifetime lying . . . but never to himself. To himself, he was only unfailingly honest. He was no phoenix reborn from the ashes. Nefarious deeds were the only things he knew.

If he survived this night, he would likely return to that way of life. It was what he was. And yet now. In this moment. He did not have the taste for it. He had met his quota of lies for this town.

The newly minted duke loomed over him, observing him, his gaze pausing on Kellan's neck and then falling to the noose on the ground, clearly making his own conclusions. He turned to examine the crowd next. "Bloodthirsty lot, are you not?"

A few of the citizens of Shropshire had enough conscience to look down at their shoes shamefacedly.

"His crime is punishable by death," Mr. Pedersen chimed in defensively, pushing the spectacles higher up on his nose.

"Should that not be left to a court to decide?" the duke asked.

"You're the law of the land around here!" a voice cried out in the crowd. "You decide!"

The solicitor seemed to find agreement in this. He punched a fist heartily through the air. "That is correct. This falls under your purview. You are the wronged party here, Your Grace. No one would look askance at you for settling this matter as you see fit."

The duke cocked his head, clearly pondering that for a moment. "I am . . . the law here . . ." He uttered the words as though he were testing them out for himself, acclimating to his sudden role as a powerful figure—not only in this village but in the country. Who knew what manner of man he had been before, but currently there were few more powerful than he in the land. The Duke of Penning could decide Kellan's fate here in this moment with one word and no one could oppose him.

Several people echoed the solicitor's sentiment. "Aye! He wronged you! Mete out justice, Your Grace! 'Tis your right."

Kellan could scarcely breathe, but he said not a word. Pleading would not endear him to anyone, nor was it in him. He was not one to beg. He'd done what he had done and he would accept this day's outcome.

He held his breath, gazing steadily at the man whose life he had stolen—at least for a duration—and wondering just how deeply Penning's hunger for reprisal went. He supposed the good citizens of this town were not wrong. It was the duke's right as lord of the manor, as the grand liege lord of these lands. This was his little fiefdom to rule and Kellan and his father had tried to usurp it from him. Kellan's fate would be whatever Penning decided.

Into the silence of bated breaths, a soft voice spoke. "Please. Do not hurt him."

It was Gwen Cully. Again she was making a plea on his behalf.

For some reason, in that moment, it annoyed him. He knew he had done nothing to deserve her compassion. And yet she was offering it fullheartedly.

The Duke of Penning looked at her then, and it was a look of marked interest, a slow head to toe appraisal that made Kellan bristle for some reason, pricking his annoyance further. "And who are you, madam?"

"I am Gwen Cully."

"And who *are* you, Miss Cully?" he pressed, gesturing around them with a light flick of his fingers. "What involvement do you have in any of this?"

She hesitated only a moment, moistening her lips. "I'm the—*a* . . . blacksmith here. In Shropshire. Please don't harm him. He—" She stopped abruptly amid her fragmented speech, glancing at Kellan again rather feebly. As though he might offer her some assistance.

"But why not? Apparently it is what he deserves." The duke gestured vaguely around them. "That is what everyone is telling me, what everyone appears to want. But you don't agree." He narrowed his gaze thoughtfully on her again.

"No. I do not." Her chin went up and she was that fierce Viking queen again.

"She's only saying that because she is in love with him!" It was the young Miss Blankenship.

She was back, charging into the fray and still in high fury. She had escaped her father, who trailed behind her, panting and trying to seize hold of her arm. "Daughter! Come away from this at once. You are only distressing yourself."

"Oh. Fascinating." The duke looked at Miss Cully with even more interest than before. "You are in love with him, lass?"

She inhaled and nodded once. "I am."

The right and proper duke looked between Gwen Cully and Kellan with keen curiosity. "And how do you feel about her, sir?"

Kellan swallowed thickly. "I love her, too." The words felt like marbles spitting from his mouth. Now, here, with the question put to him so plainly, this particular lie for some reason felt more wrong than all the other lies he had spun in his life. And he had spun many. Countless. Except never that one. Never *that* lie.

For some reason, in his less than noble history, he had never falsely professed to love someone, even when it would serve him to advantage. A person had to draw the line somewhere, and for him that had been the line he would firmly not cross.

"He has me." She patted his chest. "Please don't hurt him. I . . . I need him."

The big, burly man from earlier—Kellan believed his name was Meyer—snickered in the crowd. "You needn't tie yourself to this criminal simply to have a man work your forge."

Several other men guffawed, and Kellan did not miss the emphasis he placed on *work your forge*. He did not think the man was only talking about the task of blacksmithing and he wanted everyone to know that.

Gwen scowled at the man. "You know nothing about this. Mind your affairs, Meyer!"

"Enough." The duke sliced a hand through the air. The simple gesture served to work. Everyone fell silent again. "Well, then. You are in love. I see." His gaze turned thoughtful, contemplative as he alternated looking at Kellan and Miss Cully.

What did he see?

Meyer erupted, clearly impatient. "Enough of this rubbish!"

The duke looked at the man coolly. "I don't know who you are—"

"I'm Digby Meyer, Your Grace, the village blacksmith." The man's barrel chest swelled with self-importance.

The duke pointed at Gwen. "I thought she was the blacksmith."

"I am!" she insisted.

Meyer waved a meaty hand in dismissal. "She has a little shop she *calls* a smithy, but I have a much larger operation that I own with my two sons." He motioned to two bull-necked young men beside him. "Ask anyone here. I have the better—"

"Don't you dare say it." Gwen's face reddened in outrage. Clearly there was some unfriendly rivalry between the two blacksmiths that had nothing to do with her actions right now.

"As I was saying," the duke cut in, his voice deep and authoritative. Whatever he had been in the past, before he claimed his title, he was clearly a man accustomed to command. "Far be it from me to stand in the way of love." There was something in his voice, something vague and fairly ominous.

The hairs at the back of Kellan's neck prickled in warning. He peered at the nobleman steadily, trying to decipher his intent, but his coolly imperious gaze revealed nothing.

"I can't believe any of this," Meyer blustered. "I came out here to see a hanging, not suffer this nonsense."

The duke looked down from his perch atop the horse to the man. "Not another word from you."

Meyer's fleshy face brightened to a shade of purple. Clearly he was unaccustomed to being spoken to in such a manner, but he knew better than to oppose a man who so considerably out-ranked him.

The duke looked back at Kellan and Gwen Cully inquiringly. "Now there. What was I saying?"

Kellan shook his head, uncertain. He had no notion what the man was working up to, but he knew well enough to know something was happening. Something was afoot.

"Ah. Yes." The duke snapped his fingers. "You two are in love." He looked out at the crowd. "I don't know about all of you, but I would much rather stand witness to a marriage than a hanging."

"Marriage," she echoed softly beside him.

He snorted, certain the man was jesting.

The duke did not miss the reaction. He narrowed his eyes on Kellan. "You find that amusing? You love each other, do you not? You have both professed as much before all of Shropshire. Why would the notion of marriage be so objectionable?"

It was a test then.

"It isn't. I am not objecting," Kellan quickly protested.

"What would you prefer? Marriage to this lovely woman whom you profess to love? So that you might build an industrious and honest life together? Or the alternative?"

He watched the man, surmising what that alternative was, but waiting to hear it nonetheless.

"Marriage?" the duke suggested. "Or hang for your crime?"

Kellan looked away from the man offering him a choice between death or marriage. He smiled humorlessly, thinking that some people would say there was no distinction between the two.

All the blood had leached from Miss Cully's face. Gone was the pretty color marking her cheeks. She didn't look nearly as proud or indignant as she had before, only moments ago, fighting on his behalf.

Suddenly she looked terrified and apprehensive, her eyes large and unblinking. He knew she was thinking. Weighing her choices and doubting everything she had done up to this point, clearly questioning whether she should have started this game at all.

Before she could reconsider, before she could fully absorb her regret, he announced in a strong voice that harbored no misgivings, "Marriage."

Chapter Five ❧

*G*wen was not well acquainted with the new vicar. He'd only moved into the position a fortnight ago. The former vicar had stepped down after presiding over the village for several years, ever since Gwen was a little girl. Back then, she had lived a much more carefree and contented life. Her father and uncle were strong, invincible men who ran their prosperous smithy without a whiff of the hardships to come.

Old Mr. Bates had moved in with his daughter and her husband. They lived in a beautiful new house just outside of Shropshire. Gwen could have used them here now. *Any* one of them. The old vicar, Imogen or her husband would have injected a much-needed voice of reason into the chaos— and likely had more clout than dear Mrs. Dove, the only other person to speak out.

"Are you certain of this?" The new vicar stood before them, in the shadow of the church, the parchment he had readied only moments before, their full names boldly writ there alongside their declaration to wed, clutched in his hands.

Kellan Fox.

The swindler had given his true name. His subterfuge had come to an end and now she knew his
name. The entire village of Shropshire was privy
to that information now, presuming, of course,
that he was to be believed on this point.

The vicar looked at Gwen and Mr. Fox. This
man whose name she had only just learned
whom she was on the verge of marrying. It was
ludicrous. She had declared to all and sundry that
they were in love with each other—a man whose
name she had not known. It was absurd. Laugh-
able. *Terrifying.*

The words had popped out of her mouth. At the
time it had seemed the only way, the only thing to
do, and it seemed her instinct was correct. They
had been in the process of hanging him before the
Duke of Penning rode up. Her lie had saved him.
It was the only reason he was not dangling at the
end of a rope presently.

But it seemed the cost would be high. It would
be her life, apparently. Her very freedom.

Gwen gulped down a panicked breath. She was
not one to swoon, but she felt very near the precipice right now, her toes just inching the edge.

Most females wanted a husband beside them
in life. At least most of the females she knew in
Shropshire. She had never known her mother. She
died from a fierce ague when Gwen was just a

babe, during a particularly bitter winter. She had thereby never been schooled in the ways of drawing rooms and embroidery and fashion. She had never been taught to prioritize such things. The longing for motherhood, to *be* a mother, had never been instilled in her. Marriage was not a particular aspiration of hers.

Gwen did not need a husband to take care of her. She could take care of herself. Also, she had lived alongside two of the very best of men: her father and her uncle. She had yet to meet a man who came even close to either one of them. At least a man who was not already attached to a woman.

Her friends Imogen and Mercy appeared to be married to strong, good, handsome men. Perhaps the only two remaining such men in Shropshire, and now they were taken. There were no others who came even close to their caliber. But there was no going back now. She had to carry this ruse to fruition and marry the blasted man.

She glanced at the man occupying so much of her thoughts, noting that his wrists were still bound. "For heaven's sake, someone untie him," she snapped, glancing around.

The Duke of Penning stepped forward. "Allow me."

He had shadowed them to the church and kept close, as though he doubted they would see this thing through. Reaching inside his jacket, he pulled out a pocketknife. With little effort, he cut through the bindings.

"Thank you." Her husband-to-be rubbed his raw wrists.

Husband-to-be.

Good God. How could this be real?

"Miss Cully?" The vicar, a much younger man than the former vicar, recaptured her attention. "Are you certain you want to do this?"

Of course, she was not certain, but she nodded resolutely. No backing out now. She was up to her neck in this with this stranger. Not only to save face—she could still feel Meyer's glare on her from where he stood in the front churchyard—but because it was the one thing keeping him alive. She could not back down. Whatever he had done, he did not deserve death. "Yes. I am certain of this."

A lie, but she managed to get it out past her lips. She was certain she did *not* want to do this, but she was even *more* certain that she must.

The vicar turned then, and with his slim, elegant hands he pinned the marriage banns to the door for the world's perusal. "There you are." He pushed the pin in securely through the parchment and into the thick wood and waved a hand with flourish. "In three weeks' time, you two will be married." He smiled nervously. "God willing."

The crowd murmured in reaction.

Gwen schooled her features to reveal none of her horror. She nodded stiffly. Three weeks. Twenty-one days to be precise.

God willing indeed.

The Duke of Penning clapped his broad hands together once and she startled at the sudden sound. "I am glad we have that settled in a satisfactory manner. I look forward to your nuptials."

"Not *everything* is settled," Mrs. Dove spoke up. "Where do you intend to—" She stopped suddenly and glanced at the banns printed on the church door, squinting as though the print was too small for her weak eyes to decipher. "What is your real name, sirrah?"

"Kellan," he spoke up, motioning to the parchment. "Kellan Fox."

Kellan Fox. She let that roll around in her head again. Now, presumably, she had his name, this stranger she was to wed. How very . . . *strange.* Her name was joined to his on the door of her church, declaring their intention to wed three weeks hence.

"Mr. Fox," Mrs. Dove continued, looking at him fixedly. "Where do you intend to reside during these next three weeks? You cannot stay overnight in the same house with your bride-to-be. That is the height of impropriety." She puffed up her rather impressive bosom like a hen ready to battle.

"He can sleep in the smithy. In my shop," Gwen

offered. "There is a cot in the back room where the apprentices sleep." When they *had* apprentices. When times had been better for the business. Before Da died. Before Meyer showed up.

Her father had taken in apprentices on occasion. They would work for her father in exchange for training. Gwen had taken on an apprentice for a short time, as well. The lad had not remained very long. He'd decided blacksmithing was not for him and departed to find less arduous work in the city.

Mrs. Dove considered Gwen's proposition for a moment and then nodded once, apparently appeased. "I s'pose that will be acceptable." Gwen did not know why Mrs. Dove had appointed herself the protector of Gwen's virtue. Gwen doubted that her virtue was under threat. Yes. There had been that kiss, but it had only been pretense. A kiss to convince the world that they were something real.

A tumultuous kiss that singed her lips like a fiery brand. And not just her lips. She had felt it everywhere. Her entire body had caught fire when his lips landed on hers, when his tongue had slipped inside her mouth.

It had been the most wicked, delicious thing she had ever experienced.

And it was wrong. It had to be wrong because *he* was wrong.

Any intimacy with him, with a man like him, the wrong kind of man, had to be a mistake. It didn't matter how good it felt. It didn't matter that she relished every moment of it—of his larger body against hers.

He was the perfect wall of solidness, of strength and power. Never in her life had she felt so feminine. Her breasts tingled and grew heavy at the memory of that pressure, of his hard chest against the aching mounds. It was a pity it had not been an authentic act of passion. A pity that it had only been a performance, a show for their audience.

Or perhaps not a pity at all.

Perhaps it was good to know. Safer and healthier to keep things in their proper perspective since it had been so wrong. Since it could not happen again between them.

He was not the kind of man you kissed. He was dishonest. A trickster. A man you steered your virtue clear of lest you wanted a bastard babe in your belly and a heart reduced to broken shards.

"Very good." The duke intruded on her thoughts and nodded in approval at Mrs. Dove. "Thank you, ma'am, for sorting that."

"Indeed," the vicar seconded. "We would not wish anything untoward to happen and pose a risk to both their eternal souls."

Gwen's head was spinning. Everything was happening so quickly. Too quickly.

This morning she had risen from bed never having even met this man. An hour ago she had been working in her shop, with no thoughts other than catching up on her overdue orders.

"Oh, there won't be any wedding," Meyer called out belligerently. "Mark my words. You all shall see! Once a thief, always a thief. This scoundrel will vanish one night soon after pilfering everything of value that isn't nailed down in her home and shop, and we will all know she lies. There is no love between them." The blacksmith looked immensely satisfied with himself, and his words prompted several nods from bystanders and murmurs of agreement. "We will know then that Gwen Cully is little better than a criminal herself and no one should take their business to her. She cannot be trusted!" He waved his arm wide as though he were preaching dramatically from the pulpit.

She flinched. Of course Meyer would use this to malign her and promote himself among the community. She had not thought that far ahead, but the blacksmith's prediction could very well come true. Her stomach sank. It could very well happen. A man like Kellan Fox, a proven swindler, would likely be gone in the morning, all her valuables with him.

Her neighbors and friends would know then.

She gulped against her thickening throat. *Everyone* would know she had lied. That she had let a man boldly kiss her in public. She would be ruined.

At best, the townspeople would whisper behind her back. The worst scenario? They would punish her by refusing her business. By treating her with cold indifference or even openly ridiculing her.

What had she done?

She had barely been eking out a living these last weeks. Now she had sunk her ship even deeper.

She felt ill.

Mrs. Dove swatted a hand in the air in the direction of Mr. Meyer. "Oh, shoo, you! Did you not see that kiss? That was love. There was no artifice in that. These two are the genuine article! Do you hear me? The genuine article . . . and they will marry soon."

Meyer scoffed. With one last glare for Gwen, he roughly shoved his two sons ahead of him. The trio took their leave, departing down the lane.

At this point, most of the villagers followed suit. There was to be no hanging. The allure of spectacle was over. The dinner hour was approaching and she knew they were all eager to head to their tables.

The duke and his valet mounted their horses once again. Standing between the vicar and Mr.

Fox before the front doors of the church, she watched them rather numbly. The duke returned his hat to his head and tipped it in her direction. "Many felicitations on your upcoming wedding, Miss Cully. I look forward to it." He turned his flinty gaze to Mr. Fox then. She thought she detected an unspoken threat there. "You are quite fortunate you have such a devoted betrothed, sir."

Kellan Fox did not so much as blink. "Indeed, I am, Your Grace."

All of this was undoubtedly a test the duke wished to impose on Kellan Fox. A test that was not over. It had just begun. It would continue until his next move—until Mr. Fox either stayed or slunk away in the dark like the thief he was.

Mr. Fox took her hand and tucked it in his arm as though it were the most natural action in the world. She resisted the impulse to pull her hand away. That would not do. Clearly he was not oblivious of the precariousness of his situation, and he wisely wanted to present the best impression. He addressed the duke. "Thank you, Your Grace. We shall see you then."

Three weeks.

He acted as though that wedding day would actually come. As though it would arrive and they would both be back here exchanging vows in front of the village that had only just been clamoring for his blood.

As the duke rode away, Fox turned his steady, unreadable gaze on her.

Gwen swallowed.

She was a practical woman. A realist. And that was how she knew. No matter how he behaved, how he pretended and lied, she knew the truth.

Their wedding day would never come.

Chapter Six ❧

Twenty-one days until the wedding . . .

𝒦ellan had gotten himself through innumerable predicaments over the years with no significant cost or injury to himself. That was the nature of his existence. Swindling and charming and thieving his way through life. Certainly, there had been countless near misses, close scrapes, but always he had managed. Always he had emerged. Always he had survived. Persevered without any real harm or long-lasting consequence to himself.

Until now.

This time he had not scraped by precisely.

Never before had he come this close to danger. This time he had nearly found himself hanging at the end of a rope. Miraculously he lived, all credit due to the intrepid Miss Cully. He lived, but not *without* consequence. And the consequence of his most recent deceit?

A wife.

A bloody wife.

Or very nearly a wife.

He was to be married to a stranger in three weeks. That was what that parchment pinned to the door of the church proclaimed to the world.

He, Kellan Fox, chronic bachelor, was promised in marriage. And from the pallor of her face, he would say that his bride-to-be was not enthused about it either.

True, she had saved his life. That was the most important thing. He owed her for that, but his head was spinning. Did he owe her the rest of his life? Did he owe her himself? All of his days?

He pressed a hand to his aching head. Perhaps it was his recent loss of oxygen from that wretched rope squeezing his neck. He gave his head a small shake, but that only made the spinning worse.

He gulped and then winced. Blinking several times, he hoped that simple action could clear his head.

"You look like you could use a bed."

He lowered his hand and looked at her appraisingly.

Her face colored brightly, twin flags of color staining her cheeks and he knew she, too, was hearing that as it sounded. *Bed.*

The word alone made him remember that kiss. Her lips. Her taste. The slide of his tongue against hers. And those breasts. *Bloody hell.* He had to force his eyes not to lower to those magnificent breasts of hers for further consideration.

His cock twitched to life in his trousers just thinking about that, remembering their delicious fullness, the weight of them on his chest. He dropped his hand in front of his trousers to hide his wholly inappropriate response to her. Hopefully it was a casual pose, blocking any visible swelling of his cock to outward viewers.

"I meant to say," she said with heavy emphasis, "you must be fatigued from the trials of the day."

"I understood your meaning." He was certain the moment his head hit the pillow he would be out for the night. "It has been quite the day," he agreed. A day in which he had almost died. Perhaps that was why he was suddenly entertaining randy thoughts. Nothing like amorous pursuits following a near-death experience to remind one what it felt like to be alive.

"Let us go home then." She discernibly cringed and stepped back, disengaging from him, severing the contact of his hand on her. "To *my* home," she amended, as though he might be confused into thinking her home was now his and that she actually, in reality, wanted him there. He harbored no such confusion. He never had a home before. He doubted he would ever be in one place long enough to call it home.

They walked side by side. She moved stiffly, keeping several feet between them. She was going to have to relax and not appear as though he were someone she wished to avoid. He felt eyes on them, peering from windows. Of course, they were still a sight of interest.

He inched a little nearer, closing the space between them. She started to inch away and he reached for her arm. Grasping her elbow, he murmured, "Try not to look as though you wish to be anywhere but with me."

She glanced to him and then straight ahead. "Oh. Of course."

She led them the rest of the way, tracing their steps back to her shop. Once inside, she doused her smoldering forge with several shovelfuls of ash. She worked efficiently, her body strong for a woman, he noted. Hell, for a man. She was strong by anyone's standards.

"Is there anything I can do?" he asked rather lamely, not comfortable standing by idly as she worked.

"Almost done and then we can go." She returned her shovel to the tool stand and dusted off her hands. Finished, she turned and closed the windows. He watched her, still ill at ease with his sense of uselessness. "Come now. I will show you to your room."

She strode to the back of the shop. He followed, glancing at the corner where he had earlier hid— where they first met. Only a short time ago. He smiled derisively. Had that only *just* occurred? It could have been only an hour ago . . . and yet it felt longer. Days. Weeks. A lifetime.

She turned down the latch of a door and pushed it open. Stepping inside, she motioned around her. "Here you go."

The space boasted two naked cots, each one pushed against opposite walls of the room. There was a small dresser, table and two chairs, and a grate. She motioned to that now. "In case you get chilly at night. It's going to become colder soon. In the coming weeks . . ." Her voice faded away.

He glanced at her and she quickly looked away, not holding his gaze, and he knew. He knew she was suddenly thinking that he would not be here long enough to experience the cold of which she spoke. She believed he was going to leave, and she was not wrong in that thought.

Why would he stay? At the first chance, why would he not sneak away? The notion of staying, marrying her, and settling into domesticity? It was absurd. It was not him and he doubted that she wanted him for a husband even if it was. He had nothing to his name and only an ignominious reputation.

She had only sought to help him. She did not deserve to be stuck with him for the rest of her days for her altruism.

He nodded. "Thank you."

"It is by no means fancy."

"It is more than acceptable."

"Not like Penning Hall though, is it?"

He winced. "I think we have established that Penning Hall was not for me." The world had just proclaimed that loudly enough to him. Of course he had known that from the moment he assumed the role of a duke's son. He had never felt right within his skin whilst he lived the subterfuge. He had stayed out of concern for Da, and because of his vow to his mother, because he could not turn his back on the only family he possessed in the world.

She nodded, her awkwardness only seeming to grow with each passing moment. "I shall show you to the house now. And get you fresh bedding for . . . your cot." She motioned to the bed that would barely hold his frame.

He followed her out of the shop. At the front door, she closed and locked it with a key she lifted from her pocket. He waited patiently.

She sent him another quick, wary glance. "It's not London, but the town is growing. Can't leave our doors unlocked anymore."

"Of course." He knew something about the criminal element that existed in the world, even in seemingly safe villages such as these. "You can never be too cautious."

"Indeed."

There was a pregnant pause, ripe with the

awareness that she was talking to a scoundrel. She knew it, and so did he. She was likely envisioning him scaling walls, breaking into houses and businesses, something he had actually never done before. He was not a burglar in the traditional sense. No, he liked to think himself too sophisticated for that.

The setting sun tinged the sky pink as she left her smithy behind and led him toward the house next door. A modest two-storied cottage with a thatched roof and white walls. Colorful flowers bloomed in boxes before the windows.

He had spent the last few weeks in a grand mausoleum with multiple gardens and too many liveried servants to count, but it had never quite felt natural to him. It never felt like a home. Indeed not. His flesh had itched and felt too tight from the moment he arrived at Penning Hall and fell in with his father's mad scheme. He'd felt in his bones that it was a bad plan and he had told Da that. It had not mattered. His father was dedicated to the charade, and when he had his mind set on something there was no swaying him. Kellan could do naught but ride out the deception alongside him. Abandoning Da had not been an option.

For the greater part of his life, it had only been his father. No one but his dear Da. Kellan remembered his mother only slightly. She had possessed a kind and lyrical voice and cool hands that brushed his forehead when she put him to bed.

He distinctly recalled the day she died though. That was one memory he could not shake if he wished it.

His father had ushered him into the room and then had to excuse himself, too overcome with emotion. Kellan had climbed up on the bed with her, something he had done countless times. He'd lain beside her frail frame, not much larger than his own. She had stroked his head where he rested it on her shoulder.

"Promise me, Kellan. You will take care of your da," she invoked in her lyrical voice. "He is not as strong as you are. He is going to need you."

It had not occurred to Kellan she was doing anything unreasonable in obtaining such a promise from him. He had been seven years old, but it felt perfectly acceptable. Even now, when he could absorb that it was an unreasonable promise to extract from a young child, he still could not shake his sense of obligation to look after his father.

Da had brought him up the only way he knew how. He'd never treated him as a child, but rather a comrade. A partner. He'd trained him in how to survive. By the age of five, Kellan could lift a pocket undetected. By the age of ten, he could act better than a Drury Lane performer and pull off a complex ruse the most skilled knuckle couldn't bring about.

Da was not the most paternal figure, but he'd seen Kellan was fed and clothed and had a roof over his head. By the time Kellan reached his fifteenth year, it was clear he had other charms to be utilized. His father put those to good use, planting him in places where he could charm the ladies with fat purses.

They were artisans. Knuckles. Scoundrels. The most experienced kind of pickpockets. Charmers. Rogues. His father always said that, always insisted that what they did was a skill, an art, and they should feel no shame in it. And he never had. Until lately.

And never before quite as profoundly as today when another, a stranger, risked herself, her very reputation, for him.

Today he had fought for his life, surviving only by the grace of the female beside him, and he felt a measure of remorse over that. She had stuck her neck out for him, and he was going to fail her.

There was no other possibility. He could not be a proper husband to her—to any woman. He did not know how to do that, how to be a man that settled roots in one place and attached himself to a single woman. That was out of his experience, out of his depth. He would not delude himself into thinking he could be that person.

Somehow he would have to explain that to her and figure out a way to extricate himself from this impossible scenario without shame to her. He owed her that. A fate with preferably no scandal attached to it.

He walked behind her as she advanced up the stone-paved path, nearing the house they would enter together. Alone. Perhaps it was that fact which had him thinking all manner of lascivious notions.

He stared at the back of her, absorbing the sight. She was quite the tallest woman he had ever met. No taller than he, but then few men were. She moved sensually. Her hips had a sway that begged a man's hands to grip them. The trousers did not help—or they *did* help, depending on one's perspective. They fit her like a glove and did nothing to hide the fact that her teardrop arse was a work of beauty. This woman in trousers was a lethal thing, and his cock stirred thinking of her *out* of those trousers. How her long legs might look, shapely and toned with muscle. He knew they would be. She was no demure lady that swooned at the faintest activity. Her legs would be strong as they wrapped around a man's hips. Even her luscious backside would flex enticingly as she worked herself on a cock. *His cock.*

He swallowed thickly and hastily adjusted his member where it swelled against his breeches.

He could not imagine how she came to be unattached. She must be close to his age of eight and twenty. How could she have reached such a ripe womanhood without forming an attachment? He supposed he should only be glad of it—relieved that she was free to proclaim their love and save his life.

Clearly she had no husband . . . but no lover? No suitor?

He gave his head a quick shake and told himself that it mattered not at all. The particulars of her life were not his business—despite what that parchment pinned to the church door proclaimed. It was just one of many lies to span across his life. Another invention.

As soon as he could manage it he would be gone from here and her and this town.

Chapter Seven ❧

*G*wen entered the still and quiet of her house, keenly aware of the man's presence behind her. She felt him like the forge in her workshop, an immense radiating heat at her back. He was like that. *Fire.* And she had just brought him inside . . . into the sanctuary of her home where he could incinerate everything. Herself included. She was a blacksmith. She knew all about the risks and dangers of fire and how to treat them with caution.

This? This was not caution. This was utter madness. Something only the very daftest of women would do, and she was doing it. An image of the banns pinned to her church door flashed before her mind. She gulped past the painful lump in her throat.

Swallowing thickly, she vowed that this—*he*—would not burn her. Somehow she would sort this all out. She could not marry this man. There had to be another way.

She quickly lit the lamp in the small foyer of her house, telling herself that she would find a way out of this impossible situation.

She could not marry a man she did not know. She did not even want to marry a man she *did* know.

The warm glow from the lamp instantly infused the familiar space. For quite some time she had entered her home alone at the end of the day. Ever since Papa's death and her uncle took to his sickbed, her days had been spent in solitary toil.

She was accustomed to the aloneness of it all.

Her youth had been different. From the age of eight, she had spent her time in the smithy alongside her father and uncle, enjoying watching them, learning the ways of anvil and hammer and longing for the day when it would be her turn at the helm, when she would manage things.

In those days the three of them had entered the house together at the onset of evening, the inviting aroma of dinner in the air, the fireplace in the living room crackling in welcome. They had a housekeeper then. Odette lived with them. She was the closest thing to a mother Gwen had ever known. Gwen's own mother had died before her second birthday. It was Odette who explained all the little lessons that a mother imparted to her daughter. Now she was gone, too.

In her cheerful youth, Papa and her uncle had been robust. Their smithy had been prosperous, and they'd had dear Odette who kept house and cooked for them and always made certain fresh linens were on the beds.

Those days felt long ago. A lifetime ago.

Papa was dead. His heart had failed him whilst working in the smithy. He'd been too weak after the attack to do much of anything except keep to his bed. His normal routine and life had been over from that moment. He'd suffered two more attacks before the final one that took his life. Now her uncle was dead, too. Odette was not dead, but living with her niece in Bristol.

Life had indeed changed.

It was always changing, and she was not so naive as to rail against the inevitability of it all. Apparently today was yet another change that she must learn to accept. Another *unfortunate* change. This evening she found herself, for the first time in a long time . . . *not* alone as she entered her home. A man accompanied her. She winced.

Not just any man. Her betrothed. *Betrothed.* The word alone stuck in her throat and she had not even attempted to voice it out loud. Her mind had great difficulty wrapping itself around the notion.

Heavens above, how had such a thing come to pass? This was one change she could not have foreseen when she woke in the comfort of her warm bed this morning.

She slipped her stocking-clad feet into her waiting house slippers.

She had left her dirty boots outside by the front door of her house like she had done countless times before. Kellan Fox had followed suit. At least she had not needed to instruct him. Not that his Hessians were in any way unclean. He'd been respectful at least to copy her actions.

"What manner of name is Kellan?" she asked, proud at how natural and even her voice sounded to her ears. "And is that truly your name? Kellan Fox? Or another lie?"

She snuggled her toes into the warm fur lining of her slippers. They were a birthday gift from her uncle last year—even on his sickbed he made arrangements and saw to it that she had a present and a cake. The slippers were by far the most luxurious thing she owned.

This year there would be no cake or presents. She had no family left. She had friends, but no one close enough to make a grand occasion of her birthday. It would slide past, simply another day to be unremarked upon.

"Yes. It's my true name. My mother named me after her father. He was Irish."

She nodded as though that meant something. "And where is your mother now?" How did she fit in alongside him and his thieving father? Did she join them in their misdeeds? Would she show up pretending to be the duke's aunt, unaware that they had been caught in their ruse?

"She died when I was young."

"Oh." She rubbed her perspiring palms over her breeches, thinking about that. About him. A motherless boy raised by a reprobate father. That could not have left him with many choices—

No. No. *No.*

She would not make excuses for him. He was a man now. No one forced him to pretend to be the Duke of Penning's heir and perpetuate a sham on the world.

"Mine, too." Shaking her head once as though that cast out any amount of commiseration she might feel, she gestured ahead of her. "Shall I give you a tour of the house?"

He nodded tersely and fell in behind her as she led him into the parlor, the heart of the house. It was a cozy room. A sizeable mullioned window offered a view of the street when the drapes were pulled back as they were now. A large sofa and a pair of wingback chairs sturdy and deep enough to hold the likes of her father and uncle— not small men, by any means—sat before the fireplace.

Her family had spent countless evenings in this room. Several knitted blankets were folded neatly over the furniture. She would often tug one down and snuggle beneath its soft warmth as her father read to them. Many a happy scene had been played out in that room.

He surveyed the parlor, nodding as though in approval.

She motioned to the bookshelves. "You can help yourself whilst here." It was not an insignificant library. They were in possession of many fine books—all of which she had read multiple times.

"Thank you."

She moved on then, guiding him from the room and out into the corridor. She showed him to the dining room and kitchen. Following that, she led him up the narrow steps to the second floor.

There were three bedchambers in total. She occupied the largest of the three. "And here we are. This is . . ." Her voice faded.

She did not bother to step inside the space, merely stood in the threshold and motioned vaguely to the large four-poster bed. Papa had insisted he would never sleep in a bed if his feet hung off the end. Thus all the beds in this house were customized to comfortably sleep warrior-sized men. The Cullys were always big people. Papa said their ancestors had been Norsemen who came over in the Viking raids. She didn't know how he could know that for certain, but it was a fanciful bit of lore that she had enjoyed hearing from him in the parlor after dinner.

And yet this bed now loomed larger than memory served. It could sleep *two* warriors. Not just one. Not just *her*. It could easily sleep Gwen and the man standing beside her. Her *betrothed*. In three weeks, her husband. It was a thought she could not seem to escape.

Her face flushed hot and then cold. Except it would *not*. It could *not*.

Her bed would remain hers alone. She might have proclaimed her intention to marry this man today in some wild turn of events even she could not yet fully understand, but that did not mean they would be husband and wife in the truest sense.

He must know that.

She shifted uneasily on her feet, acutely aware of the imposing man just to the side of her. The stranger. A lawless man with nothing to recommend him. It was impossible to forget that her neighbors had wished him dead over an hour ago and now he stood in a room alone with her. What was to stop him from harming her? Putting a less than gentle hand on her now . . .

Her lungs suddenly felt constricted, the air trapped and unable to flow freely.

This man in her house was bad enough, but his proximity to her bedchamber made her queasy. She pressed a hand to her stomach in an attempt to quell the roll of nausea.

"Your room?" he prompted, finishing for her and motioning around them.

She looked at him sharply and answered him

even more sharply. "Yes. This is my room." She stepped from the threshold and led him to the bedchamber that had been hers as a girl.

"You can use this room to freshen up before dinner, if you like. Your room in the smithy does not have a washstand." She gestured to the washstand. "After we eat, you can carry that down with you so that you needn't return here to wash every day."

He peered inside the chamber. "I see. Very good." From the tone of his voice she was not certain he did *see*. He looked at her steadily—so much steadier than she felt.

She expelled a breath. "We should discuss matters. Why don't you change and we can meet downstairs for dinner in half an hour?"

He glanced down at himself and held out his arms. "I stand before you in everything I possess."

She looked his considerable person up and down. "You have no belongings?"

"I arrived at Penning Hall with a horse and a valise full of belongings, yes, but I don't think anyone is inclined to return me my things."

"Ah." She nodded at that likelihood. "Well. I am sure you are hungry. I will meet you downstairs shortly and we can talk about . . ." Her voice faded away. She did not even know what to call the situation she found them in.

She left him then, her feet eagerly carrying her

into her bedchamber where she closed the door and leaned against the solid length of it. She sighed and rubbed both hands over her face.

She looked toward the ceiling as though she could see her father and uncle looking down at her. She wondered what they thought of the man she had so publicly betrothed herself to. What did they think of Gwen?

They never hid that they wanted her to meet someone, to find a partner in life—to marry and have her own family. It was important enough to them that they mentioned it on more than one occasion in their boisterous way, tossing one of their burly arms over her shoulders as they did and giving her an encouraging squeeze. They had even gone so far as to play matchmaker a time or two. Those efforts had ended abysmally, of course. Not that they had been deterred. They had continued to try. They would be trying still if they were here. Only death had stopped them.

Our lass deserves a man worthy of her. Love and family . . . and a houseful of babes like your dear mother wanted.

They may have wanted her to be a wife with an army of children, but they had treated her as an equal, raising her to be strong and independent. They trained her in blacksmithing like any lad brought up in a smithy. Poor darlings. They had not realized they were fashioning her into a decidedly ineligible female. Men did not particularly relish tying themselves to women who were taller, stronger and more robust than they were.

Gwen knew that better than anyone else.

She supposed her fate would have been different if Papa had remarried or if her painfully shy uncle had ever summoned the bravado to court a lady, thereby bringing another female into the family. But Papa insisted he could love no other save his first wife, Gwen's mother, and her uncle never appeared to long for anything other than his bachelor existence.

She quickly changed out of her work clothes, and washed herself off at the basin. Refreshed, she donned a simple dress, one of the few she possessed, and then slipped a well-worn pinafore over her head. She might perform her work in trousers—it was just safer to do so—but in the evening she enjoyed the ease and flow of a dress.

A quick glance in the mirror confirmed her hair was still well in order. At least well enough to dine with her unexpected houseguest.

Her father must be rolling in his grave. He might have always hoped she would find a gentleman to marry, but he would not have condoned the manner in which today's events occurred.

She suddenly realized Kellan Fox did not have water in the basin in his washstand. She had been the last person to occupy that room and that was some time ago. Hurrying from her chamber, she went downstairs and fetched a pitcher of water. After carrying it upstairs, she paused outside his closed door. She knocked once. At his call to enter, she closed her hand around the latch and pushed it open. Stepping inside, she held the pitcher out before her. "I thought you might need this for washing, Mr. Fox."

Thankfully there was quite some distance between them.

He stood near the window, peering down into the small garden she kept in the back that was in dire need of her attention. She had been so busy in her shop lately, trying to catch up, trying to get ahead on her orders, trying her best to keep her current customers and regain those who had left, that she had not been giving it the necessary attention. It was unfortunate as she would need that food in the coming weeks for her table.

Shaking her head, she pushed away such thoughts. Such thinking led to despair. Despair froze a person and made it impossible to move ahead, and she was doing her best to keep moving, to keep working and doing all that she could.

He turned to face her. "I think we are past formalities. You may call me Kellan, if you wish."

"Kellan," she murmured with a single nod, hugging the pitcher to her stomach. "I am Gwen."

"Well, Gwen. I have yet to say it. You saved my life today and I am in your debt."

She shifted on her feet, uneasy with his gratitude. "It may not have come to that."

He gave her a look. "It *did* come to that."

"I think the Duke of Penning's arrival helped more than anything I did."

"He only finished what you started."

He meant her *lie*. The lie she had started. The duke carried it through to fruition though, whether he realized it or not. She presumed the man did not realize it . . . but he *suspected*, and then he carried her lie to conclusion when he suggested they marry.

He continued, "I owe you my thanks . . . What you did today impacts you." He blew out a breath. "Significantly. I am sorry for that."

She shook her head. "I could not let them kill you."

"Everyone else seemed able to do that." His mouth lifted up at a corner. "And I don't think it's because you love me."

She huffed a breath. "No. Of course not. I never even met you before today."

"And yet somehow you were very convincing in your declaration."

"As I said, you did not deserve to die for what you did. It was not a just punishment."

"And so this is a just punishment? Marriage to you?" Those dark wolf eyes prowled over her.

She laughed lightly, pretending not to feel as though she were trapped alone in a room with an unpredictable animal—one who made her breathing hitch erratically. "It shall not come to that."

"No? The banns nailed to the church door state otherwise."

She winced at that and had no response.

He was correct. The banns were posted, proclaiming to the world that she and this man would be bound. It was a problem. One for which she had no solution at the moment. If he left here before twenty-one days, she would be revealed a liar and ruined. Meyer alone would see to that.

And yet she could not marry him. She *would* not.

It would take some careful thought.

Kellan glanced around the modest bedchamber, and she felt assessed in that survey. Judged. He was evaluating not only her, but also her home . . . her modest life. "It is just you alone here then?"

She hesitated for a moment. No sense denying it. Mrs. Dove had made it clear that she was a woman alone. "Yes."

She despised how vulnerable that admission made her feel. There was nothing wrong with being alone, with being a woman living alone. A woman was not somehow *less* because she was not married. She was not lesser than other women because she did not choose to populate the world with offspring. She should not be at risk because of her unmarried status. She should not . . . and yet she knew the world viewed things differently than that.

"It's a nice home you have."

She studied him for a moment, attempting to read if he was being sincere. He'd just come from living at Penning Hall. Whether such a grand place belonged to him or not was immaterial. He had been staying there quite comfortably, residing in palatial splendor with servants waiting on him hand and foot. Her home was humble by comparison and there would be no one to wait on him here.

She surveyed him in his posh garments, rumpled and torn from the day's deeds. "I think I have some clothes that will fit you," she offered, feeling a bit awkward. It was simply a magnanimous offer. He had nothing on him save the clothes on his back. Of course, he would need something else to wear while he was here.

She'd cleared out a great many of her father's belongings, removing them from the house, but not all. She had packed most of his clothing into a chest. She didn't know why she saved the garments at all, but she had. She supposed it was sentimentality, which was not an emotion she would assign to herself. Now it seemed some good would come of it.

"Do you?" He cocked an eyebrow and she knew he was wondering what man she had lived with who had been close to his size.

She nodded and gestured to the washstand. "After you refresh yourself, you are free to use them until you can retrieve your own things from Penning Hall."

He winced. "If they have not been destroyed."

She shrugged, unable to speak to that. "At any rate, they're fairly humble garments. They're likely not to your standard, but you are welcome to them."

"A fresh change of clothes would be appreciated. Thank you."

She stared at him for a long moment, feeling deliciously warm under his dark eyes . . . and oddly breathless. A man in her house that was not blood related was an unusual thing. It had been many months since she'd had anyone beneath this roof with her and *never* someone like him.

With a swift internal shake, she warned herself not to be charmed by his solicitousness—or mesmerizing dark eyes.

He had to know the power of his eyes, the richness of his voice. The way he presented himself. It was all an act. His weaponry. The arsenal he used to scheme and perpetrate shams for God knew how long. Likely all his life. Something told her that he and his father had years of practice. One did not wake up one morning and decide to commit a fraud that would result in death if caught without a great deal of confidence.

She gave herself a small mental shake from her musings. "I will fetch them for you."

She left his room and located the chest in the other spare room, where her uncle had once slept. She opened the lid and quickly gathered the appropriate garments, something for him to wear tonight and tomorrow.

Satisfied, she cradled the clothes in her arms and returned to the chamber where she had left him. The door was still slightly ajar, as she had left it. She gave it a gentle push, and it swung inward with the softest creak.

Stepping inside, she glanced around the room . . . and gasped.

Chapter Eight ✧

*O*nce inside the chamber, Gwen's eyes found Kellan Fox standing before the washstand. He had made himself at home, and she stilled in shock at the evidence of that.

He had removed his jacket and vest and shirt and stood naked from the waist up. Her mouth dried at the impressive swath of his muscled torso. Gwen brought the clothing she held up to her chest, hugging it closely as though suddenly needing the shield.

She watched as he dipped a sponge in the basin and then lifted it, running it over his chest in a slow, tantalizing circle that her eyes tracked.

He looked up, asking casually, "There you are. Are those for me?"

She nodded jerkily, trying not to focus on the way the rivulets of water trailed from his collarbone, finding the path of least resistance down the center of his broad chest and abdomen, disappearing into his trousers.

She wet her lips, desperate for moisture there. She'd never seen a man built so formidably. Were all cheats and thieves and scoundrels fashioned like brick houses?

She had cared for her uncle in his final years. She was familiar with the anatomy of the male body . . . but this was no frail, old man's body.

He's no blood relation either.

This was a man who had kissed her. And she had kissed him back. It had been a feverish, consuming thing. And that was with restraint, for they had not been alone. The entire village had been there.

And now they were alone, without an audience.

And they were betrothed.

Her gaze devoured his form, and her mind could not help thinking about . . . clinging to the knowledge that he was her husband-to-be. Her thoughts seized hold of that. His body was hers by rights—or very almost hers. She could explore it, touch it, taste it. There could be more kissing. He might be sleeping in the shop at night, but they would be alone ample times. Such as right now.

She could do that *thing* that women did with men they desired.

Such passion could not altogether be wrong. She knew good women. Imogen and Mercy. They were newly married to handsome, virile men. There was nothing platonic about their marriages, to be certain. They enjoyed their marital beds. They enjoyed their men. They did not need to tell her for her to know this. She saw the long glances they shared with their husbands. The lingering brushing of hands. And of course . . . Imogen was large with child now. There was that evidence.

Gwen shifted her feet in agitation, adjusting her weight from foot to foot, all of her body warm and humming, like tongs placed in the hottest part of the forge.

Her gaze followed the trail of that sponge over his big, muscled chest, wishing it were her hand instead, wishing she could feel his skin for herself. The man was dangerous. A feast of temptation. Suddenly, she understood why half the women in town had set their caps for him—the fact that they thought him an heir to the dukedom aside.

She took a step closer and set the clothes on the bed as though they were precious things. "There you go," she said in a thick, guttural voice she hardly recognized.

"Thank you."

His hands drifted to his trousers as though preparing to remove them, and her face caught fire. "Wh-what are you doing?"

"Making myself presentable."

She averted her face and her hand flew to her eyes, shielding the sight of him from her gaze. "That is most unacceptable. You can please wait for me to leave the room before you make yourself . . . er, comfortable."

He snorted derisively. "Nothing about any of this is what I would call comfortable." Evidently, comfortable or not, he was continuing his washing. "You've just proclaimed to an entire village that we are lovers."

"I did not use those words!"

"Do not mistake me. I am grateful. You saved my neck." There was more splashing. "But it was inferred that we are lovers. By those that believed us at any rate."

She shook her head, sputtering for the proper words as she dropped her hand from her eyes, facing him directly again. "However true that might be, there is no need to make things *more* uncomfortable between us. We know what is true between us."

His gaze held hers. "Indeed. We are strangers bound together."

"Indeed," she echoed.

"Likely not the first strangers whose names have been joined together on banns, but perhaps some good can come of it yet."

She let out a breath. "Perhaps." Another nod. "We should discuss that."

"Perhaps we can make the best of this situation."

Hope fluttered warily within her. They required a proper understanding between them in order to accomplish that.

"What can I do for you?" he asked. "I owe you . . . something. What do you want? Name your price."

"Price?"

"Reward," he amended. "You deserve it for your altruism."

Her gaze went back to that magnificent chest of his again. What did she want?

She let that roll around in her mind, considering the question. She was clearer on what she did *not* want. She did *not* want a husband—never had.

What *did* she want?

She wanted independence. She wanted to keep her home. She wanted her livelihood to prosper. She wanted to be the blacksmith everyone in Shropshire valued above all else.

She studied the man before her, seeing him for what he was—what he offered. She stepped forward and stretched out an arm, reaching for his chest, stroking her fingers between the muscled ridges. His lips parted ever so slightly, but not a sound escaped. His skin contracted, reacting to her touch.

"You're strong," she announced, and while it was the most obvious thing in the world, she absorbed it in a way she had not before. Her gaze moved to his face thoughtfully. He was strong. A strong, able-bodied man.

He nodded once, his jaw taut, a muscle feathering beneath the skin.

She flattened her hand on him and swept upward, marveling at the muscled swell of his shoulder, feeling a ragged breath escape him. "What I could do with this body . . ."

His throat worked as though fighting for speech. "Oh?" he asked in a strangled voice, leaning forward slightly, pressing deeper into her touch.

She nodded, perfunctory and decisive. "Indeed." She dragged her hand down his arm, flexing her fingers and squeezing his bulging bicep in approval. "I don't imagine you tire easily."

"Uh . . . no?"

"You last for hours, I suppose."

He looked utterly bewildered now . . . and something else. His eyes seemed darker. The irises and pupils indistinguishable from each other.

"Very good." She lowered her hand, pressed her palm against her side to resist touching him again. Any more would be unwarranted . . . even salacious. She had simply been measuring him, assessing. She was finished with her appraisal and quite satisfied with her findings. "Why don't you finish in here and join me downstairs for dinner?" They had much to discuss.

He stared at her in consternation, clearly bewildered.

Without waiting for an acknowledgment, she turned and started for the door. She stopped on the threshold, and looked back at him questioningly, taking a bracing breath. "Why did you kiss me?"

The question had been burning in her mind since it happened. She had to ask. Had to know before they went any further in this charade.

"Why?" he echoed.

"Yes. Why?" She held her chin aloft, clinging to a facade of dignity even as she asked a question that made her feel utterly vulnerable.

He rubbed at the back of his neck, looking uneasy himself. "I don't know. You claimed we were in love and I thought it felt like the thing to do."

"The thing to do?" she echoed, realizing that was all it was for him. A ploy. A tactic. It was not passion.

Not real. Naturally. *Of course.* He was an expert at doing things that were *not* real. He had been fighting for his life. He would have kissed a rhinoceros if it would have kept him alive. That deflated her a bit even though it should not have. She should not feel anything save umbrage with him for daring to kiss her.

"Yes," he replied. "The final thing to convince everyone."

"Oh. That was clever of you. Indeed. It did help do that." She was rambling and knew it. "You were very convincing." She could not help herself. Her gaze drifted to his lips, remembering that kiss.

"So were you," he returned. "Quite convincing."

And then they were left staring at each other, each of them clearly thinking about that kiss which had managed to convince a mob of villagers that they were in love. Well, with the exception of a few villagers. Meyer was still not convinced, but she could not summon even a fraction of concern for what that wretched man thought.

It had looked real. It had *felt* real. Real to her at any rate.

Unlike Kellan Fox, she did not know how to fake something like that. If she did not know any better, his kiss would have convinced her. After all, she did not possess a wealth of experience when it came to passionate kissing. In fact, his had been the first kiss to ever stir her.

Staring at this man with his handsome face and bare chest and big, strong body that made her feel womanly and desirable in a way she had rarely—perhaps never—felt, she cautioned herself. She did not know how to fake an amorous kiss. But this man did. It was what he did. He was accomplished at deceiving.

She had to take care to remember that and not let herself be charmed or seduced by him again. Especially if the wild idea taking hold of her became a reality.

She edged back from the threshold. "Join me downstairs when you're ready."

Chapter Nine ❧

*D*inner was a simple affair. Unsurprising considering the distractions of the day. *Distractions.* She winced. That was a gentle euphemism.

Dinner was a simple affair most nights. Ever since Uncle died, she had only herself to look after. Many an evening meal consisted of what she had on hand in the larder or sometimes meals were offered as payment for services. Many a pie or pot of stew had been exchanged for a repaired wagon wheel.

Gwen placed a plate of cheese and dried fruits on the dining room table. Usually she ate alone at the small table in the kitchen. The kitchen was a cozy room. The old wood stove emitted warmth into the intimate space. It was enough for her. She was comfortable there. Sitting at the large table in her dining room felt silly. *She* felt silly doing that so she didn't.

And yet tonight there was nothing silly about it. She felt the need to be a little more circumspect. A wide width of table between herself and Kellan Fox felt right and proper.

She arranged the plate one way, and then angled it differently. As though that mattered. She plucked a slice of dried apricot off the plate and popped it in her mouth before moving into the kitchen to fetch a hearty loaf of bread. She had picked it up from the baker's shop yesterday, but it was still fragrant. She knew the crusty exterior hid the soft inner crumb.

Returning to the dining room, she placed the breadbasket in the center of the table as though it were the focal point of a grand meal—a magnificent rack of lamb with mint sauce—and not a mere loaf of bread. She felt a stab of embarrassment over the simple fare that she would be offering this man who had just come from Penning Hall where he had no doubt consumed things like lamb and fresh langoustines and exotic fruits. She told herself she was being impractical. Foolish, even. She should not feel such a way, but she did. She had come by the food she served him honestly. The food he had dined on at Penning Hall had not been his to rightfully enjoy.

The man was safe with a roof over his head, a bed for the night and food in his belly. A much better fate than that *other* fate he would have faced today if not for her intervention.

His footsteps thudded on the stairs in a steady tempo. He was coming.

She hurriedly wiped her palms over her skirts, marveling at their sudden dampness. He made her nervous. Naturally. He was a stranger in her house. A stranger of dubious morals. A stranger she had kissed. And yet it was more than that. The idea brewing in her head left her anxious. It was no doubt a wild proposition, but this entire day had been one wild escapade.

At the last moment, her nerves got the better of her.

What if he laughed at her? What if he said no?

She dashed from the dining room back into the kitchen. She took several deep breaths, pressed her hands to her overheated cheeks, and glanced around as though needing an excuse to be hiding out in the kitchen. She spotted a bottle of wine someone had given her and snatched it up. Pasting a neutral smile on her face, she returned to the dining room feeling more revived now. If there was ever a time that called for spirits this was it.

He was waiting politely, his hands locked behind his back as he looked out the window. She surveyed him, looking him up and down. Papa's clothes fit him fairly well. They were of comparable height, and Papa had been a bit heavier in his final years so Kellan's more muscular frame did not strain at the seams of Papa's clothing as one might think.

His gaze locked with hers as he brushed a hand down the front of his shirt, wiping off some invisible piece of lint. "Thank you again for the clothing."

"Of course." She motioned to the table, setting the bottle of wine beside the pitcher of water. "Are you hungry? It's not lavish. I did not have time to prepare anything—"

"It is plenty." He moved ahead and pulled out a chair, gesturing for her to take a seat.

She hesitated at the courtesy. She managed to school her features to reflect none of her surprise. She had been on her own for so long, but before that she had been rarely treated to such gentlemanly manners. The men in her family had always viewed her as one of them—treating her like a son and a nephew. Not a female to be coddled. The majority of time she traipsed about town in trousers. Doors were not usually held open for her and just as rarely chairs were not pulled out. It was something she had never considered before— not until now that she was presented with such gallantry.

She sank down into the chair, watching him warily as he rounded the table and took his seat across from her.

"Wine?" she asked as though she commonly imbibed with dinner.

"Please." He lifted his glass and allowed her to pour.

She then filled her own glass. Taking a sip, she eyed him over the rim, letting him drink, hoping it relaxed him and made him more amenable to what was coming. She certainly could use a little fortification.

Motioning to the food before them, she invited him, "Please. Do not stand on ceremony. Help yourself."

He didn't need to be told a second time. He loaded his plate with cheese and fruit and then tore into the loaf of bread, spreading it with butter. "This looks delicious."

She could not help herself. She made a snort of derision.

He paused at the sound. "What?"

"I am sure you are accustomed to far grander dinners at Penning Hall."

He tore a bit of buttered bread and popped it into his mouth. He chewed for a moment and then inclined his head. "I believe last night was sole and smoked duck canapés."

"That sounds delicious."

"Yes, well. That is in the past. And that dinner was never intended for me, was it?"

"I suppose not."

"Now I am here and enjoying this fare you have kindly prepared for us." He motioned to the table.

"Indeed." She reached for the bread. "Now you are here."

And they had to figure out what to do about that.

Her head spun and the proposition burning in her mind rose to the tip of her tongue. She warned herself to broach it carefully with the man. She did not want to frighten him away. There was already a good chance he was biding his time until he could escape this place—and her.

"And what shall we do about that, eh?" he asked as though he read her mind.

She cleared her throat and dabbed at her mouth with a napkin. "I have an idea."

"Do you?"

She nodded and took a long sip of wine, suddenly needing more time. And courage.

"Firstly though," he said as she continued to drink. "I have to know. Why did you do it?" He studied her as he cut a wedge of cheese and placed it over some bread. Taking a hearty bite, he waited for her answer.

"Do what?"

"Save me."

"Oh." She paused and thought about that. "You don't think I was dazzled by your handsomeness?" she quipped, attempting levity . . . and a little buttering up never hurt. It always helped her get her way with her father at any rate. "Could that not have motivated me to save you?"

He snorted. "Hardly. And no one else was motivated by my *handsomeness*."

"How can you be so sure I was not so moved? You don't really know me."

He dragged a hand through his damp hair. He must have washed it in the basin. She had an image of him in that room upstairs again, bare-chested as before, rivulets trailing down his torso as he dunked his head. He really was an impressive specimen. A man among men.

He ate in silence for a few more moments. "Whatever your motive, I know you were the only one in that crowd determined to save my life."

She resisted squirming under the unwavering directness of his stare. "Yes. I suppose I was the only one." Let him absorb that. It could only help soften him toward her upcoming suggestion.

"I shan't forget it. As I said, I am in your debt."

"Yes. You have mentioned that." Hopefully, he would remember that when she posed her idea. He would remember it and agree.

She squirmed a little, her stomach aflutter. She could not help it. It was this man. His nearness. The fact that they were together in her house—*alone together*—and she could only recall that singeing kiss of his and how it had stirred something inside her that she had not felt before.

She had tried to feel those things once years

ago. She had reached out to a man she found attractive and had only been met with stinging disappointment and rejection. She had learned her lesson and never gone looking for singeing kisses or butterflies in her stomach again.

She especially would not be so foolish as to expect anything of a romantic nature from this man.

"You don't owe me for doing the decent thing, but . . . I do have an idea."

"Oh?"

"Yes." She nodded and forced a bit of bread down her throat. It felt like dust on her tongue, but she knew she needed to eat something. She would only find herself hungry later when her stomach settled and the urge to retch subsided. *If* it ever subsided. It had to. This would not be forever. She would not be bound to this stranger forever.

With that reminder, she broached the subject that was swelling like a storm between them. "Our . . . betrothal." *Bloody hell.* The words stuck on her tongue. "I have an idea."

"Yes, you mentioned that. What do you think we should do about this situation?" He winked at her wickedly and reached to pour himself a glass of wine. "Should we go ahead and marry, you think?"

She blinked. He must be jesting. He had to be jesting and yet . . .

He stared at her intently, calmly, still eating with a faint smile as though the simple fare was indeed the most delicious of meals.

"Actually," she began, moistening her lips, "I don't think that marriage is an altogether terrible idea."

Chapter Ten ❧

𝒦ellan fell back in his chair at her pronouncement, the smile he had been wearing vanishing. "I beg your pardon?"

She scooted forward a little in her seat and cleared her throat. "I know it seems ridiculous, but hear me out."

"You have my most riveted attention."

He watched her with keen interest . . . and a fair amount of wariness.

Women had wanted to marry him before. Women who thought they loved him, but they also thought they knew him. They did not. No one really knew him. They only knew whatever role he was playing. They loved the fiction he created. They loved what did not exist.

And yet this woman perhaps knew him the best of all because she knew him to be a fraud. She saw him as he was, sitting across from her, a man caught at his game and nearly hanged for it today. He still bore the marks on his throat to prove it.

Nothing about him was a catch. He was not an eligible gentleman. He was a man from nothing with nothing. He had nothing to offer and she undoubtedly had to see that. Marriage to him? Madness.

She tucked a fair strand of hair behind her ear. She seemed almost nervous, which was at odds with the brazen creature manhandling him upstairs. He swallowed thickly and told himself not to think of those moments. The last thing he needed was a hard cock at the dinner table.

"First things first." She nodded once as though this were an official meeting. "Do you do this kind of thing often? I mean . . . it's what you . . . *do*?"

"You mean frauds? Schemes? I'm afraid so." He took a sip from his wine. "Although this undertaking was a bit bigger of a connive than I typically prefer. I opt for discretion. There was no way to be unnoticeable in this charade. I tried to warn my father, but he was quite enjoying himself in the role. I urged him to give it up weeks ago. I think he was a bit addicted to being the Duke of Penning by then. He couldn't quit it . . . until we were caught, then he had no choice."

"But then he left. Without you."

"Yes." He nodded slowly, grimly. "He got away. Without me." That still stung. Even if he did understand it. Even if he knew his father. It was the nature of their occupation. Every man for himself. It would not have done for them both to be captured. What good would that have served anyone?

"That must be a difficult thing."

"We live by different rules."

She nodded. "Clearly." The word was said without judgment, but he felt judged nonetheless.

Good people . . . a good person like *her* could not understand. He lived as he was brought up, and he was brought up in the art of the swindle.

She peered at him closely, so deeply that he was certain she read the secret sense of abandonment he harbored. Despite what he professed, it was there, buried within him. His father had escaped without him and left him to hang. He could not suppress the sting of that.

It would not be the first time his father let him down. And yet he could not do the same to his father. Understandable or not, whether part of their code or not, his loyalty ran too deep. The promise he made to his mother could never be forgotten.

He took another drink from his glass and then set it back down on the table with alacrity. "Back to what you said. You were jesting, I assume. About us. Marrying." He grinned.

She sighed and settled both her elbows on the table beside her plate. "I am certainly not looking for a husband." She cast him a wry look. "Any more than you are looking for a wife . . ." He inclined his head in agreement. "However, going forward with the marriage has its advantages."

"Advantages?" he echoed. "Do elaborate." He

smiled rakishly then. "It's me, is it not?" He waved a hand like a wand over his person. "You cannot resist all of this."

She stared at him in horror as hot color stained her cheeks. "N-no," she stammered. "I—I mean to—"

"Please, Miss Cully. I am only teasing you." *Flirting*, he mentally corrected. It was what he did with attractive women, and she was every bit that. The habit was as natural as breathing to him.

"Oh." She returned her attention to her food, eating sparingly, picking at her meal and shooting him unsure glances. Clearly flirting was not a natural act to her. She reached for her glass and took a gulp of her wine.

"Indeed. You cannot wish to be stuck with me. I am not the sort of man for any good woman to attach herself to, and I am very aware that you were cornered into agreeing to marry me out there today. I will not hold you to that, of course."

"Hmm." She nodded. "Of course. Except if I do not hold you to it, if we do not, in fact, wed in twenty-one days' time, I shall find myself quite humiliated. Perhaps even ruined." Her lip curled at the notion, but it was more of a grimace and decidedly *not* humorous. "As Mr. Meyer said."

"Ah. I see." He steepled his long fingers together. He had not fully considered the ramifications to her before. He had simply been eager to escape the rope tightening about his neck. Unfortunately doing so had put her in a difficult situation.

"Truthfully, I don't care very much what people think of me."

Not surprising. He could believe that. The woman was a blacksmith, after all, and wore trousers. Obviously if she cared what others thought she would be married to a blacksmith and not *be* a blacksmith. Married and in a dress with a herd of youngsters clinging to her skirts.

She continued, "I do, however, care about my business. If I lose customers . . ." Her voice faded away, but he understood. She did not need to explain further. If her reputation became so tarnished, she would lose all her customers to that Meyer brute. His conscience pricked at that notion, and his thoughts churned with what he could do to alleviate her situation.

"So perhaps you can stay . . . for a time," she suggested in a cautious voice.

"And marry you?" he asked, needing that clarification.

Marriage was forever. Was she not considering that? She made this sound temporary.

"Perhaps you would not mind taking a respite from your, your . . ." She waved her hand in a little circle in the air.

"Thieving ways," he supplied.

She snorted in humor. "I did not say that."

"You did not have to, and it is the truth. And what you're offering me, no? A hiatus from my criminal ways."

She nodded. "Well. Yes. Just for . . . a year." She leapt upon this as though it were the perfect amount of time. "You could stay here and work. Help me."

Help her? "I don't know anything about smithing."

"I could show you . . . or you can help with the garden. Or the stable. Or the house." Her words gained speed in her eagerness. "The tasks are endless. There is so much to do around here and there is just me to do it all. For a year, you can help me. You're capable and strong." Her gaze roamed his shoulders, and he suddenly understood why she had examined him so thoroughly in the bedchamber upstairs. He had thought she had been appreciating his body in an amorous manner. Apparently not. He snorted lightly. She saw his value merely as a laborer.

She pressed on, "With your help my business could be back on the right path in a year. Then you can go on your way after that. No one will think much if you leave after some time has passed. I'll be thriving by then. If anything, I will be the object of compassion. A woman abandoned by her husband." She stared at him with hope brimming in her eyes.

"But we would be married. There is no undoing that once it is done. What if later in life you meet someone and decide you want to marry him?"

She shook her head resolutely. "No. I don't want to marry. Ever."

"You say that now—"

"I'm not a child. I'm eight and twenty. A woman grown. If I wanted to marry I would have done so already."

He took a slow sip from his glass.

"Oh. I see." She leaned back in her chair. "I suppose you may want that option for yourself. How foolish of me that I did not consider that."

"Me?" He pointed to his chest. "Marriage? No, no, no." He shook his head with a chuckle. "That's never been something in my future."

"Well. If we marry and live together for a year it won't ruin either one of our futures then. Of course"—she cleared her throat—"this would be a strictly platonic arrangement."

"Oh?" He wasn't going to lie to himself. The thought of sharing a bed with her for a year had its appeal. Apparently that would not be part of the arrangement though. Unfortunately.

"That would be for the best. So neither one of us becomes confused and starts viewing our marriage as something it isn't . . . as something real."

"You've given this some thought."

"Actually this only just occurred to me upstairs." Her gaze skated over him again. "You're in very fine form. You've already the look of a blacksmith to you."

Except he was not a blacksmith. He was not a man to make his living in such an honest and diligent manner. He could not settle into such an ordinary and tame existence.

But he owed her. He was in her debt. He had said as much. A great sigh expelled from him.

It would just be another role to play. A hardworking husband. For an entire year. Except he would be himself. Kellan Fox. And everyone here already knew what he was—what he did. No more lies. There would be some relief in that.

She shook her head. "Oh, never mind. It's madness. Why would you want to stick around here for a year? That's an unreasonable commitment. There is nothing in it for you—"

"I'll do it."

She blinked. "What?"

"A year. I can do that. I mean . . ." He angled his head thoughtfully. "I owe you that. At the very least. It's only a year, after all."

"I . . ." She stopped. "You are being sincere. You will do this?"

"I don't lie."

She looked at him sharply and he chuckled. "That is to say, I don't lie to friends."

"Friends?" She paused. "Oh. Is that what we are then?"

He nodded. "Yes. You saved my life. If I can't call you a friend then who can I call a friend in all of this world?"

Warm color stained her cheeks. "Then we have a deal?"

He extended his hand to her across the table. "You have my word, my friend. I'll marry you, Gwen Cully. And stay a year."

She hesitated before accepting his hand, wrapping her cool fingers around his. She told herself this would be a good thing . . . and she was not making a pact with a scoundrel that she would come to rue for the rest of her life.

Chapter Eleven ✦

Twenty days until the wedding . . .

Gwen was up with the roosters every morning. Unfailingly. That was the way of things when her uncle and father had been alive and that had not changed now that they were gone. *Especially* not now that they were gone. It was just Gwen and her failing business. Gwen and her desperate need to persevere. Gwen in solitary toil. There was no pardon for sleeping late. She could not afford to be lax in her duties.

Which made sleeping in today so very wrong. Inexcusable.

She opened her eyes slowly, sleepily, dreamily, gradually absorbing the cheerful wash of sunlight.

"Wah!" she cried out and surged from her bed, her legs getting caught in the tangle of bedding. She hit the floor of her bedroom. Hard. The collision of her body on the wood floor reverberated through the house. She reached down and hastily freed her legs, cursing herself for her clumsiness . . . for her laziness. For sleeping away half the day.

Hopping to her feet, she peered across the room to the clock. How could she have slept so late? What must Kellan think of her? And after she had expressed her need for his help? He probably thought this was how she lived her life and conducted her business. Like a sluggard. A sloth. Someone who deserved her decline in business.

She was all movement then, quickly changing into work trousers and a shirt, muttering under her breath, calling herself all manner of unkind names. Until she blinked, stilled as she processed what she had just thought. What did it matter what Kellan thought of her? It wasn't as though she wanted to impress him.

Plopping down on the bench before her dressing table, she stared reproachfully at her reflection. For once her eyes looked remarkably rested—or *un*remarkably considering how late she slept.

Her stomach felt queasy. She pressed a hand there, rubbing and trying to quell the rioting butterflies. She glanced to the window and the sunlight streaming around the edges of her drapes.

The agreement she had entered into last night with Kellan Fox felt long ago. It felt dim and vague and she wondered if it was truly real. Now, in the light of day, could it all be true? Did Kellan Fox intend to stick around and marry her and stay for a full year? Had she asked him to do that? Had he agreed? She was assailed with doubt.

Despite their conversation the night before and the agreement they had reached, there was nothing keeping him here. No bars on the door. No chains. No guard stood watch.

It was doubtful that honor and obligation had kept him here through the night despite their pact.

He was likely gone and that stung.

She attacked her hair with her brush, dividing it into chunks and then plaiting it. Her fingers worked nimbly, coiling and pinning the plaits to her head. Somehow she would cope with the consequences of his departure. She always managed.

Of course, he had left.

Hopefully, the town would not turn on her as Meyer predicted. Perhaps they would not believe she lied. Perhaps they would think she had been deceived, duped, taken in by a pretty face. They'd think her a fool. She winced. They would pity her, but she doubted she would be ruined. Not a great thing. But humiliation trounced ruin.

It was the only hope she had as she sprang from the table and hurried downstairs. There would be no breakfast. No time for that. She'd slept through any chance for breakfast.

At the front door, she slipped on her boots. She exited her house and walked next door to her smithy, her hurried pace slowing. Suddenly she was not so eager to face the truth—to confront the likely reality that Kellan Fox was gone.

Her stomach knotted as she advanced on her smithy, knowing what she would find. Or rather what she would not find. *Who* she would not find.

Slipping the key from her pocket, she unlocked the door to her shop and stepped inside. She left the door open, welcoming the fresh air into the stale space. She lifted the latch on the shutters and opened the windows. She knew the next step was to get the fire started in her forge, and following that, she needed to tend the horse in the stable and put food out for the cats that hung about the place.

She had done all these things countless times, but she could not bring herself to move through the paces of these most familiar acts. Not yet.

Her gaze went to the door in the back of her shop. It was closed as usual. That did not mean anything. It did not mean he was here. It did not mean he was gone. She always kept it closed, to keep the ash and grime of the shop from getting inside the room. However unlikely, a part of her harbored the hope he was still here . . . in that room, that he had honored their agreement. Perhaps he was sleeping late, too.

Determined to find out at last, she walked across the space of her smithy, her stride swift and purposeful. At the door she stopped, lifted her hand in midair and then paused, hesitation stealing over her again. Deciding she needn't knock, she lowered her hand to the latch and pushed the door open to view—

An empty room.

The bed was tidily made. She had not necessarily expected that. She did not think a man sneaking off like a thief in the night would be concerned with such a thing as making up his bed. He was gone.

She exhaled.

He was indeed gone.

Disappointment mingled with relief.

Perhaps it was for the best. Even if his departure stung. Even if the village turned on her.

She inhaled. Her feelings were complicated. Whether he was here or he had left, he brought unrest to her life. Nothing would be easy about any of it.

A new thought suddenly occurred to her. *How did he leave?*

On foot he would not have covered much ground. He could not have wanted that. He would not wish to be pursued. He needed a horse. A horse he did not have.

But she did. She had a horse.

No no no no.

Her heart hammered in her chest as she sprang from where she stood on the threshold and out the door of her smithy. She rounded the building for the stables, plunging inside breathlessly.

"Bloody hell," she cursed once she burst inside to see her horse gone.

He took her horse. *No.* He *stole* her big bay. The wretch!

She collapsed back against the barn wall, a sob threatening to overcome her. It felt a double betrayal. Not only had he left after vowing to stay, but he had stolen something important from her. She should not feel so hurt. That was what he was. Who he was. Somehow she had forgotten that.

She groaned and buried her face in her hands. It was too much. That horse was the only one she owned. She needed Sally to go anywhere, to pull the wagon she used to deliver items to customers. She didn't possess enough funds to go out and buy another one. She was destitute.

Her stomach roiled. She pressed her hand there. She was going to be sick. Things were bad enough when Papa died and then her uncle became sick, but after her uncle died it seemed like everything she touched fell apart. She was alone and nothing she did seemed to help. Not herself or the smithy.

Meyer's face materialized in her mind's eye, his voice in her ears.

A female like you can't be too choosy. You've no money. No beauty. In fact, I've heard of your debts. Not many men would take on a woman like you. But my son will. My son will have you.

She lifted her face, and struggled to compose herself . . . and stave off the urge to retch. She was not one to surrender to tears when she could be doing something productive. She had work waiting for her. She would busy herself whilst she tried to come up with a way to get her horse back . . . or find a way to acquire a new one. Perhaps she could work out an arrangement, a trade of some sort with Imogen to borrow one of her mounts. Even if it was just when Gwen needed to transport materials.

Oh, curse that wretch! Her hand curled tightly at her side. She would like to see Kellan Fox now, directly in front of her. She would plant her fist into his face to show him just what she thought of his treachery. He had said they were friends, and like an idiot she had believed him.

The sound of hooves beat in the air in a steady clip and she turned, searching for the source. There, riding up the narrow lane between her house and the smithy was one thief, Kellan Fox—the sole subject of her most heated ire.

Wretched man, indeed.

He stopped in front of the stable and dismounted in one fluid movement.

She walked a hard line for him, the heels of her boots biting into the earth.

He tipped his hat at the sight of her, opening his mouth to speak. His stupid, lovely mouth.

The words never emerged, whatever they were. She did not care. She had no wish to hear him speak, to spout undoubtedly what would be only more lies.

Her fist flew, and landed on his mouth, knocking him off his feet and onto his arse with a satisfying thud.

She towered over him, quivering in outrage. She folded her fingers, curling them inward until she felt the sharp cut of her nails into her palms. The sting helped, kept her in check when she only wanted another go at him.

"What was that for?" he demanded, picking himself back up, gingerly touching his lip. "Bloody hell. I've had men who've struck me with less force than that." He gave his head a little shake as though to clear it.

She inhaled deeply. "You stole my horse." *Along with my pride, my dignity.*

She had believed him. She shook his hand as though their agreement were something real. He must have been laughing inside, thinking her the greatest of fools.

He motioned wildly. "I wasn't stealing it. I was bringing it back."

"We had an arrangement. We shook hands," she said with a hiss, as though this last bit were the ultimate intimacy and thereby betrayal.

He pulled back his hand from his face to the sight of blood smeared on his fingers. "I'm bleeding."

Her stomach plummeted at the sight, but she shook her head, refusing to feel guilt. Not when she felt this crushed. "I should have known. You are a thief as everyone said. You would not know how to be honest."

His face tightened in anger. "I keep my vows. You were still in the house, asleep, I presume. I knocked. Should I have beat down the door? I did not wish to disturb you."

He had presumed correctly. At the reminder that she had spent half the day in bed she felt a fresh wave of embarrassment.

He continued, "I returned to Penning Hall to claim my belongings. Since the duke was so decent to me yesterday I thought he might be willing to return them to me."

She glanced to her horse, noting the double satchels attached to his mount stuffed full with what must be his possessions. "Oh."

I was bringing it back.

He had not run off then. He had not abandoned her.

The breath shuddered out of her, and suddenly

she flushed, mortified and regretting her impulsiveness. Papa always did say she was hotheaded.

"Oh," he echoed sardonically, touching his split lip again, fingering it lightly. "The duke even offered to return my own mount to me. He's having a groom ride it over shortly." He cocked an eyebrow at her. "In the future, I will not need to avail myself of your horse and risk your wrath."

Now her flush of embarrassment deepened, turning a degree to shame. Perhaps she had been quick to judge . . . and react. *Heavens.* She had struck him, not thinking at all. Only feeling. Feeling much too much after so short a time of acquaintance. After vowing to a relationship without physical congress.

"You can understand how it looked to wake and find you gone," she attempted to explain.

"Perhaps," he allowed. "But I did not think I would face the fury of your fist . . . and that it would hurt quite so much."

"Oh, don't be a baby," she admonished.

"A baby?" He wiggled his fingers stained crimson. "I'm bleeding."

She waved a hand in dismissal. "I am certain you have faced worse."

He snorted. "You know I have."

Her lips twitched. Indeed. Only yesterday.

"And how is your neck this morning?" She stepped forward and put her hands on him as though it were the most natural thing in the world to do so. As though she was in the habit of touching virile and dangerously beautiful men.

Her fingertips went to the still very raw flesh. The skin had even scabbed in places where the rope had torn the flesh and drawn blood in spots. She should have cared for it yesterday—for him. She had been a poor host in that regard.

"You could use my balm." She stepped back, wondering at the sudden tightness of her chest and the breathiness of her voice. "Come inside. Tend to my horse first and then meet me in the house. I'll tend to your neck."

"Perhaps, while you are at it, you have something for my poor mouth you have most viciously attacked," he called after her, a twinge of humor in his aggrieved voice.

Her lips twitched. "Cease your whining. You best thicken your skin, Mr. Fox."

"Why? Do you intend to hurt me again?"

"Not as long as you behave," she called, a smile playing on her lips as she departed the stable and hastened to the house and her bedchamber. She quickly retrieved her basket of salves and poultices from her armoire, but stopped before returning downstairs, before meeting him in the kitchen.

She took a moment for herself in her bedchamber, leaning against her door and breathing in and out. In and out.

She flattened her palm over her chest, marveling at her galloping heart. That happened around him. She wondered if that would be the case for the next year.

He had not left. He had not abandoned her to ridicule and ruin. He had stayed and she felt buoyed. Her spirits high. Their agreement still stood. Perhaps he was in possession of honor and there was something of a gentleman to him, after all.

A gentleman thief. *Ha.* She would not be so naive. Yes, he had stayed, and he had promised her a year. A year was a long time though. She knew the odds of him staying for that duration were slight.

But he had not left. Not this time. Not yet.

He was here. He had kept his word to her and she was not facing ruin or ridicule just yet. She was spared for now, and perhaps best of all . . . she had a big strapping man at her disposal.

Chapter Twelve ❧

𝒦ellan waited for her in the kitchen, fingering his abused lip and fighting a smile. She packed a hell of a punch. Of course, she did. His lady blacksmith was no delicate miss.

She strode into the room with her basket and paused at the sight of him. "You're wearing a demented smile on your face. Why?"

His smile widened a bit at that. He could not help himself. She was amusing in unexpected ways.

She gripped her basket with both hands, holding it in front of her as though it were a shield. "Are you laughing at me?"

"I would never do that." He forced his expression into something serious and unsmiling. "You might strike me again."

She gave him a reproving look and set her basket down on the kitchen table. He watched as she started rummaging through it.

"Your neck is still a very angry red. The last thing you want is for the skin to fester."

He nodded, wondering if anyone had ever

fussed over him before, and then knowing the answer to that. No. No one had. Not since his mother. His memories of her were few, but he knew she had been the fussing kind. Mothers who sang lullabies fussed and she had always sang to him.

"We do not want that," he agreed as she unscrewed the lid to a small jar and dipped two fingers into it. She scooped the pungent salve and applied the cool substance to his throat.

"Gah. That stuff smells bloody awful."

"But it works."

He swallowed and tried to ignore the gliding sensation of her fingertips against his skin.

"Why must anything medicinal smell like rot?"

"I believe it is a rule."

Her fingers brushed his pulse point and he fought down a groan. He watched her face with a searing intensity that he felt deep in his bones. Her gaze was fixed on his neck and she wore an expression of intense concentration. Suddenly her gaze moved and collided with his. The air crackled between them, but he didn't look away.

He watched her watching him, her fingers still moving, gently massaging the ointment into his skin.

"How is that?" she murmured.

"Feels good . . . still smells like rot, of course. But you have a magic touch."

Her throat worked. She slid her hand away. "That's that then." She wiped her hand on a cloth and screwed the lid back on her jar of salve.

"But you're not finished."

She looked at him curiously. "Am I not? Did I forget—"

He pointed. "My lip."

Her gaze dropped to his mouth. "What is . . ."

"It needs your . . . attention . . ."

She frowned. "It's a little puffy."

"It's swollen to the size of a melon."

She snorted. "You exaggerate."

"Come now. You cannot shirk your nursing duties. Especially as this particular injury was inflicted by you."

She inclined her head. "I suppose that is true." She turned her focus to her basket.

"Since this is for my mouth, you would not happen to have something in there that smells better than death?"

"I might." She ceased her rummaging and pulled out a jar smaller than the last one.

"Who taught you to hit like that?"

"No one."

She dabbed a single finger into the concoction and brought it to his mouth, stopping an inch away as though suddenly taken aback with the task.

"No one?"

"I am a blacksmith. I wield heavy objects all day long."

"That makes you strong," he agreed, "but not necessarily knowledgeable on how to properly plant a facer."

"If you have not yet deduced, I did not have the upbringing of a lady. When my father and uncle were hale enough, we would travel to fairs to sell our goods. Those can get rowdy. There were even pugilism exhibitions. I've observed my share of men at fisticuffs."

"Ah. And you took notes?"

"Let us just say I am a keen observer of life."

He made his way through life doing much the same thing. Watching. Studying people and situations. Deciding his next move. "We have that in common."

He continued to study her. Her attention drifted, flicked to his face—so close to his own. He could see how her lashes were thickest at the roots, close to her eyelids, making it impossible to distinguish them separately.

She pulled back her arm and dropped her hand away, stepping back hastily. "Perhaps you can apply this yourself." She shoved the jar at him.

He fumbled to take it before it fell between them. "I think you would be better at it."

She shook her head. "Why?"

He shrugged. "I can't see what I would be doing. I have no mirror."

She stared at him with a mixture of trepidation and suspicion. Both valid emotions, of course. His lip didn't hurt so badly he needed her special salve. He simply wanted to feel her hand, her fingers, her touch on his mouth. Her lips there would be even better.

Reclaiming the jar, she squared off in front of him with an air of resolve. "Very well."

She glided this new sweet-smelling salve over his bottom lip, coating the swollen flesh.

He sighed.

"How's the smell?" she murmured.

"Better. What is it?"

"It's just honey."

He released a short laugh. "Really?"

"Mm-hmm. It's not just for eating, you know."

"Is that so?" He opened his mouth to taste her finger, licking the digit's sticky residue off her, drawing her finger deep into the warmth of his mouth. "Tastes delicious though."

Her eyes flared wide, darting from his face to her finger that he sucked and laved with his tongue. "There's a bee colony right outside town where a few brave souls collect honey."

"I wasn't talking about the honey."

"Oh," she breathed. Her gaze went back to his mouth where her finger had disappeared. Her eyes dilated, the pupils almost disappearing entirely into the blue of her eyes. "What are you doing?" She whispered this, her voice a faint scratch on the air.

"Tasting you."

"Oh." She swallowed again, her throat working. He could practically hear her gulp. "That is . . . uh . . . does not seem like a good idea."

He talked around her finger, his mouth nibbling on her skin. "This tastes . . . like a fine idea to me."

"We had an agreement."

"And I'm keeping that agreement. I'm still here and not going anywhere. For an entire year."

A flicker of something passed over her face. "There was more to the agreement than that. There was another part, if you recall."

She was, of course, talking about the no fornicating part of their agreement.

He would not object if she wished to reconsider those terms. The realization that he might in fact *want* her to reconsider jarred him. He normally did not prefer the militant type. He preferred his women soft and uncomplicated, certain in their desire for him. He did not pursue them. He did not need to do so. More often than not they pursued him. He acknowledged this without ego. It was simply the pattern of his life.

And yet he suddenly found himself with a pen-

chant for Viking queens who punched as hard—
harder—as a man.

Perhaps he knew all this on some level last
night when he sat at her table and struck an arrangement to live with her for a full year. Perhaps
his body already knew what his mind had yet
failed to recognize.

He had thought he was being bloody noble—
doing the right and proper thing, helping her as
she had helped him . . . *more* than helped him. She
had saved his life. A life that could be argued—by
nearly everyone in this village, to be certain—was
not worth saving. He could not even refute that. It
was not as though he had a long history of good
deeds to his credit. His life was not decent or upright or worth much of anything to anyone. Apparently not even his own father.

Very well. He was not so very noble. Because
here he was intrigued with spending a year under this roof with her . . . and passing the time
in enjoyable and intimate ways. He would hardly
describe himself as altruistic.

He pressed on further, lowering his voice sug-
gestively. "A year is a long time."

"Is it?" she softly queried.

"We could find ways to divert ourselves during that time. When we're married and I move
out of the smithy, we'll have long evenings together in the house." He swirled his tongue

around her finger, satisfied at her sharp gasp. He had no doubt she would taste this sweet even without the honey coating her finger.

Not even a day since entering into an agreement with her for a very *platonic* in-name-only marriage, and he was sucking her finger as though it was candy. His mind moved to what other parts of her he would like to suck next. Of course, he knew all those parts he should like to visit with his mouth. He did not have to ponder very hard. He'd felt those mouthwatering, generous breasts of hers against his chest. Like the rest of her, they were not insignificant. He'd like to peel off her clothes and start there.

"I don't think that is a sound notion."

"I think it is a fine notion," he countered.

An abrupt knock resounded in the air, and the back door was unceremoniously opened.

There would be no starting—or continuing—of anything apparently.

A fair-haired woman entered the kitchen with an air that announced she had done it countless times before. He recognized her. She was familiar, and increasing with child. It was difficult not to notice. Her hand went to her large belly, holding it as though her unborn child needed protection from the sight meeting her gaze—from him.

Kellan had met her before at some point, but her name evaded him at the moment. He had met

countless individuals in his time out and about in
Shropshire, masquerading as the duke's son. He
could have met this woman at any of those occasions.

"Gwen, I heard the—"

The lady stopped abruptly, her speech dying on
the air as she assessed the scene upon which she
had intruded with sharp eyes.

Gwen's finger slipped from his mouth and
she stepped back hastily, knocking over one of
the kitchen chairs in her rush as though he were
afire. It fell to the floor with a clatter that echoed
all around them in the cozy space.

The three froze in a startled tableau, eyes flit-
ting to each other.

"Imogen!" Gwen exclaimed. "You're back from
your trip. How was London?"

"Very well. Fine. Crowded. Smelly. I am glad to
be home." She pronounced each word with a stac-
cato beat, spitting out her responses as her gaze
narrowed suspiciously on him. "And you must be
Mr. Fox."

He inclined his head. "A pleasure, ma'am."

"Oh, we have met before, but then you were
introduced to me as the Duke of Penning's much-
prized heir." The lady's eyes sparked fire at him.
She did not like him. That much was clear. She
looked ready to carve him up.

He did not recognize her from yesterday. Had

she been there, in the bloodthirsty crowd, she would likely have been shouting for his neck with the rest of them.

"Ah. Yes. Forgive my lapse in memory. I have met a great many people since arriving in Shropshire." His father had not believed in keeping a low profile despite Kellan's suggestions that they do just that.

"Yes." Her lip curled in obvious distaste. "A duke's life is ever so busy . . . or rather the son of a duke. Not that it was your rightful life, but rather the one you had stolen."

He nodded once, his jaw locked tight. He cleared his suddenly too-constricted throat. He did not quite know how to respond to that. He was not sure he was expected to. The lady clearly did not like him and nothing he said in this moment was going to change that.

She lifted her cool gaze from him, scornfully dismissing him. She settled her attention on Gwen Cully. "Gwen. What is happening? I heard—" She stopped for a breath. "I saw the banns on the church door."

"Ah, yes." Gwen smoothed her palms down her trousers. "It is a bit complicated."

"It is fairly straightforward as I am hearing it, and there is little else to hear since I arrived home. The village is abuzz with the story, incredible as it seems." The woman sent another accusing glare Kellan's way.

He turned his gaze to Gwen, as well, wondering what she would tell her friend, as it was clear the two were friends. Good friends. And good friends told each other everything.

"We are to be married." Gwen donned an unconvincing smile.

He almost laughed in the face of it. She was a shit liar. How had she convinced an entire village that they were entangled in a torrid love affair? She would have to work on that if she was to continue convincing people they were a loving couple. Perhaps he would give her some lessons. He was an expert, after all.

Apparently her friend was not convinced either. "Oh. Indeed?"

That fake smile of hers grew even flintier. "Indeed," Gwen returned.

"Funny how you never mentioned any of this before. I didn't even know you two knew each other." Again with the suspicious expression and sharply narrowing eyes.

Because we do not know each other.

Gwen's cheeks pinkened. "Well. I am a private person, as you know. I told no one."

"So allow me to grasp the fair gist of this. You and this *person*"—she said *person* as though it were a dirty word and flicked a hand in Kellan's direction—"have been engaged in a clandestine romance whilst he was parading about as Penning's heir. And why was that such a secret, may I ask you? Is that because when he was pretending at being a haughty nobleman and duking it about the village he was too good for a mere blacksmith like you? He wasn't too good for Emily Blankenship. He openly courted her."

Kellan fought back a cringe. None of those facts painted him in the best light. When she described it like that . . . he felt a proper cad. Even though none of that was true. In this one thing, at least, he was not guilty. He had not met Gwen Cully before yesterday. But if he had . . .

She would have fascinated him from the very start.

There was something about her that attracted him and drew him in and had him committing a year of his life to her. That was the truth of it.

Gwen looked perplexed. She bit the bottom lip of that lovely mouth of hers and sent him a quick uncertain glance before facing her friend again.

He decided it was time to play the role of besotted suitor . . . or rather, betrothed. He had managed to do that yesterday successfully enough. Certainly he could do so again. He stepped beside his wife-to-be and took her hand, resting it on his forearm and covering her fingers with his own. Her fingers trembled against him. "I can only say that I am glad the world knows the truth."

"The truth?" Gwen's friend snapped, launching it like a barbed arrow at him. "That's an interesting choice of words. From *you*."

Indeed.

Gwen turned to face him, patting him reassuringly. "Why don't you give me a moment with Imogen? I am certain you can find a task to occupy yourself. The stables could use some attention."

"My attention?"

"Yes. Rub down the horse. Muck the stalls."

"Ah. Yes." He nodded as though he were familiar with all those things and had not spent the bulk of his life in London, paying someone else to tend to his horse at the end of the day. He would figure it out. He nodded politely. "Of course." Kellan started for the door but stopped at the sudden words to crack over the air.

"Oh, Mr. Fox, if that is even your real name—"

He turned. "I assure you, it is my real—"

"I do not care for your assurances." She swiped a finger through the air in a rather frightening manner, reminiscent of a stern schoolmaster. "Just heed me well in this. If you hurt this woman . . . if you lie, cheat or steal from her, I will deliver pain upon you."

He blinked. She was not jesting. Not even exaggerating in the slightest.

An awkward beat of silence fell.

He finally found his voice. "Fair enough. I understand your meaning perfectly." He nodded once, and then turned to go and muck the stable, leaving the two women alone to talk about him and all the ways he was going to ruin Gwen Cully's life.

Chapter Thirteen ⟨⟩

"Did I happen to walk in on him sucking your finger?"

It was not the question, worded in sharply affronted tones, that Gwen was expecting to hear from her friend. She had almost forgotten that Imogen had witnessed *that* in the face of Imogen's rather severe interrogation.

She flushed warmly from her face to her toes. Gwen had *not* forgotten about the way his mouth felt on her, however. Nor would she ever. Her finger still tingled. Along with other parts of her body.

She opened and closed her mouth, considering how she wanted to explain Kellan Fox to her friend. She was still struggling to explain him to herself.

Normally she and Imogen were quite forthcoming with each other, but this did not feel like a confidence she wanted to share with her. Partly because she knew her friend would declare her mad, and their scheme mad. Their approaching nuptials mad. All of it . . . madness.

And partly because Gwen felt like this was something personal, something private between herself and Kellan. Their arrangement was no one else's business. Not even Imogen's, the one person in this village she usually confided in.

That had always been Imogen's role. Advisor. Mentor. As the vicar's daughter, she had been the town's shepherd—or shepherdess. Especially during the last few years. Her father may have still been the vicar then, but he was not a young man anymore. He was feeble and absentminded. It was Imogen who had done everything. Imogen who had tended to the villagers of Shropshire. Imogen who gave everyone counsel—including Gwen.

But she was married now and expecting her first child. Naturally her priorities had shifted, and Gwen would not unburden herself to her.

"Gwennie, did you hear me?" Imogen shook her head, looking quite worried, even distressed. "What is happening? What are you doing?"

"You read the banns." She donned a neutral smile. "We are to be married. Mr. Fox . . . Kellan and I. Such things happen to people when they develop feelings for each other. I am certain you can understand that as someone who has not been married for very long yourself."

Imogen's eyes grew large in her face. "Of course, I can, but I was in love with my husband when—"

"From the very start?" Gwen snorted. "Come now, Imogen. I know that is not true and so do you. You knew each other for years and I recall you were not always overly fond of him. In fact, you quite despised him."

"*Despise* is a strong word, but very well. It was not love from the beginning. Love grew, but we always had attraction. Always that. It was always there. A fire between us—"

Gwen laughed and pointed to the door. "Have you seen the man that just left my kitchen? Why would you not believe there is genuine attraction between us? Apparently every female in the village has been panting after him since his arrival."

"*You* are not *every* female."

For some reason, perhaps unfairly . . . *certainly* unfairly, Gwen heard these words as: *You are not female.*

She knew she was projecting this onto her friend. Just as she knew that had to do with her own concerns and apprehensions. Spending her life in a smithy, working in a profession that was typically reserved for men had almost canceled her as a woman in the eyes of her community. It had never mattered before though. She had never cared. Gwen almost preferred it. Somehow it had spared her from societal expectations and the pressures placed upon those of her gender. In some manner, it had left her free.

Now although . . . she cared.

It stung. She did not appreciate the disbelief everyone was treating her to when it came to the notion of attracting a man as virile and handsome as Kellan Fox.

"I am not so different from other females. Rest assured, I am a woman with all the usual working parts." *With feelings and desires.*

"Of course, of course!" Imogen shook her head, her expression earnest. "Granted he is exceedingly attractive . . . as are you! But I do not trust him and certainly you cannot trust him either."

Gwen studied her friend, thinking about that and what she truly meant. "Oh. I understand. It is *his* attraction for *me* you doubt." Alongside everyone else.

Imogen flushed. "Gwen! Why, no! I did not say that."

"You did not have to. I mean . . . it is what everyone else, the entire village, thinks, too."

"It was not my intention to imply that you are undesirable. Of course not. You are perfectly lovely. It's only—"

"Only that I am a spinster who has never been courted. A female blacksmith no one wants. It would be an embarrassment for a man to have me on his arm." She did not count the insulting proposition from Meyer as courting. That was something ugly and rotten. Not courting. "And why should an attractive man want me? Is that not the right of it?"

There was a time when Imogen had been a spinster, too. When everyone in town viewed her as someone relegated to the shelf. Gwen had thought her friend would be more understanding . . . more supportive. Why should she automatically believe the worst? Even if the worst was true.

"Oh, Gwen. No." Imogen shook her head miserably. "I am not saying that, but please. This man is not to be trusted. Clearly. I worry for you with him."

"You should not distress yourself over me. Not in your condition."

Imogen glanced down at her swelling belly, smoothing a hand over the bulge. "I cannot simply shut off my worry for you."

"You think our betrothal is a farce." *Because it is a farce.* She should not be offended by Imogen's suspicions considering the truth of that. It was irrational of her. And yet it stung her pride.

She felt a moment of indecision. It struck her that perhaps it would be easier to go ahead and confess the arrangement she had struck with Kellan Fox to her friend, but then she quickly quashed that idea. She could indeed unburden herself to Imogen and confide the truth of everything, but reading the pity in Imogen's eyes was the ultimate deterrent. She could not tell her. Pride stopped her. The truth stuck in her throat. Imogen would not approve. Her friend would likely never leave her alone with him once she heard it.

Imogen stared at her intently with her far-too-wise eyes. Wise and probing. "You think it is *not* a farce? It is truly grounded in affection and commitment to one another?"

Gwen fidgeted under her friend's focus and moistened her lips. Rather than answer, she said, "You needn't worry for me. He's not going to murder me in my sleep."

"Do you *know* that?" Imogen shivered as though she believed that scary prospect to be possible.

"Imogen," she chided, reaching for her friend's hand and giving it a squeeze. "You worry too much." She pointed to Imogen's belly and said in her kindest voice, "You have more important things to concern yourself with."

"You are worth worrying about. Letting this man into your life . . . there are definite concerns I don't think you are considering—"

"They are *my* concerns, Imogen. I am capable of managing myself." She nodded in the direction of the door. "And him."

"You think you can manage him?" She waved to the door through which Kellan Fox had departed and laughed harshly. "That swindler? That criminal? Gwen, he makes his living fooling people. He is fooling *you*."

"He has been exposed for what he is. He cannot dupe me. I know what he is . . . or rather what he was," she corrected.

"What he still *is*! You think he is done with those ways? You think he can never lie to you again? Never hurt you because his fraud has been revealed? Do not be naive, my dear friend. He is still that person who lies, cheats and steals."

"I did not interfere or speak out when you decided to wed Butler, and at the time I would have had just cause. I would appreciate it if you would simply be my friend and respect my decision, as well."

Imogen gazed at her for a long moment before nodding once with seemingly grim resolve and squaring her shoulders. "Of course." She exhaled. "I respect your good judgment. You've only ever been sensible, after all."

"Thank you."

"But promise me you will take care of yourself, and remember you can come to me for anything." Imogen stepped forward and embraced Gwen, the large bulge of her belly between them. "I will do my best to keep my nose out of your affairs until then, but you know me. I am a busybody. Not one to stay out of people's affairs. I will be lurking about . . . dropping in from time to time."

"I would expect no less." Gwen chuckled.

"Papa may have stepped down from his position, but I still see the people of Shropshire as very much my concern and that includes you, my friend. Now." She smiled brightly. "I shall leave you to the rest of your day. I know you are busy. You always are."

"Thank you."

Gwen escorted Imogen from the house. She closed the back door behind them both and waved her farewell. She started down the path to the stable to check on Kellan. He had not looked too certain of himself when she had directed him to muck the stall.

She heard the rhythmic scrape of the shovel even before she entered the space. She peered into the stall to find him working as diligently as any farmhand. He was shirtless, sweat glistening off his broad chest. His arms were thick bands of muscle rippling and straining as he worked the shovel, scooping dung into a waiting wheelbarrow. It should not have been a mesmerizing sight. Nothing about the scene should have stirred her.

He looked up and caught her staring. He paused, a light smile taking hold of his face. "Is this what you had in mind?"

"Yes. You are doing fine." This gorgeous beast of a man was shoveling horseshit for her. *For her.* She had never seen a more beautiful sight. It was the nicest thing anyone had ever done for her. She would take this over flowers or jewelry or any other present.

"I already fed the horse—"

"Sally."

"I beg your pardon?"

"Her name is Sally."

"Sally is fed, and I will rub her down after I finish here."

She nodded, a happy, silly euphoria stealing over her, which she quickly attempted to tamp down. This would only be for a year. Just long enough to make a difference and get her solidly back on her feet.

He held her gaze, heated promise gleaming in those dark eyes and she knew he was recalling their conversation . . . his suggestive words before Imogen interrupted them. She recalled it, too. The warm hum of blood in her veins. The low throb in her belly. His words as he sucked honey off her finger. She took a fortifying breath. If he thought, or hoped, to resume where they had left off he would be mistaken.

"The original agreement between us stands." He stared at her without commenting. "Without . . . alteration," she added because it needed to be said. "It is not . . ." She thought back to the word he had used. "Negotiable."

"Very well." Clearly he understood her meaning and accepted it. "Whatever you think best. I would not wish to pressure you or make you feel uncomfortable. Not after all you have done for me."

She nodded. "Quite so."

It was for the best and not in the least bit disappointing. Even if her entire being felt strangely bereft at his gentlemanly acquiescence. As though she had just lost something she could never get back.

Chapter Fourteen ❧

Nineteen days until the wedding . . .

*T*he following day was Sunday. That meant church for the good residents of Shropshire, which included Gwen Cully, Kellan's bride-to-be.

Bride-to-be. He shook his head at that bit of strangeness.

Church for Gwen also meant church for him. They were a couple now and that meant they did things together. He had attended church before. Naturally. Contrary to what the world might believe of a man such as himself, he was not a completely uncivilized scoundrel.

He had stepped foot in many a church and not instantaneously burst into flame. He recalled his small hand nestled in his mother's grip as she led him down an aisle and turned into a pew where they took their seats. He remembered lowering to his knees alongside her and praying for the soul of Da, as she directed him.

His father had always been the subject of her most fervent prayers. Kellan had watched her lips move feverishly, the sound of her soft pleas a whispered hush on the air as she bowed her head in prayer, begging for the salvation of her beloved husband.

She might have been married to a ne'er-do-well, but she knew him for what he was. She loved him for all his many faults anyway, but nothing could erase that she had been a God-fearing woman. That meant attending church and offering up all the necessary prayers.

Later in his life, after his mother had died, he frequented church far less, but his father had once courted the spinster daughter of a wealthy merchant out of Brighton who was a rather devout and pious man.

For several months they had attended church regularly with the lady and her father . . . during which time Da had fleeced his unsuspecting prospective father-in-law out of several hundred pounds under the ruse of an investment.

Kellan frowned at that memory. He had not thought of that particular lady in quite some time. He had just been a lad then, no more than ten years of age, but she had been kind to him, always sneaking him sweetmeats, treating him as a mother might. He supposed the notion that he would be her stepson had been in her mind and she had taken a liking to him. Da was courting her, after all. She had believed he wished to marry her.

He hoped the lady had met someone else who treated her properly, someone much more deserving than his father. He winced. He knew she would not have had to look very far to find such a man.

"This is a terrible idea." Gwen's feet stalled several yards from the church beneath the canopy of an oak tree.

He turned to face her. She did not wear trousers today. She was attired in the same modest blue wool dress she wore to dinner the previous two evenings and he could not help wondering if this was her only dress. Her hair was pinned, as usual, in tidy plaits around her head. "Do you or do you not usually attend church services on Sunday?" he asked.

She nodded rather bleakly. "I do."

"Then we should continue to do what is normal for you, should we not?" They would have to present themselves as a couple in this village, to these people, to her neighbors with regularity. She would have to overcome her aversion to going out in public with him.

She swallowed visibly. "I suppose so."

He motioned toward the doors of the church. He was already quite familiar with those doors. They loomed open presently. The banns were posted there, pinned to the thick wood, his name boldly displayed, binding him to the woman beside him.

A steady stream of villagers flowed through the doors. No one had spotted them yet, but it was only a matter of time. Only a matter of time before all eyes were fixed upon them. Then Gwen Cully might lose her nerve completely.

He grasped her elbow before that could happen and murmured encouragingly, "Come along now. Let us do this."

This was her town, her people, her past, current and prospective clients. He did not wish her to feel alienated. Especially as he would be the reason for such alienation. With that thought running through him, he forced himself to maintain a mien of utter cheerfulness. When he did look at Gwen Cully again he made certain that he looked perfectly besotted.

She nodded resolutely at his words, reminding him of the confident lass he had first met when he invaded her smithy. "Very well." She moved ahead, walking with her head held high and her shoulders squared back.

The good vicar spotted them first as they approached. His face lit up with a bright smile. "Good morning, Miss Cully and Mr. Fox."

Others turned to gawk at them. Kellan recognized a few of them from the day of his near hanging. Some of those faces looked only slightly less cross. He did not doubt that if the cry for a rope went up once again some of these people would still be in favor of that.

One face stood out in particular. Young Miss Blankenship glared at him. The entire family, in fact, treated him to hot, venomous stares. Her mother and father looked every bit as embittered as their daughter.

"Ouch," Gwen murmured beside him. "If looks could destroy." She shook her head as they entered the church side by side. "Just remember you were the one who insisted we come." Following that whispered reminder, she strode ahead of him down the aisle.

He stared after her. Gone was her hesitancy. There was not the slightest whiff of vulnerability about her now. She was once again a Viking queen. She took her seat in a pew in the middle of the church, holding herself proudly as she faced forward. He followed close and seated himself beside her.

The vicar advanced down the center aisle to take his place at the front of the church. Following his greeting, he led the congregation in song, the familiar hymn filling the air.

Upon finishing, he bestowed a benevolent smile on his parishioners, cleared his throat and began an oration on the subject of forbearance. It was a deliberate choice. Several times his gaze fixed on

Kellan before sweeping the congregation at large. Members of his flock shifted with seeming discomfort in their seats as he talked about tolerance and the act of turning one's cheek. Kellan felt his lips twitch but he maintained a stoic expression for the most part.

By the time the service came to a close the air felt notably subdued. He even noticed a few tentative smiles cast their way. He would not go so far as to say anyone seemed apologetic for their lack of control two days ago, but rather they appeared more amenable to moving forward with him in their midst.

He was to be one of them, after all. There was some irony in that. He had never belonged to a community before. He had never stayed put that long. Even in his youth, when he and Da lived in Town, they'd moved from one part of the city to another with strategic frequency. Roots meant detection. Detection meant discovery. Da had taught him that. Clearly he had not followed his own advice. He'd been enjoying himself too much at Penning Hall, reveling in his role as the duke. He'd broken his own rules and not left when Kellan had beseeched him to.

There had been times, especially lately, that Kellan longed for an end to his nomadic existence. Days where he did not have to look over his shoulder, where the ground did not feel constantly unstable under his feet, where he had roots and honest purpose in life. His father always told him they never hurt anyone—that their crimes were victimless.

Kellan only had to recall the kindly spinster from Brighton to doubt that. His father swindled other women over the years, too. Observing Da all those times, Kellan had vowed to be different—to have his own code. There were thieves and then there were thieves. Not all were without honor.

Kellan liked to think he was one of the good ones—a thief with principles. He never took from someone what they could not afford to lose. He never broke any hearts or left anyone ruined. He believed the greatest harm he had dealt was to the inflated egos of a few very wealthy, arrogant men. And he tried to give back to those less fortunate.

If he saw a struggling family, a child begging for coin on the streets, a woman with bone-thin shoulders walking home in the cold at the end of the day with a meager shawl wrapped around her, he would lighten his own pockets and give to them.

The congregation stood up from the pews and filed out of the church. Kellan did his best to keep in mind that he had a role to play, like so many times before. His performance was more important than ever because it was not only for his benefit. It was for Gwen Cully, too. Her future depended on him. He was alive because of her and he would do his best to repay her for that debt.

The one person who did not appear softened after the young vicar's kindly didactic efforts from the pulpit was the young Miss Blankenship. The well-dressed lady stood with her arms crossed near her waiting carriage, her features drawn tight as she glowered in his direction. Although he had tried not to encourage the young lady, she had been most zealous in her pursuit of him. Clearly she begrudged him for that.

As Miss Cully was waylaid outside the church by Mrs. Dove and locked in conversation, Kellan found himself . . . not alone.

Rather than the bitter Miss Blankenship confronting him, it was her father he found himself facing. He braced himself for the imminent words of outrage from this aggrieved and irate papa.

Kellan nodded deferentially. "Sir," he greeted. He could think of little else to say. He held himself tightly, waiting for whatever was to come, counting it as his due.

"You, sirrah, should mark yourself very fortunate indeed." His nostrils quivered in disapproval. Mr. Blankenship's gaze flicked to Gwen Cully. "If not for *her*, you would have quite deservedly met your end and would not be standing here now bold as you please."

Kellan inhaled and nodded stiffly, not about to argue with the veracity of that statement. "I am grateful indeed, sir."

Blankenship sniffed and turned his gaze on his petulant daughter moping nearby with her mother and a few other well-attired matrons. Clearly she wished to depart, but her mother was deeply enmeshed in her friends.

The young lady had shared with Kellan that her sister was recently wed. He had sensed the urgency in her to likewise enter into the state of matrimony and join ranks with her sister. Kellan knew he had been her target.

"Now *I* must take her to London so that she might find a proper husband like her sister before her," Mr. Blankenship grumbled. "That was a wretched experience. I detest the city."

"I am sorry to hear that."

The older man snorted. "What good does your apology do me, if that even amounts to an apology?" he asked waspishly and with such heavy accusation that Kellan felt compelled to say something—not so much in his defense but as to assure the gentleman that nothing toward had happened between him and his daughter.

"Sir . . . I promise I only ever accorded your daughter the utmost respect. I made no untoward advances—"

Blankenship waved a hand in annoyance. "I

know that . . . but I am in no less a dire state. My daughter believes herself to be in love with you. Now I have to rectify that."

Kellan winced.

Blankenship continued, "She is crushed and does not even wish to entertain other eligible suitors." He shook his head. "It is as though you have bewitched her, and ruined her for anyone else."

Kellan swallowed down the unhelpful urge to insist that he had done his best to discourage the lass. The Blankenship chit had been as tenacious as a bloodhound, hunting him down at every occasion . . . even showing up uninvited to the grand ducal hall.

One time she had been bold enough to appear unchaperoned whilst he had been strolling through the Penning's vast gardens. She had popped out from a hedge like an impudent squirrel and attached herself to his side. Fortunately his father soon joined them, saving him from what could have been a compromising and disastrous situation.

Obviously Blankenship would not appreciate that particularly unflattering anecdote, as it did not cast his daughter in the most favorable light. Calling the chit a tenacious bloodhound would understandably come across as an insult.

The truth of the matter was that Kellan's title, stolen as it had been, had bewitched the lass and nothing more. It had naught to do with *him*. It had not been Kellan himself to enamor her. Not his good looks. Not his charm or winning personality. Not the breadth of his shoulders.

If he had not presented himself as the Penning heir, if he had just been a man, a yeoman or any simple man of humble means, she would not have looked twice at him. She certainly would not have stalked him with the resoluteness of a lioness after her next meal.

"I am certain all the many diversions and charming society in Town will make her forget all about me."

Blankenship peered at him with a jaundiced, doubtful look. "You don't have much experience with the hearts of young ladies, do you?"

Kellan shifted uneasily on his feet. Before he could arrive at a suitable response, the gentleman added, "How foolish of me. Of course, you have *ample* experience . . . You simply do not care. A man who goes about seducing and having his way with every vulnerable softheaded young lady to cross his path"—*was he saying his daughter was softheaded?*—"has the morals of a satyr. I am certain you've been seducing and ruining young ladies for years now. The status of their hearts means naught to you."

Kellan never toyed with women. That was what set him apart from his father. He never manipulated the affections of ladies to land a purse or perpetrate a ruse. That was a line he would not cross. However he did not think the angry papa before him would believe that even if he was willing to listen to him. Blankenship only wanted to vent his spleen, not hear Kellan's excuses.

The gentleman was not finished with him either. Blankenship looked him up and down with a curling lip. "How do you live with yourself? You're a scoundrel through and through. Rest assured, if I was not convinced that my daughter was still in possession of her virtue, you would have met your end already."

Kellan nodded stiffly, accepting the man's vitriol as his due.

Upon delivering that resounding denouncement, it seemed Blankenship was finally finished with him. He turned away abruptly and moved on to rejoin his family without a backward glance.

Kellan stared after him. A slight sound had him looking over his shoulder only to discover Gwen standing there, watching him, obviously listening.

Apparently she had overheard the entire exchange and that only made him feel low. Embarrassed even . . . embarrassed *mostly*.

No doubt Gwen Cully thought him the lowest of vermin and was regretting the day he burst into her shop. Regretting the day she had followed after him when a mob hauled him from her smithy. Regretting the day she ever risked her reputation for a thief like him with a lie. For some reason that stung the most. He did not like the notion that she regretted saving him, that she thought him deserving of Blankenship's embittered words.

Clearing his throat, he turned forward to face her and gave a circumspect nod as though she had not just witnessed that. "Are you ready then?"

She considered him, not speaking and that was almost worse because it left him imagining what she thought—and none of it was good.

He reached out to take her elbow to escort her. They had not walked very far from the churchyard before she murmured, "Well." He tensed amid the heaviness of her pause. "I would say that Mr. Blankenship did not quite grasp the spirit of the vicar's sermon. It did not put him in a forgiving and charitable mood at all."

He laughed slightly, relieved at her levity. Relieved that she did not look at him like he was something to be scraped off the bottom of her shoe. "No, it did not."

His footsteps crunched beside her as they trod over fallen leaves, and he heard himself speaking. The words were not planned, but he had to get them out there between them. "It's not true what they say, you know."

She slid him a puzzled look. "What is it that *they* say?"

"What they say about me . . . what Mr. Blankenship said is not true." He knew she had heard the man's bitter words. "I have not had my way with every woman in the village."

She stopped and stared at him for a long moment. As he waited for her reaction, he realized her opinion mattered to him a great deal.

"I am sure I do not care." She shrugged mildly as though it truly did not matter to her. "One thing you should know about me . . . I do not place a great deal of stock in the opinions of others. If I did, I would not be who I am." She pulled a face. "A female blacksmith? Come now. How would that come to pass if I cared what others thought of me? Do you know how many times it has been suggested that I sell the smithy, don a dress—every day, mind you—marry and produce a brood of children as a proper woman ought to do?"

"People say that to your face?" He felt outrage on her behalf.

She nodded vehemently with widening eyes. "Oh, yes. So many *kind* and *well-meaning* people have said that to my face . . . and more. I have lost count. Rest assured, I do not listen to what others say."

"I suppose not." He chuckled. "So you do not believe me as wicked as a seraph then?"

She looked at him archly. "Oh, I did not say that. I will have to decide that for myself."

"Fair enough."

She smiled tentatively and motioned beyond them. "Shall we go home now?"

Home. The word jarred him a bit, but he nodded.

They were not the only people leaving the churchyard on foot. He gently clasped her elbow. That simple touch felt right. What a betrothed couple ought to do. Nothing too intimate. Perfectly acceptable behavior in public. And he liked touching her. There was no denying that.

Ahead of them a trio of young girls cast unsubtle glances back at them. Their parents strolled far in front, allowing them their space.

Their giggles and whispers were not discreet. Nor were they technically whispers.

Gwen's jaw locked tightly as their voices carried on the air.

"Can you believe it? She is a giant. Her hands are bigger than my papa's hands."

"He can't really love her. He said that to save his neck."

More laughter ensued. He shot Gwen a quick look. She heard every word. Of course. Her cheeks burned brightly as though someone had slapped her. That was some irony, of course. Only moments ago she had claimed not to listen to what others said, but she heard these young ladies now. Clearly.

The levity had dissipated from her face as she listened and absorbed every cutting, brutal word.

"Can you imagine working and living as a blacksmith? How mortifying!"

"I hate to say it, but she should stick to trousers. She looks ridiculous in that dress!"

A small sound escaped Gwen. It was soft. A warble on the air that was almost animal-like. Nearly inaudible, but he heard it. He heard it and he recognized the pain in it. A flash of anger overcame him. Gwen did not deserve such unkindness.

"I was not there to witness it, but I heard he kissed her!"

"Oh! I saw it. It was clearly a sham. He looked as though it sickened him. Poor fellow."

Poor fellow? Apparently they were not part of the faction that had wanted him dead.

He glared at the little brats, but they did not appear to notice. When they looked back it was only to gawk at Gwen. They no doubt saw the hot wash of color staining her face from their nasty remarks and it clearly fueled them.

He tugged her a little closer to his side, covering her hand with his own and giving it a comforting squeeze. He wanted to do more than that, however. He wanted to lash out and inform those little pests just how very desirable he found Gwen Cully.

"*I saw it, too. He most definitely looked repulsed.*"

That comment triggered more obnoxious giggles. The three of them sent a long deliberate look over their shoulders at Gwen. They knew Gwen Cully heard them and they relished it. He realized they wanted to affect her. They wanted to see more than her blushing face. They wanted to see her break. The wretched girls wanted tears.

They were clearly doing what they were doing, saying what they were saying, to witness her reaction. They wanted a spectacle.

He was only too happy to give them one.

Chapter Fifteen ❧

*K*ellan said her name firmly. "Gwen."

She dragged her gaze away from the snickering girls. "Yes?" she asked distractedly. The wounded look in her eyes cracked something in him. A surge of protectiveness swept through him.

He placed a finger under her chin. As tall as she was it was not necessary to tip her face up to him that very much, but the contact alerted her to his intent. Her distracted air vanished and her eyes flared wide as he dipped his head and placed his lips over hers.

He intended to deliver a sweet, chaste kiss that effectively silenced the vicious run of remarks coming from the trio, but the instant his lips touched hers that was forgotten.

The kiss was no longer for show.

It was no longer to silence a few bullies.

He forgot himself. He forgot what was proper and kissed her as a man kissed a woman when they were alone. When they were free to engage and surrender to their secret longings . . . when those secret longings broke free from the binding darkness.

He increased the pressure of their lips, deepening the kiss as his fingers slid around her neck, caressing the soft skin of her nape, positioning her face for him at just the right angle.

Her gasp filled his mouth and then her hand was on his chest, pushing him away.

He lifted his head and stepped back.

Her eyes were wider than ever, locked on his face. Her lips moved, clearly searching for words. "What are you doing?" she hissed.

"Smile," he softly advised. "We have an audience."

Her gaze whipped from him to the girls that had been tormenting her only moments before. They had stopped and turned to gawk fully now.

Gwen glanced around them then, clearly assessing their surroundings to see if they had attracted any further notice. No one else seemed aware of their public gaffe, so there was that bit of good fortune at least.

A shaky smile curved her lips as she turned her attention back to him. He reclaimed her hand and nestled her fingers in the crook of his elbow.

"What were you thinking?" she asked through clenched teeth. She started walking. He kept pace with her.

"I was thinking only of you and silencing those little monsters."

"They are *children*! You should have ignored them."

"As you were ignoring them?"

The color returned to her cheeks. "Yes. I was. I *am*."

He snorted. "Children or no, you were not un-affected by their words."

Gwen Cully was not the crying type. He already knew that about her. And yet she had been hurt.

"Whatever *I* was, it was not *your* place. They were just words. I told you I don't care what others think of me—"

"That's a lie. I saw your face. Your eyes."

She visibly swallowed, her throat working. "I flinched perhaps. Be that as it may, I don't need you saving me from them—or anyone."

"As someone who was recently rescued—by you, in fact—it is not a terrible thing." He tipped his head as though in contemplation. "It is not a crime to accept help, you know. It's not *bad* when someone lends assistance." He moistened his lips and added, "It reminds you that you are not so alone in the world."

She stared at him blankly. "What are you talking about? Lend assistance?" She shook her head in bewilderment. "You *kissed* me. In public. Again."

He chuckled. "Is that what is so distressing to you? No one witnessed except the girls. Even if they tell others, I suspect their story will be taken with a grain of salt. From the sound of it they do not seem to be a reliable source in any matter." They deemed Gwen Cully repulsive. That alone marked them as delusional.

"But how was that assisting me? You cannot continue to kiss me to prove that we . . . *love* each other. That is not how it works." She whispered *love* as though it were a foul word.

His lips twitched. "I think that is *exactly* how it works when two people are infatuated with each other. They kiss. Frequently. At every opportunity." He nodded in the direction of the now-retreating girls. "It put a stop to their taunts, did it not? Now they see you as you are."

"As I am?" she echoed indignantly.

He paused, suddenly feeling as though he were exposing himself with his next words. And yet he was unable to refrain from saying them. "Beautiful," he said gruffly. "You are beautiful and tempting. Nothing about you is repulsive. Far from it. And they should see that—they should know."

She looked astonished. As though, unbelievably,

no one had ever said that to her before, and that seemed the true crime here, surpassing even his own misdeeds. No one had told this woman that she was beautiful before.

She averted her face, looking away from him as though uncomfortable with the praise, uncomfortable with his intent scrutiny. The wind rustled the tiny fair hairs framing her face and he resisted the urge to brush a finger along there. She was extraordinary to behold.

After a moment, she turned, composed and bearing a neutral expression. They continued down the lane, passing the storefronts all closed for the day and turning off High Street onto her lane. He marveled at that for a moment. What if he had not taken a left in his flight from the angry mob and bolted down her street and dived into her shop? What if he had taken a right? Or proceeded straight ahead?

If he had never sheltered in her smithy they would not have met. They would not now be playing out this charade. He might even be dead. The true Penning heir would likely have arrived in time to stop that, but perhaps not. He shook his head slightly. Strange how a sudden and unplanned decision could affect the course of one's life.

Her shop and house loomed ahead, beckoning.

"So what if those girls were talking about me?

It's not the first time. It won't be the last time. As you are going to be staying awhile, you best get accustomed to people talking about me. You need not defend me. I am not made of glass. I will not break, Mr. Fox. So if you please, keep your pity kisses to yourself."

Pity kisses? Is that what she thought? That he received no pleasure from the performance and it was a simple duty for him?

She removed her hand from his arm and stepped back, the actions jerky with agitation.

"I cannot promise to cease trying to protect you. That is what a husband does."

"You are not my husband. Yet."

He inclined his head once in acknowledgment. "I imagine a betrothed would behave in much the same manner as a husband when it comes to protecting the woman in his life."

She blinked several times. "Perhaps. But I am not accustomed to anyone . . . to someone . . ." Her voice faded away, but he heard the words she left hanging, unspoken on the air. They spiked anger in him at the pure unfairness of it all.

It should not feel so strange to her to have someone looking after her. Perhaps his outrage was more personal than it should be because he knew what that was like. Kellan understood what it felt like to be alone—to not have anyone that would support you through life's hardships.

No one had looked out for him save his mother and that was a long time ago. He and his father had functioned more as partners than father and son. More often than not, he had felt like the parent in their relationship. Except he would not have abandoned his father. Not as he had been abandoned when he most needed an ally.

He swallowed against the sudden tightness in his throat. "Caring? Giving a bloody damn? Looking out for you?" he demanded with a shrug that belied his intense feelings. "You did that for me when I was a mere stranger. You should not object to me doing the same for you."

She inhaled a ragged breath. Her chin came up a bit. She opened her mouth and closed it several times before saying, "The impulse was kind of you. I'll give you that, but I do not need a protector. I have been looking after myself for quite some time. Even before my father and uncle passed away. I am a capable person." She waved about them. "You're here to help me. Help me in the house, with the garden, the stables and the smithy."

They turned down the front walk leading to her house. "But do not step in if someone is mean to you. Or bullies you?"

She gave him a forbearing smile. "I can handle that on my own. I always have."

He gazed at this stubbornly independent woman

and wondered if he had ever before met a female who resented someone wanting to champion her.

"Very well. Understood." What else could he say?

Of course it would not change how he behaved in the least. If she could save him, then his pride demanded that he return the favor.

She could say what she wanted, but he would not stand by and let someone hurt her.

Chapter Sixteen ⟨⟨⟩

Seventeen days until the wedding . . .

A distant crash woke her.

Gwen sat up in her bed, disorientated for a moment, thinking herself caught in a dream.

Then she heard it again. A very faint banging sound in the otherwise quiet night.

It was coming from outside. Shaking her head, she slipped her feet over the edge of her bed and bolted from her room and down the stairs. Flinging open the door to her house, she stood in the cool night for a moment, listening, straining for a hint of sound that something was amiss. The lane was empty save for a lone dog trotting about its nocturnal business.

She heard it then. A thud and muffled shout coming from her shop.

She sprang to action, not even bothering with her shoes. Rushing to her smithy, she could see one of the windows was busted open, the wood shutters smashed.

Someone had broken into her shop. They had

not even attempted to go through the front door. She'd left her key, so she rushed to the gaping window and peered into the shadowy confines of her shop—to spot two figures wrestling on the floor, bumping into objects and tools, creating chaos and disarray in the normally tide workspace.

She couldn't identify them. It was too dark.

Gathering her nightgown with a fist, she carefully swung herself over the windowsill, mindful of the splinters of wood jutting from the frame.

"Stop, there, you brutes! You're wrecking my shop!"

She dropped down on the ground, but soon realized that was risky as pain lanced the bottom of her feet. With all the debris littering the floor, it was a dangerous endeavor to walk through her smithy in bare feet—especially as these two were wrecking the place.

She peered through the darkness, her gaze acclimating to the murky air. She recognized Kellan's shoulders and barrel thighs . . . and the way he moved, strangely graceful for a man of his size. She'd made a thorough study of him in recent days as he'd worked so diligently and without complaint to every task she set before him. He never even grew out of breath as he labored. His warrior body was made for a life of toil.

She did not know the other man he tussled with. She could see no more than the blur of his face.

"Kellan!" At her shout of his name, he jerked and turned in her direction.

The stranger took advantage of his distraction and bolted for the window. He charged past her, roughly bumping into her. She wobbled unsteadily, trying to regain her balance. Her feet staggered a bit, and her left foot stepped down on something piercingly sharp.

She cried out in pain.

Kellan was at her side then, his arm wrapping around her waist, propping her up. "Gwen?"

"Who was that?" she demanded as she twisted around, trying to identify the blur that was fast disappearing out the window of her smithy.

"I don't know. I caught him breaking into the place."

"Bastard," she mumbled beneath her breath. "Did he steal anything?"

She caught the motion of his shaking head. "I don't know. 'Tis doubtful. Everything seems in place. I caught him at that set of drawers against the wall. It could not have held anything too valuable . . . nothing large at any rate." He motioned to the old drawers she used to store her assortment of nails.

She knew instantly. "Nails," she muttered, biting back an oath.

"What?"

"Nails. They are a commodity. They fetch a

steep price and are often stolen because they're so easy to pocket and transport."

"Oh. Is that what he was after then?"

"More than likely."

It could have been Meyer, of course. Or any member of the mob who objected to her championing of Kellan Fox. There had been quite a few unhappy individuals.

The notion that she had created enemies in her own town gave her a headache. She shook her head and sighed. There was nothing to be done about it now. Perhaps in the future she would consider better security measures. Bars on the window, for instance. Shropshire was not the little village it once was. It was growing, and that meant there would be more instances of crime. It was unfortunate, but times were changing and that meant she had to adapt, too.

She hopped once on her good foot, attempting to disengage herself from Kellan, only clutching his shoulder for better balance. "Please. Light the lamp. Over there." She lowered her foot to the ground, putting the barest weight on it, and then let out a sharp squeak as cutting pain shot up the sole of her bare foot.

He glanced down. "You are not wearing shoes, you daft lass!"

"I didn't have any time to—" She let out a yelp. "What are you doing?" she cried out as he swept her off her feet. One of his big burly arms scooped under her knees whilst the other one supported her back.

The shock of being carried left her floundering for speech, blocking out all the other little surprises of the night. Such as having her smithy robbed and her foot injured.

"Put me down." Her fingers curled into his meaty shoulder. "I'm too heavy."

"Rubbish," he retorted, and she had to acknowledge that he was not out of breath. He did not sound in the least strained or winded. Perhaps she truly was not too heavy for him. She did not think to ever meet a man capable of hauling her off her feet and carrying her about as though she were no heavier than a feather, but apparently she had.

He carried her several strides and set her carefully upon her worktable in the middle of her shop, treating her as though she were something precious.

He stepped back and lit the lamp, illuminating the space, and at that moment she saw the full destruction wrought by Kellan's skirmish with the burglar. "Oh, brilliant," she muttered.

Kellan glanced around. "Nothing that can't be set to rights."

She sighed. "I suppose."

She started to push off from the table, determined to get started on that very task, but he darted in front of her, holding his hands up in the air before her as though to stop her. "What are you doing?"

"Well, if we are to get any work done on the morrow all of this has to be picked up."

"Yes, by me. I will do it. You're injured, lass." His fingers circled her bare ankle and she gave a little jump at the warm contact of his fingers on her skin.

"You?"

"Yes. Me. I'm capable of tidying this place up."

She blinked, staring at him whilst digesting what he was saying.

He continued, "Have I not proven myself capable these last few days? I can manage. I've got a sense of where most things go."

"I . . ." He had eased her workload, helping her about the smithy and stables, and even working in the garden, with nary a complaint. "Capable? Yes. You are that."

"Well, then." His fingers flexed on her. "Relax."

"Wh-what are you doing?"

"Let me see the condition of your foot."

"That is not necessary—"

"Give over now, lass. Stop arguing. Your foot, please."

She relented, girding herself and letting him examine her foot, his fingertips probing her skin delicately. His fingers left a trail of fire that she felt to the core of her.

"Not too deep a cut," he pronounced, "but we should clean it thoroughly and apply that salve of yours and bandage it."

"You needn't fuss—"

His dark eyes flashed at her with a mixture of humor and exasperation. "And you needn't be so stubborn. Were you not the one lecturing me about the importance of not letting a wound fester? What is the matter? Has no one ever taken care of you before?"

She tried to tug her foot out of his grasp, but he would not permit it, his fingers tightening on her heel ever so slightly.

Has no one ever taken care of you before?

The question reverberated through her, stinging and leaving her a bit shaken. She thought about that for a moment, pondering it. Her father. Her uncle. Odette. But only when she was very little. They had loved her and cared for her. It had been years though since anyone had taken care of her like he was trying to do.

She swallowed against the sudden thickness in her throat and told herself she ought not to let that addle her thinking. She must not fool herself into believing that he cared for her in any real and lasting way. A year would come and go.

And so would he.

"Now. Are you going to permit me to help you?"

She nodded once, knowing she looked like a grump. "Yes. If you insist on treating me like an invalid, forcing you to clean this place up by yourself, who am I to refuse?"

"Thank you, oh, gracious one."

A smile twitched on her lips. She started to slide down off the table, but he stopped her, sweeping her up in his arms. Again.

"Kellan, this is not—"

"Necessary. Yes, yes. I know." He managed to unlock the smithy door while still holding her. It was a rather impressive testament to his agility and strength.

He stepped outside and started toward the house. It wasn't complete darkness. The moon cast enough of a glow to light the air around them. He carried her along the short path to the house. "Your kit?" he inquired. "With all your ointments? Is it still in the kitchen?"

"No. Upstairs in my room."

She had left the front door of her house open in her hasty departure. He passed through it, nudging it shut with his shoulder, and then marched her up the stairs to her bedroom as though it were the most natural thing in the world for him to do so.

He set her down on her bed and then turned for her lamp. A warm glow soon suffused the room.

She scooted back against her pillows, hastily arranging her nightgown so that it properly covered her legs. Only her toes peeked out.

He glanced around them, clapping his hands once efficiently. "Now where is that kit?"

She pointed. "At the bottom of the bureau."

He followed her direction and opened the doors, removing the kit and approaching her once again on the bed. He sat on the edge as though it was wholly appropriate. The springs squeaked in slight protest at the additional weight, but he paid it no mind as he picked up her foot and plopped it on his lap. Heat suffused her face as she reflected that it had been some time indeed since two people occupied this bed. Certainly she had never thought to share it with another person.

She held her breath, watching him as he proceeded to clean and tend to her wound, eyeing it carefully. Again, she could not recall the last time anyone had made such a fuss over her. Her stupid heart warmed and tripped beneath his kind attention.

"I don't think it is going to require stitching, but you should stay off it for a day. Keep it clean and allow it to close properly," he pronounced after careful study.

"Oh, that is not possible. I can't stay in bed all day. That's indolent." She laughed dryly. "There is too much to be done."

"And I will see to it."

"You?" she asked, trying not to squirm beneath his careful ministrations. Who knew a giant of a man would have such a gentle touch?

His gaze locked on hers. "Again, do I not seem capable?"

"You are not a trained blacksmith."

"I can do other things to help. In the house. The stables. The garden. Bookkeeping. I'm good with numbers. Make me a list of the things you need done and I will see to it."

She sighed. "I really can't. I have orders to fulfill."

"And we will get to those. One day in bed won't hurt."

"Easy for you to say." She watched as he wrapped her foot in binding.

His fingers stilled on her ankle when he finished. "There now."

"Thank you," she murmured, wondering when he would unhand her ankle.

"I will go downstairs and set your shop back to rights then."

She shook her head. "It's the middle of the night. Get some sleep. It can wait until morning."

"Are you certain of that?" He looked amused. "Or will you be unable to fall back to sleep because you will be plagued with the thought of the mess left in your shop?"

Was she so transparent? Or did he already know her that well? She forced a stoic expression on her face. "I will sleep like a baby," she lied.

He laughed. "As I've mentioned, you are a terrible liar."

She winced and then covered it quickly with a pert smile. "Perhaps you can school me as you are such an expert at lying."

"Oh." He shook his head with a smile and pressed a hand to his chest as though wounded. "That is rather harsh."

She giggled. It struck her then that she was laughing in the middle of the night with a man in her bed. Such a circumstance was beyond her imagination.

His fingers flexed, playing lightly over her skin, each touch sending a crackling spike of heat up her leg.

"A list," she said abruptly. "That is a fine idea. I shall make you one."

He held her gaze for a moment before nodding once and twisting around on the bed, searching. Spotting what he was looking for, he rose from the bed and marched to her desk, lifting a pencil and piece of paper off the surface. He brought them back to her.

"Thank you." She quickly started jotting down tasks for him to do. Finished, she handed him the paper. "Here you go."

He took it from her, scanning it quickly. "Very good. I'll see to it."

And she knew he would. It had only been a couple of days, but she already knew him to be a hard worker.

He pointed a finger at her. "Now you stay off that foot. I'll check on you in the morning and fetch you something to eat and see if you need any other help."

She would not be needing any help from him. "Thank you."

"This is why I'm here. To help you." He held her gaze for an awkward moment. In the silence of her chamber, she was achingly reminded of how very alone they were . . . and how late it was. It felt like they were the last two people on earth.

"Thank you," she said tightly. "Good night, Mr. Fox."

He blinked and pulled back slightly and she knew it was due to her formality. It had the necessary effect. A proper reminder that their arrangement was simply an arrangement. Nothing more.

He rose up from the bed stiffly. "Good night."

He departed her room.

She listened to his tread as he descended the stairs. The front door creaked open and thudded once after him. The house went silent again, holding its breath, it seemed, until he returned.

Chapter Seventeen ❧

Sixteen days until the wedding . . .

*K*ellan looked down at the list in his hand. He was halfway through it and it was already morning. He woke early. He had not slept well. After the incident with the burglar, he could not fall back into easy slumber. His blood pumped too swiftly and he'd stared wide-eyed into the dark, wary of the smallest sound. He'd risen before dawn and started on the tasks before light even streaked across the sky.

He tucked the list into his pocket and finished preparing her breakfast.

Gwen Cully underestimated him. On multiple counts. It should not irk him, given how they had met. Why should she think well of him? And yet it did irk him.

She had thought he betrayed his promise and left the morning after they struck a bargain. He supposed it only natural she thought so little of him, but he had given his promise to stay a year with her. He had promised he would help her and he would. In time, when the days rolled into weeks and months, she would see that he wasn't going to slip away in the night. Eventually she would see that she could trust him.

Holding the tray, he took the stairs to her bedchamber. He would have to convince her that he was not eight years old and he could do more than the three items she assigned him. A little teasing might be in order. Perhaps he would even make her smile again, as he had done last night. Her smithy might have been robbed, but he had made her laugh. Before she caught herself and killed all attempt at lightheartedness and fun. Before she had turned all stern and called him Mr. Fox like he was some stranger on the street and not a man she would soon marry.

If that even happened.

They had made an agreement he intended to keep, but he wondered if she would. Would she back out?

It was her idea, true, and she had expressed sound reasoning as to why they should marry, but she was an independent female, rooted in self-sufficiency. He did not envision her releasing her independence so easily. Saying you were going to do something was entirely different from actually doing it.

He knocked once on her slightly ajar door before entering with her tray.

She was already awake and dressed.

He frowned. "I hope you do not bear weight on your foot."

"I hopped on the other one. Promise." She put down the book she was reading and pushed up a little higher on the bed as he approached, eyeing the food on the tray. "Thank heavens."

"Hungry?" he asked.

"Bored."

"Is your book not interesting?" he asked as he settled the tray of food on her lap.

"I've read it before. I've actually read everything in the library at least once."

"A village this size does not have a subscription library?"

"Not yet. Although there is Mr. Gupta. He has an extensive library and is kind enough to loan out his books."

"Perhaps you should prevail upon him."

"No point. Tomorrow I will be up and about and have no time for reading."

"Do you never have time for relaxation and fun? It's important to make time for diversions. Life should not be all toil."

"Um. Leisure time?" She cocked her head to the side as though considering his question. "Not in a decade at least."

He sobered. "Well. I'm here now, Gwen Cully. We will see that you have a little more fun. Life can't be all work. There must be some pleasure to be had between birth and death or what is the point in it all?"

"You're very philosophical." She stared at him for a moment looking thoughtful. Then she blinked and looked down at her food. "Thank you for this. It looks delicious."

"I've always been good with eggs. My da always said it was important to know how to make a proper egg."

She forked a bit of the fluffiness into her mouth. "Well. You have succeeded in that." She followed her bite of eggs with a crunchy bite of toast that he had taken the liberty of spreading jam across. "So that is what your father taught you? The proper way to thieve and the proper way to cook an egg?"

He nodded. "That would be accurate. Yes."

She smiled as she skirted her fork about her plate, chasing a bit of egg. "You know tomorrow I am getting out of this bed."

"We shall see how that foot looks in the morning."

"Nonsense. It's fine now. I shall show you." She set the tray down on her bedside table and flung back her coverlet to demonstrate.

"Oh, no, you don't," he admonished, moving in front of her to block her.

She pushed up to her feet, bringing their bodies

flush, but he gently pushed her back down on the bed, his hands covering her shoulders. His hands remained on her, lingering on her shoulders through her nightgown, appreciating the warmth and shape of her. He loomed over her, his hands still on her, holding her there on the bed.

He couldn't move.

The air between them turned charged, the scant inch or two between them filled with their mingled breaths.

Suddenly he remembered the taste of her, that kiss they had shared in front of a horde of people who wanted to kill him.

He could not help wondering if the heat between them had been an aberration, something brought on by the direness of the situation, the fear of his looming death and desperate need to feel alive.

Doubtful, given the way he was feeling now . . . and had been feeling ever since he'd come to stay here.

But there would only be one way to find out with any certainty.

He lowered his head and closed that tiny space separating their lips. He brushed his mouth over hers gently at first. Once. Twice. Three times. Soft, featherlight kisses, testing, questing, each one growing a little longer, deeper, bolder, granting her abundant time and opportunity to stop or pull back—to make her wishes known. If her wish was *not* this.

That did not happen.

With a groan of satisfaction, his lips fused on hers until he was easing over her, coming down on her on the bed, sinking into the delicious curves of her body.

She was kissing him back, her hands spearing through his hair, her lush body arching up off the bed toward him. Clearly she had forgotten her insistence that their arrangement be without intimacy because her tongue was in his mouth, as eager as his own.

All of her was eager, rubbing against him hotly, singeing him. He felt on fire. Burning for her. His hard cock pressed against his breeches, begging for her.

It was everything he remembered and more. Except this time it was wild and without restraint. It was the two of them. Alone and together in this house, in this room, on this bed . . . it felt as though they had been barreling toward this moment ever since they met. Since the moment he had burst into her shop.

They twisted, rolling until she came atop him. Her hands moved from his hair to his face, holding him there as though he were the most precious and necessary thing in the world.

He had kissed many women in his life, but

no one had ever touched him like that. His cock pulsed, throbbing against her hip, compelling him to thrust. He rolled his pelvis, driving into her yielding flesh.

She moaned, straining against him, attempting to turn, fighting against the tangle of her nightgown, trying to twist around and get him right where they both wanted him to be, between her thighs.

The sound of a bell intruded into his consciousness. He lifted his head from hers with a groan at the insistent clanging. "What is that?"

"The bell. Outside the smithy," she panted, her palms still cupping his face.

"Oh." He breathed hard. "Someone is here."

"Yes. A customer." She stared into his eyes, and he read the flickering emotions there: desire, frustration, disappointment . . . hardening resolve. The resolve took over, pushing out the fire, dampening her visible ardor. She blinked as though coming free of a spell. "You have to go."

He froze, watching her transform into a horrified maiden before him.

Her eyes went a little wild then, dismayed as they skimmed over him. "This isn't right." She shoved at his shoulders, rolling off him. "We can't! Get out of my bed, my room . . . go!"

Groaning anew, he dragged himself from her bed. "Very well. You needn't be shrill. I heard you."

"Do not touch me again. No more kisses!"

His chest lifted on an angry breath as the bell tolled again outside. "Do not pretend this was all me." He pointed at himself. "You wanted this. If we had not been interrupted by that bell I would be inside you right now and you would be reveling in it."

She flinched. "Well, thankfully we were interrupted and I have soundly returned to sanity."

He laughed once, a mirthless bark. "Until the next time, you mean."

"Oh!" She grabbed her pillow and tossed it at him. It bounced lightly off his chest. "There will not be a next time, you beastly man!"

He tried not to flinch at her words, but he felt them as effectively as a well-aimed arrow. He should not have taunted her. It was poorly done of him. She owed him nothing. Certainly not her body. She was an innocent. That much was evident. An innocent who was alone with no family to shield her from the likes of him. She was a good person. She had saved his life. Of course she was too good for him.

She continued, "Our arrangement does not involve you in my bed, do you understand? If that is why you are sticking around, then you best go ahead and leave."

He gazed down at her grimly. "I understand perfectly. I gave you my word. I am staying for the year." He was not so without honor that he had to force his attentions where they were not wanted. He motioned to her tray. "I will come back for this later."

"You needn't do that—"

"I will be back," he said, disappointment pulsing through him. Disappointment in himself . . . and disappointment that he was still not in that warm bed with her, enjoying the obvious delights she had to offer. He doubted he would ever not feel disappointment over that loss. He accepted her rejection, but that did not mean he didn't ache for her. "To check in on you later." He pointed to her foot. "Meanwhile rest that."

Turning, he left her bedchamber to attend to whoever was so insistently ringing the bell outside the smithy.

Chapter Eighteen ⊱

Fifteen days until the wedding . . .

𝒢wen was up on her feet again the following morning, and Kellan Fox had not vanished in the middle of the night. He was still here. He had remained. He held true to his word. She should not feel such surprise over that anymore. It had been several days now, but each morning she released a small sigh of relief to find him up and moving about the place.

She had seen Kellan two more times after their tryst yesterday when he had checked in on her and brought her food. No further *incidents* had occurred. It helped that he had not insisted on examining her foot again. Touching her seemed to be where things went wrong.

Although wrong had never felt so right or so good as when they were tangled together on her bed. It was going to be difficult resisting him. Especially if he continued to kiss her. And yet she must. She must resist him. She would. Consummating their marriage—or betrothal—would only complicate things. She might become confused into thinking they were real . . . that what they had was real. That he could be something permanent in her life.

She dropped her hammer in repeated movements, her breath falling in steady, exerted gusts as she shaped a piece of metal into a sickle. A farmer outside town had placed an order for half a dozen sickles. He needed them for harvesting. She hoped to have them ready by tomorrow. Now that she had help with her other chores that felt like a real possibility.

She banged the heated metal with her hammer until it started to cool and become less pliable. At that point she turned back to her forge, momentarily leaving the sickle resting on the anvil.

She worked the bellows, breathing air into the forge to increase its heat. Satisfied, she picked up her tongs and placed the sickle back in the fire, nestling it into the hottest part of the burning coals. Satisfied that it was again hot enough, she returned it to the anvil to finish shaping the blade.

She worked at a brisk pace, the tendrils framing her face growing damp with perspiration. It felt good to be busy. She was already producing at a quicker rate simply because she did not have to stop to attend to the tasks Kellan was assuming.

He was working in the garden today. He had been occupied there the last few days, planting for the next season before he began harvesting the fall vegetables. It comforted her to know that was being handled and she would not starve in the months ahead. It was one less thing she had to do.

She felt free as she worked in the smithy, her movements and steps lighter. For the first time in months, mayhap longer, she felt as though she was accomplishing something instead of falling further and further behind.

The door to the smithy suddenly opened, banging into the wall unceremoniously. She glanced over her shoulder, partly expecting to see Kellan striding across the threshold, but somehow doubtful of that. Sometimes he checked in on her, curious about her work and to apprise her on his progress. He would never enter a room so brashly and with such heedlessness. He would have more respect for her property. She already knew that much about him.

Indeed, it was not Kellan.

Dread filled her as she lowered her hammer and stepped away from her anvil, facing her caller. "Have you never thought to ring the bell? You cannot just march in here as you please."

Mr. Meyer sauntered into her workshop as though he owned it—which she clearly knew he wished to do. *Her smithy and her.* He made no qualms about that.

He stopped beside her worktable to examine

her labors. Bending, he picked up one of the sickles she had already made. He gave a slight nod in seeming approval of her craftsmanship and returned it to the table. Brushing his hands, he surveyed her domain before turning his attention to her. "Clearly you've made a mistake, lass."

She did not need for him to explain his meaning. It was some surprise that he had not called on her sooner, the very day after the banns were posted, to taunt, gloat or generally torment her.

He continued, "You lost your head and made a mistake. Understandable. It happens to those of your sex from time to time. You're not the most logical creatures. God did not fashion you that way."

She breathed in and out through her nose, fighting for her composure. "I don't think so. There has been no mistake." She gave him a small deprecating smile and motioned to the door as though to suggest he should take his leave through it.

He went on as though she had not spoken. "No shame in making the mistake. The shame would be in not correcting it when you have the chance." He shrugged a mountainous shoulder. "You let pity guide you, and a female should have a tender heart. To be honest, it's nice to see you have such tender sentiment in you. It is quite flattering. You ought to be soft. No man wants a hard woman. I certainly would not wish for that in the mother of my future grandsons."

She flinched. "I am *not* the mother of your future grandsons."

Certainly he was no longer laboring under the delusion that she was marrying one of his sons? Even if her previous rejection had not penetrated, the events in the town square yesterday should put the matter well to rest in his mind. She was no longer eligible.

And yet here he stood, reminding her of the last time he paid her a call and stood in her smithy. She frowned, her gut twisting at the memory of that unwelcome visit.

Of course she had not forgotten. It had been a fortnight ago. He had delivered a rather insulting and unappetizing marriage proposition, offering her either one of his sons. She had sent him away with a stern no and a caution to never cross her threshold again. For all the good that did as he was here now.

She folded her arms across her chest. "I told you. I am not interested in marrying either one of your sons—"

He waved a thick sausage-like finger in her face. "This offer won't be extended indefinitely."

"You promise?"

His face reddened at her quick retort. "Make all the jests you like—"

"Oh, I am not jesting." She fixed her face into the most stoic expression she could manage. "I heartily wish you would stop haranguing me on this matter and leave me be. I am not even unattached anymore. Now I am betrothed."

"Pfft." He waved a meaty paw. "You are not truly betrothed. It is nothing that cannot be undone. It is not as though you are already married." He looked around. "Is the miscreant still here or did he steal away in the middle of the night with all your valuables?"

She stiffened, loathing how close he came to her secret fears with that question. "He is still here, of course," she huffed. "Why would he not be?"

"Indeed. You claim yours is a love match." Mockery dripped from his voice.

"That is correct." She fought to hold his gaze as she uttered this lie. This was not the time to recall Kellan's insistence that she was a poor liar. She needed to project confidence.

She shook her head. "Why are you doing this?" She waved her arms wide. "By your own admission, your smithy is doing well." She knew the amount of customers she had lost to him. He was doing more than well. "Why do you need me?"

He tsked. "There are still those who stubbornly maintain loyalty to you. Your family's roots run strong here. If you merge with us, then your roots would become ours. There would be no limit to our success. Don't you want to end this feud between us?"

"So . . . you're frightened of a little competition? Of me?" she challenged.

He did not like that. Not at all. His nostrils flared. "I am not afraid of *you*, lass. I want your smithy and you. Plain and simple. I want strong grandsons." He leered at her, looking her up and down. She was grateful her leather apron covered her body from his insulting inspection. "You're built for breeding."

She swallowed back a surge of bile.

It was his turn to smile now. He knew he'd offended her and it pleased him. It seemed he wanted to offend her some more as he added, "Both my boys are quite taken with you. They squabble over who has rights to you."

"Neither of them do!"

"You should be flattered. They are fine lads, my boys." He blithely went on, nodding to himself. "Aye, my eldest son thinks he should have first rights to you as he's my firstborn, but he's concerned you have been sullied."

"Sullied?" she echoed indignantly.

"Yes. Ruined. Besmirched. Despoiled. It's a fair concern." He sank back on his heels and looked her over appraisingly for a long moment. "The question needs to be asked. Did he bed you?"

She knew instantly to whom he referred.

"Oh!" Outrage quivered through her, and her palm tingled with the urge to connect soundly with his face. The gall of the man! How dare he barge into her shop and ask such a thing of her? As though the status of her virtue were any business of his or his son. "How dare you even—"

"I hope you were not so weak and foolish as that. He might stay with you for a bit and sate himself beneath your skirts, but then he will leave you. Before your wedding day. Mark my words. He shall leave you used up and sullied, possibly with a babe swelling in your womb."

His words were disgusting and unwanted . . . and hit far too close to the mark for her peace of mind. Not that Kellan and she had crossed the line and become lovers, but there had been their brief tryst in her bedchamber. That had not been done for the benefit of others. No audience needed proof that they were in love then. She had kissed him because she wanted to do so. Because he made her ache.

She shook her head. "You presume too much. Get out." She fought hard to keep herself from shaking and revealing just how much he had rattled her.

He glanced about her shop as though evaluating it before he continued, "If you are carrying his bastard, the offer of marriage is revoked."

"Revoke it! Revoke it now!" she snarled. "I will never change my mind."

Meyer went on as though she had not spoken. "As long as no bastards come of your little adventure, we can look the other way when it comes to an end. Damaged goods or no, I long to see our smithies merged." He shrugged and looked her up and down in a lascivious manner, making her wonder how safe she would be from him if she were desperate and mad enough to marry one of his sons. The man's attentions made her decidedly uneasy. "And with your impressive stature, I can only imagine the strapping boys to come out of you. You will give us strong sons."

The urge to retch came over her again, but she managed to keep it in, fighting back the bile. "You're a revolting man."

He tsked. "Come. Don't be so proud, lass. I've offered to take you with or without your virtue. How many of the good people in this town would say such a thing? You should be more gracious."

"And what is it *I* get from this *magnanimous* arrangement?"

"Why . . . security, of course. We shall merge our shops and you will have nothing but the children to concern yourself with, which is how it ought to be. Your father should never have brought you up in the smithy. That was his mistake. It's no place for a woman. You belong in the house, raising babies and preparing fine meals for your men."

"Do not speak of my father." She pointed an imperious finger to the door, eyeing the tongs she had left heating in her forge, tempted to take them to his hide if he did not obey. "Leave!"

Ignoring her command, he sighed and craned his neck, glancing about with a curious expression. "Where is the scoundrel?" He continued to look about as though Kellan's big frame could be hiding somewhere. "You are certain he has not abandoned you already?"

"I am right here. And no, I have not."

Gwen snapped her gaze to Kellan. He stepped over the threshold, stopping just behind the brute, Meyer. Tugging off his gardening gloves, he slapped them rather forcefully in his palm.

Meyer turned slowly, seemingly unaffected at his arrival. "Oh, there you are," he murmured drolly. "Enjoying your stay with Miss Cully?"

"It is not a holiday," she snapped.

Meyer shrugged. "I am certain he is enjoying his leisure time here."

"It is not a leisurely holiday. We are betrothed. He will be here longer than a stay." Indeed. An entire year.

Kellan held Meyer's stare, looking him over, equally as scornful. It satisfied her greatly to see that Kellan emitted a fair share of menace as he loomed over the similarly big man.

"Gwen?" Kellan said her name softly, and his

voice was loaded with inquiry. "Are you . . . in need of assistance?"

Meyer snorted. "Ah. You're playing the hero. Is that not chivalrous?"

She took a breath, feeling not so alone in this moment. She felt supported by Kellan's presence. It was a refreshing change. "Mr. Meyer was just leaving."

Kellan arched a brow inquiringly at the man, clearly waiting to see the evidence of that.

Meyer huffed and smiled in a way that was decidedly without mirth. "I'm leaving." He narrowed his gaze on Gwen. "Think on what I have said."

She crossed her arms. "I shall forget you and your words the instant you depart."

Meyer's expression tightened. For a moment he looked prepared to say something more, but a quick glance at Kellan and he refrained. He walked stiffly from the shop.

Kellan faced her. "Are you . . . Did he upset you? What did he say?"

She shook her head, unwilling to repeat his ugly words. She would like to forget them, as she said she would, but she doubted it would be as easily done as that. The man had been a threatening presence ever since he arrived in Shropshire. "'Tis nothing. He's a boor. Nothing more."

Kellan nodded, peering at her closely, looking unconvinced.

"Thank you for coming in when you did," she added. "But I am fine."

"Of course. That is part of the agreement. I am here to help you. That includes helping you manage bullies like that." He nodded his head in the direction Meyer had just departed.

She gazed at Kellan and tried not to let him see how his words affected her, how warm and safe they made her feel. No longer so alone. No longer lonely.

It was a dangerous thing . . . liking that feeling, liking *him*. She did not want either of those things. *Liking* could turn into *needing*, and she could not let that happen. He would not always be here. She would not always have him to intercede when someone like Meyer harassed her. Or a group of young girls taunted her. Or a burglar broke into her shop in the middle of the night. All these things she had to cope with on her own.

She had always been self-reliant and strong, and she intended to stay that way. Strong with him, and strong without him.

Chapter Nineteen ⟡

$\mathcal{F}$ive minutes passed before Kellan slipped out from the smithy and caught up with Meyer before he reached High Street. Gwen thought he was returning to work in the garden. And he would. But not yet. First he would do this. He had to do this.

He knew Gwen would not approve, but he could not let that bastard leave without speaking to him. Not after seeing how rattled she was over the encounter. She had pretended she was not upset. Stubborn lass. She did not want Kellan to know she was shaken, but he did. He knew and he would not do *nothing* about it.

He would speak to Meyer.

"A word, please, sir." Despite the politely worded request, Kellan was not asking the man. He was telling him.

Meyer turned at the sound of Kellan's voice. His lip curled into a sneer at the sight of Kellan hurrying up behind him. "Oh. You."

Kellan smiled tightly. "Yes. It is I."

"What do you want?"

He stopped and squared his shoulders. "I want you to leave her alone."

Meyer blinked and spread his feet a bit wider, bracing and readying himself as though this encounter might become physical. "Oh. I see. Getting territorial so soon, are you? I suppose that is reasonable. You landed yourself in a fine arrangement and do not wish for me to muck it up."

"You know nothing of my situation."

Meyer went on, "I cannot say I blame you. Although it is a step down from a dukedom. But a step up from hanging, to be sure."

"You know nothing of what you speak."

And nothing of me.

"I know a scoundrel when I see one."

Kellan nodded slowly. He would not disagree with that. He was a scoundrel, but he was also determined to do right by Gwen. Not that he would waste his breath convincing this bastard of that. The only person he cared about convincing was Gwen . . . and words were not going to persuade her. It would be his actions and only with time.

"Gwen Cully is not your concern."

"Oh, but she is yours now? Is that it?" Meyer chuckled mirthlessly.

"That's right."

"Oh, that's rich." Meyer shook his head. "You'll tire of this place soon enough. And of *her*."

"I would not count on that," he replied with a surprising amount of ferocity . . . surprising even to him. The urge to plant his fist in the man's face overwhelmed him. He curled his fingers into fists at his sides.

"Come, man. This place is not for you. You're not the manner of fellow to thrive in domesticity. You must be eager to get back to Town and all its buzz and diversions and excitements and beautiful women. Eh? Women who know how to be women. Who dress in gowns and smell of perfume." He waggled his eyebrows. "Why don't you let me help you with that particular endeavor so that you can return there?"

Kellan hesitated, digesting that and not fully understanding. He frowned. "Help me?"

Meyer continued, "Would you not wish to leave this dull place? I can help you with that."

"Are you offering me . . . a bribe?"

"Clever fellow."

Kellan could only stare. Could only absorb what the thick-necked brute was proposing to him.

Meyer elaborated, "What do you need? A horse? Some clothes? Obviously money." He smiled in a very pleased way. "Ah. Money. Of course, that. I could give you enough to get a start on to your next adventure. Come, man. This life is not for you." He motioned around them. "You're not the manner of man to lead a quiet life . . . married to a woman blacksmith." He made an exaggerated sound of disgust.

"You know nothing of the manner of man I am."

"What say you? I can have a horse saddled and waiting for you outside Shropshire tonight, with enough funds packed to get you comfortably through the next fortnight. You can be gone before anyone wakes."

He thought about that for a moment. Thought about Gwen waking to find him gone. She had done that once before and he had been dealt a facer for it.

He knew she would care. But would she . . . *miss* him? Or would she only be worried about the adverse effects on her reputation?

He gave his head a small shake. It mattered not. He would not do it, of course. He could not. Perhaps he once would have, perhaps he would have once pounced on the offer, but no longer. The very notion of accepting the offer and abandoning her to the ridicule of her village and the likes of this wretched man was distasteful to him.

He shook his head again. *No.* It was not even up for consideration.

Certainly Da would have taken the offer. He would have gleefully seized the opportunity. He could hear his father's voice in his head, calling him ten kinds of fool for declining what he would perceive as serendipitous.

Meyer waited, watching him, smiling expectantly.

"I cannot do that," Kellan finally answered.

Confusion flashed across Meyer's face, but he clung to his smile, clearly not ready to give up. "Whyever not?"

"I have not," Kellan began slowly, not about to reveal the workings of his inner thoughts, "finished with harvesting the garden."

Meyer's pleased smile slipped. "Wot?" he blustered. "You're worried about gardening?"

Kellan nodded, smiling slowly, enjoying watching the man unravel before him.

"Gardening?" Meyer repeated, his voice almost shrill with incredulity.

Kellan continued to nod in satisfaction.

"Ah. I see, I see." Meyer rocked back on his heels, his gaze sharpening. "You're enjoying yourself here then," he snarled. "She must be quite the fuck. At least my son has that to look forward to once you finally leave."

Kellan's smile vanished. He grabbed the blacksmith by his jacket with one hand and brought his fist up beneath his chin. Bloody spittle flew.

Instantly they were locked together, tussling, thrashing, delivering blows anywhere they could reach. The man was older, but he was thick and strong like a bull. He landed a blow to Kellan's ribs with a meaty fist that robbed him of breath, but Kellan kept going.

They fell against the side of a building with a crash. Kellan got in another good cuff to the side of the man's head.

Suddenly they were forced apart. A pair of men wrapped their arms around Kellan, dragging him from Meyer. He surged against them, his arms swiping, longing to smash the bastard's face.

"Enough!" one of the men bellowed, squeezing between them.

Meyer shrugged off the man holding him back. "I'm fine." Blood streamed from his teeth. He jabbed a finger in Kellan's direction. "*You!* You'll get yours."

"Stay away from Gwen," he snarled.

The blacksmith tugged his rumpled jacket into place, grimacing as he noted the tear at the seams of his shoulder. With a final glower, he turned and stalked away, turning down onto High Street.

Kellan's breaths fell in ragged pants. It was more than exertion. Fury still pumped through him. Fury at Meyer's words. Fury that he would speak of Gwen in such a manner . . . fury at the notion of the man's son ever touching her.

Gradually, he became aware of the other men staring at him. They looked him over appraisingly, taking his measure. He thought he read what seemed to be respect in their gazes.

"Are you well?" one of the men asked.

Kellan nodded. "Fine," he said gruffly.

"Don't pay that arse any mind." The man stuck his hand out for Kellan to shake. "I'm Calvin Fredericks, Miss Cully's neighbor."

Kellan shook the man's hand, managing not to wince at his sore knuckles. "Pleasure to meet you." He motioned to himself and in the direction of the retreating Meyer. "Sorry for the—"

"No need to apologize. You were taking care of your own." Mr. Fredericks nodded. The men beside him murmured in agreement. "I'm glad to see Miss Cully has found someone with mettle. She deserves that. She's a good one."

Kellan grunted in acknowledgment, his throat thick for some reason. Even with his earlier fury still throbbing in his veins he felt a little humbled at the man's welcome. A week ago the villagers had not been nearly so approving of him. Far from it. "Th-thank you, sir."

The men waved him farewell as he turned back for home. *Home.* He did not permit his thoughts to linger over that mental slip.

He tentatively brushed a hand over his tender ribs as he walked back to Gwen's house, stifling a wince. He was still on his feet and he wasn't limping. There was that at least.

His nose throbbed and he tasted copper in the back of his throat. He swallowed against it, trying to get rid of the unpleasant taste. He lifted his sleeve to wipe at his nose, only to pull back with a streak of crimson on his sleeve. Apparently Meyer had managed a punch to his face. He had not even noticed. At the time, he had only seen red, his ears ringing from the insult given to Gwen.

As he approached he spotted the woman he had previously met, Mrs. Butler, Gwen's protective friend. *Brilliant.* And he looked like this.

The lady stopped before the door to the smithy, not lifting a hand to knock as she eyed him approaching.

"What happened to you?" she asked, her voice rife with censure. She did not trust him, and he could not blame her given the circumstances. The sight of him did not bolster confidence.

He brushed a hand down his mussed and wrinkled shirt and gave it a tug as if that helped. He must look a mess. He was not even wearing a proper vest and jacket as he had been gardening this afternoon. "I—"

Her gaze sharpened on his face. "Were you in a fight?" From the reproach in her voice, she did not find this acceptable.

"I might have had a disagreement—"

"Mr. Fox," she snapped. "I hope you are not going to bring trouble into my friend's life." From the sharpness of her gaze and voice, he suspected she would flay him alive if he did.

"That is not my intention."

"Who were you in a *disagreement* with?" The way she stressed the word *disagreement* indicated how little she thought of him and his description for what had transpired.

He sighed. "Mr. Meyer."

Her expression altered slightly. The distaste was still there, written all over her features, but the distaste no longer appeared to be directed solely at him. "That vulgar man. What did he want?"

Kellan did not respond to that. He knew she was a good friend to Gwen, but this was a private matter—it was Gwen's life—and he would not carry tales. If Gwen wanted to share with her, then that was her choice. He would not, however. Apparently, though, he did not need to answer the lady.

"Ah. I see." She sighed and looked him up and down, as though considering him for the first time and not seeing a complete rogue. "Meyer has been rather aggressive toward Gwen since he moved to Shropshire."

He nodded. He had only been here a short time, but that would be a fair statement.

She continued, "You take exception to that then?"

"I take exception to anyone who makes her feel threatened . . . or unhappy."

Mrs. Butler angled her head thoughtfully as she surveyed Kellan. "Interesting." Her lips twitched in an almost smile. "So do I."

"Then we have that in common."

"It would appear so."

Silence stretched between them and it felt as though some manner of understanding had been reached.

The door to the smithy suddenly opened then to reveal Gwen.

"Imogen, I thought I heard you talking. What are you doing standing out here—" Her voice cut off into a swift gasp then. "Kellan! What happened to you?" Gwen hastened to his side, her hands fluttering to the tear in the front of his shirt and then drifting to his face, the tips of her fingers grazing his raw nose. "Is that blood? Your nose is bleeding!"

He pulled his head away from her searching fingers, his attention still locked on the closely watching Mrs. Butler. "I am fine," he assured her.

"You don't look fine!" Her gaze leapt over him. "It looks as though you have been tussling in the streets with a pack of mad dogs."

That was a somewhat accurate description.

"He had a disagreement," Mrs. Butler unhelpfully offered, suddenly looking as though she were enjoying herself.

Kellan sent the woman a rebuking glare.

"A disagreement! With whom?"

He exhaled. "Meyer."

"Meyer!" Gwen shook her head. "Don't tell me you went after him."

He nodded slowly.

She closed her eyes in a long, pained blink. "You foolish man! What did you hope to accomplish?"

Kellan held Mrs. Butler's stare again as he answered. "It was my hope to dissuade him from bothering you further."

"Dissuade?" She gestured wildly. "And that resulted in fisticuffs?"

"He gave offense."

"Offense?" Her lips compressed in a disapproving line. "What did he say?"

He shook his head. "It does not bear repeating." He was not about to impart the lurid details and upset Gwen.

Mrs. Butler made a noise that suspiciously sounded like laughter. Gwen glared at her friend.

"What?" Mrs. Butler shrugged defensively, her lips twitching with amusement. "I must agree that Mr. Meyer is a rather offensive person."

"See there!" Kellan nodded.

"Oh, I am glad you two find this so vastly entertaining." Gwen waved inside her building. "Of course he is offensive and he gave offense. That is what the blasted man does." She shook her head in disgust. "Come now. Let me look at you and see to your injuries." She glanced back to her friend. "Are you coming inside, Imogen?"

"Oh, no. You seem to have your hands full here." That almost smile played about the lady's lips again. "I will let you tend to your betrothed."

Gwen startled a little at her friend's announcement, and Kellan imagined she felt surprise over the reference to him as her betrothed. It did ring a little strangely to his ears, too. He wondered if it would ever feel natural.

Mrs. Butler waggled a small farewell with her fingers, appearing much more relaxed and at ease than when she had first happened upon Kellan with her friend days ago. "I'll call again soon. You two have a good evening." She strolled away with a buoyant air.

"Come along," Gwen directed and led him inside the warm confines of the smithy.

He glanced around as she moved about her shop, tidying up and putting things away. He assumed she would see to him in the house. He knew her salves were still there from the last time she had tended his wounds. He grinned. Another facer then, too, but that one had been courtesy of her.

As though she could read his thoughts, she explained, "I'll close up the smithy and then we can see to you in the kitchen." She gave him a tolerant smile. "This is becoming a habit, you know . . . patching you up."

"I seem to bring out the physical nature in people . . . and not in the best manner." He did not bother mentioning he had been the first one to lose his temper and strike Meyer.

"You might want to take some time to reflect on that."

He smirked. "Indeed, I might."

She laughed lightly, shaking her head. "It's all fun and games until you are seriously hurt, you know."

"I am fine," he insisted, watching as she began banking the fire in her forge.

"You forget I grew up with a pair of men. Your kind always says that." She shook her head. "Even when it's not true. *Especially* when it's not true."

"My kind?"

"Proud men."

He joined in, picking up a shovel and dumping dirt and ash over the burning coals. He winced once, the movement pinching his sore ribs. She did not miss the reaction.

"See there." She waved at him. "You don't appear fine."

"I've suffered far worse. Trust me."

"Well, there is no need to suffer at all, is there? Not when I have healing salves."

She dunked a pair of still-hot tongs and a

hammer into a nearby barrel of water. The tools hissed, steam coming off the surface of the water.

"You don't have to stop working on my account."

"It's getting late. I have some things to do in the house before dinner." She took a breath. "And I thought we had reached an understanding."

He looked at her curiously. "What do you mean?"

"I don't need you saving me. I can take care of myself. I'm capable. Do you not remember that conversation?"

Oh. That conversation.

"Yes. I remember and I heard you. But that is not how friendship works."

"Friends?"

"Yes. Friends," he replied casually. "Do you not remember *that* conversation? I believe we have established that we are friends. Do you recall that?"

She stared at him almost resentfully, and he knew he had her there. "Yes," she admitted with clear reluctance. "I remember that conversation."

"Well, friends do not stand by and let someone hurt and threaten a friend. Not if they can do anything about it."

She fell silent then, moving to the anvil, carefully stacking several crescent-shaped blades.

He stepped closer, eyeing her work. "Sickle?"

"Yes."

He picked one up. "Nice work."

"Careful. They're sharp," she warned.

He tapped one of the blades with a finger and then made a hiss of pain, bending over as though suddenly wounded.

"Kellan!" she cried out, grabbing his wrist. "I told you not to—" She stopped at the sight of his shaking shoulders, her gaze flicking to his face. "Are you . . . *laughing*?"

He could not keep it in. Chuckling, he held up his uninjured hand, flipping it from front to back to show her it was unmarred.

She swatted his shoulder. "I thought you skewered yourself, you daft man!"

Her words might have been full of outrage, but her eyes danced with merriment and her cheeks were flush with more than warmth from the smithy.

She still clung to the wrist of his perfectly perfect hand.

"I told you." His gaze traveled her face—roaming her perfectly perfect face. "I am not hurt."

Her fingers shifted, almost caressing his skin, and he could not help himself. She looked so pretty. So . . . tempting. His gaze devoured the sight of her. She looked down at their joined hands as though surprised at the connection and then lifted her face up again to stare at him. So close. Too close.

He kissed her.

Her mouth was ready for him, soft and pliant, sweeter than honey.

She immediately opened for him, backing up until she leaned against the anvil. He dove into her, his fingers spearing through the pinned coronet of plaited hair, reveling in her damp, greedy mouth.

The kiss intensified between them, deepening until he knew he would forever remember the shape and taste and texture of her. There was no tentativeness. Just a bone-deep craving. A hunger that found its release. That snapped like an animal freed from its cage.

His hand grasped her hip, molding over the delicious full curve and yielding shape before sliding around to her generous backside, squeezing and hauling her in until their bodies were flush. She moaned into his mouth and he drank up the sound, devouring her. And she devoured him back.

Her fingers grabbed a fistful of his shirt as she lifted her leg, wrapping a thigh around him in a frantic bid to get closer.

He lifted her with a grunt, plopping her down on the anvil so that he could wedge himself in the only place he wanted to be, between her thighs. A dress would have been nice so that he could have easy access under her skirts. He made the best of it though, thrusting and rubbing his hard cock into her, feeling her heat, her dampness, even through their trousers.

"You were right," she groaned, the sound equal parts pleasure and distress.

"What do you mean?"

"You said this would happen again."

Her words reverberated through him. *He said it would happen again.*

Even though she clearly didn't want it to happen. Even though she had told him to keep away from her and not kiss her anymore.

He pulled back to look at her, feeling like a world champion arse right then. "I am sorry," he choked out, the words mangled and thick in his throat.

She blinked and some of the fire in her eyes faded. "Wh-what . . ."

He withdrew with a pained sigh. Stepping back, he turned away slightly and reached down to adjust his aching hard cock.

He was not sorry that he kissed her, touched her, tasted her. He was sorry that she did not want it and he had done it again.

He did not want to pull back from her. It was the most difficult thing he ever had to do, but he could not do this. He could not put what he wanted over her wishes. He could not take advantage of her after she had made it abundantly clear to him that this was not what she wanted.

Kissing (and more) was not part of their arrangement. He had told her he understood that and here he was acting as though he didn't give a bloody damn about anything except his own desires. He was little better than Meyer and his sons in that regard and that was a chilling realization.

"I am sorry," he repeated. "My apologies. I did not plan on doing that. You said no more kissing. You did not want this and I should not have disregarded that."

"Oh." The fire in her eyes faded and was replaced by bright spots of color in her cheeks. "Yes. Of course, you are correct. I did say that." She nodded vigorously. "And I meant that."

She slid down from the anvil, running shaky hands over her hair.

"Shall we go to the house?" He glanced around them. "Do you need further help in here?"

"N-no. I think that does it. Let's go."

"I really should finish up in the garden while there is still light left in the day." A sound excuse. He needed to be away from her right now. The last thing he needed was to be alone with her in a closed space again. Obviously he could not trust himself.

She hesitated, looking him over with a frown. "What about your injuries?"

"I assure you I am fine," he insisted, moving

to the door. "Nothing a long warm soak in a tub tonight won't rectify."

"Very well." She looked rather relieved. As though she, too, dreaded the prospect of being alone with him, examining and touching his body. He felt feverish just thinking about that. *Her hands on him.* The suffering would be real and it would have nothing to do with his injuries. "I'll have dinner ready in an hour."

He nodded. "I will be there," he replied rather lamely.

Of course, he would. Where else would he be? He could not hide from her forever.

He would take his seat across the table from her, eating, making polite conversation and discussing their chores and responsibilities for the following day whilst pretending that living with her and keeping his hands to himself, not touching her, not kissing her, was not going to be a complete torment.

Chapter Twenty 🦊

Eleven days until the wedding . . .

Miss Susanna Lockhart set the basket she carried into Gwen's kitchen on the table and immediately started unloading items. "I've brought you some blackberry jam, your favorite as I recall, and scones and meat pies. They are Cook's specialty, as you know. No one can resist them. I've caught many a footman filching them."

Gwen looked at the generous spread of food in awe. "You really should not have gone to such trouble, Miss Lockhart. This is too much."

"Nonsense. If you could see the bounty of the duke's kitchen, you would not say that."

Miss Lockhart continued unloading items. Gwen's stomach growled. She and Kellan would have a splendid dinner tonight.

"This is very generous of you, especially considering the history between His Grace and Mr. Fox."

Miss Lockhart's hands slowed in the process of unloading items. "Ah, yes. His Grace does not appear to be the spiteful sort. I am sure if he knew I was here that he would not—"

"He does not know?" Gwen stared in shock at the housekeeper and then looked at the abundance of food again in consternation.

Miss Lockhart shrugged. "He is a busy man. He has only just arrived here and is quite occupied with settling in. He has much to do, naturally. Such things as his excess foodstuff are beneath his notice."

Gwen studied the young housekeeper carefully, assessing her amber-brown eyes, imagining that she read something there.

Did she . . . *dislike* the new, er, the *real* Duke of Penning?

Miss Lockhart reached for a jar of fig compote and waved it slightly in the air. "His Lordship, ah . . . I mean Mr. Fox adores this. It was his favorite." Miss Lockhart's eyes warmed at the mention of Kellan Fox, and Gwen could not help but feel an unfamiliar stab of jealousy.

She supposed the housekeeper could have become well acquainted with him. They had been under the same roof for weeks, after all. Long enough for Miss Lockhart to know his favorite jam. They could have gotten quite close in that time. Gwen's jaw clenched uncomfortably at the very real possibility and she wondered: *What else did she know about him?*

She had known him longer than Gwen had known him—that rather eclipsed the fact that she and he were betrothed. Especially as they would not become husband and wife in the truest sense—as couples did. They would not share a bed. They would live together for a year and that would be the end of it. The end of them.

"Does he now?" Gwen asked rather lamely, for wont of anything better to say. Perhaps by the end of the year she would know his likes and dislikes, too, and could speak of them with such confidence.

Miss Lockhart nodded. "Indeed. He cares for it quite a bit. Especially on his toast in the mornings and at teatime on his shortbread." She wrinkled her nose. "He does not care for shortbread plain, insists it is much too dry."

Naturally the Penning housekeeper knew a great deal of Kellan's eating habits, but did she know of other things about him, too? His other . . . tastes? Did she know the sounds he made during a deep, knee-buckling kiss? The way his hands felt both hard and gentle when they fondled her? Gwen's breathing suddenly fell faster and she swallowed in an attempt to regulate it.

"What am I saying? You probably know all this. You and he are so very close, after all."

So very close. Indeed.

She studied the Penning housekeeper carefully. The young woman was bent over her task of arranging items onto Gwen's kitchen table. Sunlight from the kitchen window streamed into the space, striking Miss Lockhart's hair and setting it aflame. It really was her crowning glory. Not brown or red or gold, but all three. A sunset in autumn. Gilded browns, reds and golds. She was averting her eyes as she spoke. Almost as though she were too self-conscious. Or as though she were trying to hide something that was obvious in her face. Was the woman enamored of Kellan?

Outrage and jealousy ballooned in her chest, forging into one burning amalgamation. How many hearts had he snared whilst he was duking it about Shropshire? He had insisted he didn't have his way with half the women in Shropshire. And she had insisted she did not care one way or another.

And yet here she was, jealousy eating her alive over what the man may or may not have done with other ladies before they even met. She should be beyond this.

"You seem quite . . . fond of Mr. Fox," Gwen mused, attempting to sound casual and indifferent and not at all possessive of the man taking residence in her smithy. "Do you not harbor feelings of animosity toward him and his father for duping you?"

"Oh." Miss Lockhart's cheeks pinkened. "I

suppose, I should. It was wrong," she acknowledged with a sobering nod. "So many of the staff believe he should have been hanged in the town square—"

"But not you? Not even for a small moment? When you first learned of his perfidy?"

"Oh, no! Never. I would never wish him or his father harmed." She looked almost offended at the question. "Everyone went wild when the truth came out." She tsked and shook her head. "It was shameful."

"I imagine it stung a bit though," Gwen persisted. "Learning the man tossing about orders at everyone was a nobody, an usurper? I mean it had to irk you to know the man you've been waiting hand and foot on was no more deserving of such deference than a common laborer."

Miss Lockhart blinked. "Oh, but they were very kind. Always in such good spirits . . . and attentive to all. True gentlemen. Especially the young Mr. Fox. Quite the charmer." Her smile became a bit dreamy at that and Gwen could well envision Kellan Fox that way. *Attentive* would be an apt descriptor. She knew firsthand.

When she had injured her foot, he had carried her. Nursed her. Waited on her. Brought her food.

Kissed her.

And kissed her again. On two separate occasions.

She refocused her attention on Miss Lockhart, studying her speculatively, wondering if Kellan's attentions had resulted in a kiss between them, too. Or perhaps more? How many women had the blasted man kissed in Shropshire and, again, why did she care? He could kiss all the women in England. They had an arrangement and nothing more.

She had no claim on his fidelity . . . or heart. She winced. She supposed it would behoove them both to present a legitimate marriage for the duration of the year he was here. It would not do for him to go about as he had before . . . flirting, kissing and dallying with every maid to catch his eye.

Miss Lockhart continued, obviously unaware of Gwen's troubling thoughts, "I could never bring myself to wish either one of the gentlemen ill even if what they did was wrong." She paused and looked over her shoulder as though fearful of being overheard. "Although wrong or not, I liked them both. Very much. They are such likeable gentlemen." The pink in her cheeks returned. "Especially his lordship. He was very accessible. It was easy to connect with him. Such humility about him."

Of course. He was but a humble thief. Not a vaunted blue blood.

"And what of the present Duke of Penning?

Does he not know humility?" she asked, thinking it was time to talk about something other than how grand Miss Lockhart thought Kellan Fox happened to be.

The question brought fiery animation to her heretofore amiable gaze. "Oh, the new duke!" She made a huffing sound and her movements turned jerky and agitated. "He is your typical haughty insufferable nobleman. Nothing like Mr. Fox or his papa." She paused and looked ready to say more, but caught herself with a small shake of her head.

"Indeed? He seemed cordial enough. He injected some much-needed calm into the situation with Mr. Fox and the villagers. Bless him for that. If not for him, the gent would be hanging from a rope and buried now."

"Hmm. Yes." Miss Lockhart exhaled. "That was generous of him." This last was admitted reluctantly.

"I would say so." Gwen picked up and sniffed at a fragrant pear. "Given what Kellan did, His Grace could justifiably bear quite the grudge."

"Yes, that was magnanimous of him, I will allow." And yet from the tightening of her lips, Miss Lockhart did not appear too convinced of that. "You know, we really all should have known it was a sham from the start."

"What do you mean?"

"I should have guessed that Mr. Fox and his dear papa could not have been true blue bloods."

"And why is that? Is there some outward sign?"

"They were much too nice. Especially young Mr. Fox. Kind and courteous, always grateful for everything that was ever done for them. They said 'thank you' for a cup of tea, for fetching them the newspaper. Always with the thank-yous. And *that* is decidedly *un*aristocratic behavior, would you not agree?"

Gwen nodded rather helplessly, realizing when the housekeeper continued in a rush that her agreement was not really required.

Miss Lockhart continued, "Your Mr. Fox was keen on giving the staff afternoons off, too. Oh, and he would not hear of them working on Sundays! The present Duke of Penning . . ." She paused, swallowing visibly. "Ha! He is every inch the haughty, arrogant noble, expecting everything as his due."

Before she finished speaking a darkened figure appeared, bright sunlight limning all around him as he filled the threshold behind Miss Lockhart, his features undetectable. For a moment, she assumed it was Kellan, but then he stepped forward and his face was fully revealed.

It was the Duke of Penning. In her kitchen. And he had just overheard his housekeeper maligning him. Gwen winced.

Miss Lockhart must have read something in her expression. She whirled around with a gasp. "Oh. Your Grace. Hallo there."

"Good day, Miss Lockhart," he said coolly. "I did not realize you were coming to town today."

"It was an impromptu visit."

He held his housekeeper's gaze for a long moment. The two stared at each other and there seemed to be some manner of silent communication passing between them. The air fairly crackled with tension around them, and Gwen felt the irrational and cowardly urge to slip from the room and leave the two of them alone to their demons.

At last, he looked at Gwen and inclined his head. "Good day, Miss Cully."

"Good day, Your Grace. What can I do for you?"

He stepped up to the table and surveyed the bounty that came from his own kitchen. He reached for one of the pears, lifting it from the table and examining it idly.

Gwen fidgeted uneasily. What would he say? What would he do? By Miss Lockhart's own admission, he had no knowledge that Miss Lockhart had prepared the basket of goods for her. She had done it all on her own, without permission. The housekeeper's face flushed as he looked over the goods. "A fine assortment," he pronounced.

"Your Grace, I can explain—"

"Miss Cully, it is my understanding you make

house calls," he cut in as though he had not even heard his housekeeper. The young woman's face burned hotter. "I should like you to build a wrought iron fence for me. For the back garden. Is that something you can do?"

"Truly?" Her eyes widened. This was a substantial coup. For the true and legitimate Duke of Penning to use her blacksmithing services was no small feather in her cap. The Penning garden was, of course, large. The fence would be a significant amount of work. It could be the very thing she needed to reclaim her position in town as the foremost blacksmith. "I should be quite happy to do that." She tried not to look too eager, but she was fairly quivering with excitement.

He nodded. "Very good then. Come to Penning Hall at your soonest convenience and I shall show you what I have in mind."

"I will." She nodded, giving in and grinning like a fool, unable to hide her happiness.

The duke nodded again, very perfunctory. He cast a quick glance at the bounty of goods again and then to his housekeeper. "Miss Lockhart, enjoy the rest of your day about town. I am certain I will see you at home." Then, he added rather pointedly, "Eventually."

"Of course," she grumbled. Gwen watched the byplay between them with keen interest. Miss

Lockhart hardly struck a deferential tone. And yet the duke seemed coolly unaffected.

"I will leave you two ladies to your conversation then. Sorry to interrupt."

"Not at all. Again, thank you for the opportunity to work with you." Gwen walked him to the door.

He waved a hand dismissively, as though it were nothing. And to him, it likely was not. Whilst to her, it was everything. It was the difference between thriving and failure. Penury. Starvation.

The duke departed and she closed the door after him. Turning, she beamed at Miss Lockhart.

The woman muttered something beneath her breath that Gwen could not decipher.

She shoved off the door, still feeling very elated. "The Duke of Penning," Gwen began, "is a very generous man."

"Indeed, he appears to be," she agreed, the words escaping between her teeth.

Gwen eyed Miss Lockhart's face as she finished unpacking the last items from the basket with anxious hands. The woman's lips were compressed in a tight line. For some reason, another thought occurred to Gwen and she heard herself adding, "And handsome."

Her friend's gaze snapped to her face, her eyes almost wild. "I had not noticed."

Gwen smiled slowly, thinking the lady sounded

a mite defensive. "Well, he is. I am certain he will have no trouble attracting a future Duchess of Penning."

"In that, you are quite right, I am sure. I believe he already has an eye to securing himself a bride and populating Penning Hall with several heirs."

"The business of being a duke, I suppose."

"Should we all lead such charmed existences where our greatest responsibility is procreation."

Gwen shuddered. For some reason, she thought of Meyer standing in her smithy, blustering and bullying her into marrying one of his sons so that she would produce strapping future blacksmiths. As though she should not take offense at being valued for her ability to birth sons and nothing more.

"No, thank you," Gwen breathed.

"Indeed. No, thank you." Miss Lockhart nodded and echoed in agreement.

The two women sighed and stared rather vacantly at the goods overflowing on her kitchen table.

"Not that procreation is a bad thing," Miss Lockhart hastened to say. "I almost forgot you're to marry Mr. Fox. Hopefully your union will be blessed with healthy offspring. Heavens, you both will make handsome children."

She forced a smile, hoping it did not look as dubious as she felt. "Yes. I hope so, too." What else was she supposed to say? At any rate, the lie did not feel terribly . . . *terrible*.

And that was the most concerning matter of all. Alarming, in fact.

They had an arrangement—an agreement that benefitted them both. Forever bonding them with a child was not part of that agreement. And yet here she was getting flutters at the idea.

How was she to last any length of time with this man in a strictly platonic fashion if she was getting fuzzy-headed at the idea of procreating with him? And now, thanks to Miss Lockhart, she had visions of the nonexistent children they would produce. She shook her head, attempting to banish such images from her mind.

A week ago she had not even hoped for marriage—much less children—and now she was betrothed to a virile and handsome man who had kissed her. More than once now. And she suspected he would kiss her again at the slightest invitation.

Except she would not issue that invitation. She was determined to stick with their original agreement. An in name only marriage. No kissing. Well, no *further* kissing.

Four days ago he had kissed her. Again. She had kissed him back . . . and then he ended it, pulling away because she had rebuked him and told him that their arrangement did not include him in her bed.

Apparently he listened to her and took her warning to heart. She frowned. Daft man.

It was a confusing thing . . . simultaneously regretting saying something but also relieved she had.

"I best take my leave of you." Miss Lockhart reclaimed her basket and moved to the door. "I rather think the duke expects me home today." She rolled her eyes in an exaggerated fashion. "I do have his household to manage, after all."

"Again, thank you so much for your generosity." Gwen held the door for her.

"Think nothing of it. I shall see you soon about that fence when you visit the hall."

Gwen nodded. "Indeed. Very soon."

She watched the woman move down the lane and then turn, vanishing from sight. She started to move back inside when she spotted Kellan emerging from the smithy. Their gazes connected and he advanced to the kitchen.

"Good day," he greeted.

"You just missed our visitor."

"Did I?"

"Miss Lockhart was here." She motioned Kellan inside to survey the bounty of goods she brought them.

His eyes delighted as he looked over the repast. "Oh, my. What a splendid bounty."

"She is quite the admirer of yours."

"She is a kind woman." His lips twisted in a grimace. "One of the few who did not wish me dead when my perfidy was revealed."

She watched him as he examined the food, selecting a ready-ripe plum and rubbing it clean on his shirt.

Gwen sucked in a careful breath. "It must be said."

He glanced at her with an uplifted eyebrow. "What is that?"

"I know you have many admirers in this town. I would appreciate it if you keep your charms in check."

"My charms?"

"Yes. We've professed to love each other so please don't continue going about dallying with your previous devotees. It would be at odds with the story we've created."

"Devotees?" He looked incredulous. "You make it sound as though I am some deity."

"You sufficiently grasp my meaning."

"Does this have to do with what Mr. Blankenship said? I thought you did not believe him."

"In this situation, it does not matter what I think."

"It matters to me," he said mildly, lifting his gaze to her, studying her rather intently. "What do you think of me, Gwen? Do you think that I have actually tupped every woman in this town?"

"Not every single one, no. And tupping, as you say, is not the same thing as flirting and charming the ladies. That, I can believe, you are quite guilty of doing."

He stared at her for a long moment and took a deep bite into the fruit. Juice dribbled down his chin, which he caught with the back of his hand in a sensual, languorous wipe. "I believe you are jealous."

"Me?" For some reason his words ignited a flash of panic within her. "Don't be absurd. I am not jealous."

"There's no reason for it," he said in a velvety deep voice that felt like a caress on her skin. Rounding the table, he leaned against it, crossing his ankles in front of him. "You are the only woman in Shropshire to hold my interest."

"Oh," she breathed, feeling suddenly a little light-headed. Heat scalded her face. "I am merely requesting your fidelity whilst we do this . . . this . . ." Her voice faded.

"Marriage?" he finished, his eyes glinting with humor.

"Yes," Gwen snapped. She supposed that was what they had agreed to do. Marriage. In a sense. A *fake* marriage to be precise.

He bit into the plum again, his white teeth sinking into the juicy golden meat. "I've been thinking. I know what you said, but we will be together a long time. There are ways in which we might enjoy our nights together . . . should you change your mind you need only let me know."

She suppressed the sudden urge to laugh maniacally. Nothing about this was humorous. Indeed not. On the matter of letting this man in her bed, she changed her mind several times a day on that score. It was something that kept her tossing and turning in her bed every night. He would be in her house soon, sleeping down the hall from her. The temptation would be overwhelming.

"Oh, do stop talking," she snapped, willing her face to feel less . . . feverish. "Don't you have work to do? Have you finished in the garden yet?"

He took yet another bite of his plum, eating slowly as he watched her, almost as though he enjoyed her obvious discomfort. Finished, he moved to deposit it in the bin. "Yes. I have."

"Very good. Then you might begin helping me pack."

"Packing?"

"Yes. We depart for Woodcastle the day after tomorrow."

"What's in Woodcastle?"

"Their annual fair. We should begin loading the wagon with the wares I wish to sell there."

"You didn't mention anything about this fair before."

"I wasn't planning to go . . . until you arrived."

She had been thinking about the fair in Wood-castle a great deal as the date for the fair grew closer. She had hoped she might be able to attend, unlikely as that wish was. She could not manage it all alone.

Months ago she wrote to the inn where she had always stayed with her father and uncle when they attended the fair. People from everywhere came to the fair, from all over the country, so she had requested that they hold a room for her. It was a whim. A wild wish. A longing grounded in impracticality, but she could not help herself from dreaming. And then Kellan had come along.

If he had not suddenly arrived in her life, she doubted she would even be able to do it. But he had. He was here and now she could manage it. With his help.

She no longer had to care for her ill uncle, and in the short time Kellan had been here, she had managed to add more inventory, perhaps enough to make the venture worthwhile. It could be quite the lucrative undertaking. The garden was planted. There was no reason not to go.

They would leave the day after tomorrow.

Chapter Twenty-One ❧

Nine days until the wedding . . .

𝒜h, yes. I received your letter, Miss Cully. So sorry you missed the fair last year, but we are glad to have you back." The harried-looking woman smiled at Gwen whilst simultaneously waving to someone across the room.

"It is good to be back," Gwen told the desk clerk. She did not recall the woman from previous years, but she smiled anyway, simply happy to know her letter had been received and they were kind enough to have held a room for her.

Her family had consistently sold their products exceptionally well at this particular fair. From nails to tools to hair combs, her family always returned home with an empty wagon and pockets full of coin.

Once she came of age and she had started tinkering around in the smithy, she had experimented with her own creations, such as hair combs and pins. They became popular items, flying off the shelves at the fair. Every single one sold, in fact. All that Gwen could make and bring was snatched up well before their last day. Their profits from the Woodcastle Fair carried them for months. It had certainly hurt her pocketbook to miss out on it last year. She had been looking forward to returning this year and escaping out from the shadow of Meyer. As far as she knew, he and his sons did not attend.

She stood patiently—Kellan just a few paces behind her with their luggage—as the clerk flipped through the ledger. "We have your room ready."

The entrance hall of the inn was crowded. Conversations buzzed in the air. People waited in line behind her whilst several persons walked ahead of the desk to patronize the inn's lively taproom. Laughter and music spilled from the room.

"Here we are. Sign here." The clerk cheerfully rotated the ledger on the desk for Gwen to sign.

Gwen accepted the proffered quill, saying, "When I wrote you I did not realize I would require a second room."

The clerk tsked and shook her head regretfully. "Oh. There is not a room left. We held just the one for you. We could not hold a second . . . not as crowded as we are."

"Oh," Gwen said mildly, injecting none of the dismay she felt at this news.

Only one room.

She resisted the impulse to look over her shoulder at where Kellan stood, waiting, watching, listening. She swallowed and cleared her throat, hoping when she spoke her voice conveyed none of her alarm. "I see."

"The entire town has been booked for days now. You will not be able to find accommodations in all of the shire and even in the next town over." The beleaguered clerk blew out a breath. "Count yourself lucky you have the one room."

Gwen should have assumed she would run into such a dilemma, that was why she wrote to the innkeeper months ago to request a reservation for the necessary four nights, after all. The fair was always crowded, and the city brimming to capacity.

"Thank you." Nodding tightly, she signed her name to the ledger, collecting the two room keys from the clerk.

"Room 21," the clerk continued. "Forgive me for not showing you to your room. We are rather overwhelmed and understaffed at the moment. Your chamber is upstairs, third door on the left."

"Thank you," she murmured.

Turning, she met Kellan's questioning gaze and handed him one of the keys. "There you go." She kept her expression carefully neutral as she strode past him, weaving through the people crowding the reception area and heading for the stairs.

He fell in beside her as they ascended the steps. "We are sharing a room." There was a fair amount of inquiry in his tone.

She spoke in a low voice, for his ears only. "If anyone asks we will tell them we are family." He shrugged. "Cousins." And yet she doubted anyone would inquire. The city was bustling with people and activities. No one cared about one woman's sleeping arrangements.

He made a sound and she sent him a swift glance. He was shaking his head, his teeth a flash of white in his open mouth.

"Are you laughing?" she demanded.

He nodded. "Indeed. I am just wondering how many *cousins* are sharing a room and sleeping together at this inn . . . and countless others lodgings in town."

She flushed. "Very well. It is not the most innovative lie."

"No. It is not."

"Well, we cannot all be expert liars, can we?"

He grinned, not at all offended at her obvious dig. "It is a talent unrecognized by many. I am gratified you realize and appreciate that. So few do."

It was her turn to chuckle. "You are incorrigible . . . and no one said I appreciate it."

She came to the room and inserted the key. Kellan waited behind her with their luggage as she unlocked the chamber door and opened it for them.

She held the door for him, letting him pass inside before her, his booted feet thudding on the wood floor. He set their bags down in front of the bed—*the single bed*—and faced her as she closed the door behind them.

She scanned the small, cozy space, deliberately keeping her gaze from lingering on that bed.

"Only one bed," he remarked, his voice drawing her gaze to his otherwise expressionless face. "What are we going to do about that?"

She swallowed and forced a shrug. "Is that going to be a problem for you?"

He arched a dark eyebrow. "Should *you* not be the one to answer that question?"

She inhaled. "Is there a choice? There are no other accommodations to be had in town."

"There is always a choice. I could sleep in the stable—"

She winced at that. She could not do that to him. She was only able to be here because of him. Because of how much help he was to her. "And smell of horse and manure every day beside me?" She snorted. "No, thank you." She moved to her valise and began busying herself unpacking. "We can behave as responsible adults and stick to our original agreement, I am sure. We are not animals ruled by our basest impulses." She paused and looked at him. "Do you not agree?"

He nodded. "Oh, of course." He rubbed the back of his neck thoughtfully. "Although just to clarify. You mean for us to share the bed? Alone? Together? All night? You do not want me to sleep on the floor of the room at least?"

She glanced down at the wood plank floor that appeared as though it could use a good scrubbing. It would be unclean. Not to mention cold and hard. "Do you *wish* to sleep on the floor?"

Perhaps he did not wish to sleep in the same bed with her.

Perhaps he did not trust *her* to keep her hands to herself.

She inhaled. That was a rather sobering and mortifying thought.

He held up his hands in a disarming manner. "I have no desire to make you uncomfortable. You've stated in no uncertain terms that our year together shall not involve intimacy. No more kissing. No more touching. You were emphatic on that." He motioned to the bed and then waved between them. "This would be the height of intimacy. I am not certain you understand that. I don't own a nightshirt." His lips twitched. "I usually sleep naked."

She froze at this announcement, heat scorching her cheeks. She felt her eyes grow large in her face. "Well, while we are here in this room, this bed, I hope you will eschew what is *usual*!" She blinked hard, banishing the scandalous image of him naked in the bed beside her.

He inclined his head. "Of course."

She gestured to him in agitation. "You should invest in a nightshirt, sir." Especially for the next year. She did not need to happen on him during the night in a state of undress.

She looked to that bed again and then faced him, feeling more composed. "We are going to be forced into proximity for quite a spell. We might as well accustom ourselves to uncomfortable situations . . . so they can cease to be so uncomfortable. You said we are friends. Did you mean that?"

"Yes. Of course."

"Then friends should be able to share a room with no awkwardness. Friends should not feel compelled to kiss or . . . do other things."

He inclined his head, but there was still that air of skepticism about him. "Very well then."

"We are adults. Friends, as you said," she rattled on. "I am certain we can restrain ourselves from . . ." Her voice faded, an awkward flush needling over her face. She didn't need to say it. He grasped her meaning fully.

"Indeed," he agreed. "I can control myself."

"If siblings can share beds, so can we."

The moment the words popped out of her

mouth, she heard them . . . and regretted them. They were foolish and she felt foolish uttering them.

His mouth kicked up in one corner and he chuckled. "Rest assured, we are not siblings."

"No, but we have avowed to be platonic in the same fashion."

He looked at her dubiously, making her feel rather foolish again. Did he look at her and think her an idiot?

She continued, "We have made an agreement. We've discussed boundaries. We can share a bed without doing anything untoward. I trust us to behave responsibly."

"Of course. You are right," he agreed simply. "We can restrain ourselves."

His words should have provided comfort and assurance. So why did his absolute conviction make her feel somehow . . . snubbed. Slighted. As though she were no temptation at all. Merely the friend he professed her to be. Nothing more.

She hated this. Her inconsistent nature when it came to him was vexing. She loathed it. She must be constant in this, unwavering in her resolve. No more falling weak at his slightest look, at the slightest touch from him. She had to be strong. Strong and independent as she always was.

He had not touched her since that day in the smithy when he forgot himself, when she forgot herself, too. He had apologized for that. He had said it would not happen again. He took her demands to heart. It was unreasonable of her to long for him . . . to want him to long for her. She knew that. And yet she wished he could at least appear to be struggling with the temptation of her.

Instead, he treated the prospect of spending the night with her, in the same bed, as though it were of no significance.

It made *Gwen* feel of no significance.

As though they were in fact cousins and had never once shared kisses and touches. As though all those touches and kisses had never happened . . . as though *they* had never happened and they certainly would not happen again.

Chapter Twenty-Two ❦

*T*hey dined together, stiffly polite over a meal of excellent pheasant, overcooked parsnips and passable wine. They were cordial, speaking only of business. Gwen recounted the Woodcastle Fairs of the past she had attended with her father and uncle and related how they would conduct sales over the course of the next few days.

Following dinner, they left the inn and stepped outside, browsing the fairgrounds, surveying the many stalls with wares to be sold on the morrow. They eventually reached their own stall to check on the lad they'd hired to watch over their booth for the night, bringing him dinner and giving him a respite to relieve himself.

Kellan watched Gwen busy herself about the stall, inspecting their wares and making certain everything was in place to her liking and ready for the morrow.

"You will be quite well for the night, Adam?" Kellan asked when the lad returned from doing his matters.

"Yes, sir. I am not alone. My brother is two stalls

down watching a milliner's booth for the night. And that there is my cousin, Billy, across the way."

Kellan looked to where Adam nodded across the lane at another lad occupying a stall that boasted various spices and jars of honey, jams and herbs.

"Very good. We will see you in the morning." Kellan took Gwen's arm, escorting her through the cool night air back to the inn.

The first floor of the inn was boisterous. People spilled out of the taproom into the reception area, drinks sloshing in their hands. They were clearly getting a head start on the revelry of the coming days.

Kellan had been to many a fair. Plenty of plump pigeons ripe for the picking at such events. He might be familiar with them, but never had he worked one engaged in an honest pursuit. Tomorrow would be a first.

He guided her through the press of bodies, thinking how easy it would be to lift the pockets of the inebriated revelers. Too easy. And that was not what he was about anymore. The thought jarred him. Anymore? Or simply while he was with Gwen? He was not quite certain of the answer. He pushed the question from his thoughts to examine later.

Once on the second floor, he unlocked the door for them and closed it, muffling the sounds of belowstairs to a distant hum.

"Well," she proclaimed. "We have a big day ahead of us on the morrow. We should get some rest." She moved to her valise and pulled out her nightgown. Bunching the white lawn fabric in her hands as though she were strangling it, she glanced at the washstand and then to him.

He read the dilemma. "Why don't I leave you to refresh and ready for bed?" he offered.

Relief flashed across her face. "That would be most kind of you. Thank you."

"Of course." He nodded, relieved as well. He did not relish watching her undress and ready for bed. Contrary to what she thought, he did not view her platonically, and it would be struggle enough to share a bed with her without touching. Anything he could do to lessen the temptation would be ideal. "I'll be back shortly. Half an hour."

"Thank you."

Inclining his head, he departed the room, taking the key with him.

He found his way downstairs and seated himself at a vacant chair at a long table. A serving girl quickly appeared at his side and he ordered a whiskey. It would relax him before bed and he could do with a little of that. Very well, a great deal of that. The quicker he fell asleep and became oblivious to the woman in the bed beside him, the better.

The room was crowded, buzzing with conversation and laughter. The trio of fiddlers performing on a small dais prompted dancing and several people whirled in time to the lively music.

He sipped his whiskey and tried not to think of the woman upstairs waiting for him—correction. She was not waiting for *him*. He was no one. A friend, perhaps. Her partner until their arrangement was satisfied, definitely. Her husband-to-be but not in the real and genuine and proper sense. No, theirs was a union without shagging.

He took another swig of whiskey, letting the warmth slide down his throat and settle in his belly as he let all these reminders sink into his skull.

One bloody bed.

He could not have envisioned a scenario to torment him any better—or any worse. It was incredible. Like something out of fiction.

She was so confident that there was no risk—that the arrangement they had agreed to would keep her safe from his hunger for her. She might be safe, because he would never touch her against her will, but his hunger for her had not abated and would torment him for the duration of their stay here . . . and follow them back to Shropshire, no doubt. He groaned and took another drink.

It had been difficult enough keeping his hands off her when they did not share a room—when he slept in the building next door. Now? This new arrangement?

The next four nights would be a misery. Perhaps he should drink himself into unconsciousness each night. It might perhaps be the kindest thing to do to himself even if he would suffer an aching head for it the next day.

A half hour passed, but still he waited, coward that he was. He was hoping she would be tucked into bed and asleep by the time he returned.

He was many things, but never one to take advantage of a woman. He was not that big of a cad. It suited him if she was lost to slumber. He would merely slip in beside her, keep a safe distance between them, and fall asleep with nary a word between them. Not a provocative word or sound from her lips.

He exhaled. She had the most delicious voice, velvety and throaty. It would only take a murmured good-night from her to completely unman him.

He lifted his glass to empty it of its final sip when, through the bodies, he spotted a familiar head of lush gray hair.

He blinked. Frowned. Slammed his glass back down on the table, and lurched to his feet, struggling for a better glimpse.

The crowd shifted, and the sight vanished.

He strained for another view, standing on his tiptoes and putting himself well above the other heads in the room in an attempt to see . . . to find again that head of gray hair that could belong to only one man.

No such luck. He was gone. If he had even truly been there.

Kellan sank back down on his heels with a sigh and looked resentfully at his empty glass. Perhaps the wine and whiskey had gotten to him tonight, addled his mind, made him see what— *who*—wasn't there.

He had not seen his father. It had been someone else. Another man. What were the odds it was him? Da was not the only man of middle years who might look like him across the distance . . . or from behind.

Shaking his head, he departed the taproom and advanced up the steps, each thud taking him closer to the bed he would be sharing with the woman he wanted but would not touch.

The room was black as pitch when he entered and undressed himself cautiously, taking care not to collide with any furniture, easing his way through the small space carefully. From the gentle cadence of her breathing, he was confident she slept solidly, which made slipping into the bed beside her a little less fraught.

Only a little though.

He had slept with women before but never without *having* them.

There is a first time for everything.

And his life had certainly been a string of firsts lately—all attributed to Gwen Cully.

He settled his head on the cool cotton of his pillow and exhaled, letting the tension of the day evaporate. Inhaling, he caught a whiff of her skin and hair: a faintly floral soap. His eyes flared wide in the dark. Even in darkness he could feel her body so close, the length of her radiating heat toward him. Her flesh called to him.

She is not yours to have.

Stifling a groan, he rolled over, away from the temptation of her.

He recalled the room arrangement and knew he was facing the window. He thought he vaguely detected its shape in the darkened room. Hopefully when he woke, he would still be facing the window and not curled up against her.

His hand slid down the side of the mattress, gripping it as though it were a lifeline. Something to cling to so that he did not turn and roll into her and touch her tonight or any of the nights to come. *God help him.*

Chapter Twenty-Three ❧

Eight days until the wedding . . .

Gwen woke to a low persistent throb in her core. She slowly blinked her eyes open to a room washed in the deep purple of dawn. It took her a moment to remember where she was—and with *whom*.

She had gone to sleep in an empty bed, but it most assuredly was not empty any longer. Kellan's big body was sprawled over the entire mattress. Over *her*.

She was on her side and he was directly behind her, spooned along the back of her. She felt him. His hard member nestled against her bottom. He was rocking gently, rolling his hips, grinding into her. She gasped softly, her fingers clenching, fisting into the bedding bunched before her. Her body burned, aware, it seemed, even before she had been cognizant of what was happening.

She felt his breath at her neck, on the side of her face. She could turn, roll over, welcome him, draw him in. Did he even know what he was doing? Was he awake?

The throbbing pulls in her core, between her legs, was too much. It bordered on pain. She needed relief.

She turned, wiggling around until they were chest to chest. His manhood sprang between them, nudging her belly.

She made out the shadowy outline of his face. His eyes were closed.

"Kellan," she whispered in the soft air.

His eyes fluttered open and the liquid darkness there exposed him, revealed his raw need. She willingly gave herself to it, squirming on the bed until his hardness bumped directly at her womanhood. He still wore his trousers and the fabric of her nightgown shielded her, but that did not stop him from radiating heat to her.

With a groan, he rolled her to her back and dropped himself between her thighs. The clothing between them did not matter. It did not stop him. It did not stop either of them. His hips worked, grinding and thrusting into her sex.

She gasped and cried out, her hands clenching into his bare biceps. He was huge. Between her legs. Over her. In her hands.

She thrashed under him, wild as he continued pumping his cock, rubbing it over her.

"Bloody hell. You're so wet," he growled. "I can still feel you through all these bloody clothes."

She whimpered and fought for words, thinking only, *Harder. Harder. Harder.*

She must have said that. The word must have escaped her mouth because suddenly he was pushing hard against her and she exploded, shuddering as every nerve ending in her body burst in delight. She felt him erupt as well. Suddenly it was wetter between them and then he was rolling off her, dropping onto his back beside her.

"I haven't dry humped a girl since I was a lad," he choked out between breaths.

She stared up at the ceiling and into the shadows there, her own breathing fast and impossible to catch. Was that what they had done?

She turned her head to look at him. His head rolled on the pillow. "You still think we can show restraint?"

She tried to speak, but her heart had not slowed yet. "We did not . . . actually . . ." She did not know how to say it.

"Fuck?" he supplied. "I'm aware. But that nearly killed me."

He sprang from the bed then. Grabbing the rest of his garments, he started for the door.

She sat up on her elbows. "Where are you going?"

"I spotted a creek outside town. The water should be freezing. I'm going to submerge myself in it. Because this—" In the growing light of the room, he motioned to her on the bed. "This has not cooled my ardor for you one bit."

"Oh," she said in a tremulous voice.

"Tonight I'll sleep on the floor. One of us has to be honest in this relationship."

"What is that supposed to mean?" she demanded in affront.

"You claim you don't want intimacy, and then this . . ." He lifted his hand holding his boots and motioned to the bed. "I can't do this."

Turning, he left the chamber.

She dropped back down on the bed, pulling the bedding up to her throat and clutching it there, releasing a pained gust of breath, understanding his meaning. Restraint. Not kissing, touching. *Fucking*. The word was filthy, but she understood it. Her body tingled with the knowledge of it, with a deep craving for it.

She also wondered if she could keep up this restraint any longer . . . and wondered why she should.

GWEN OPENED THE stall herself that morning, sending the boy, Adam, on his way. She was instantly busy. People assailed her. They had questions about her wares. Especially the ladies.

Even as the men tested out her tools, the women adored her combs and used the mirror she had brought to test them out in their hair.

She was talking with customers when Kellan joined her, his hair damp from an obvious dunking in water. He must have done as he said, and submerged himself in the creek.

They fell into a companionable rhythm, each attending to customers. At noon, Kellan left and fetched them something to eat. The day flew by and they had sold a good many things by the time Adam returned.

"Would you like to have dinner at the inn again?" Kellan asked as they strolled between booths.

She glanced about the busy fairgrounds. "I think I would like to walk for a bit. By myself," she added. He studied her face closely and she was certain he could see her need for some respite from him.

Even as she worked through the day, she had thought of little else besides him, and his parting words from the room this morning.

"Very well." He nodded. "Have a care. There are some rowdy people here. Spirits do not always lead to good judgment and there are a goodly number of drunkards about."

"I can take care of myself."

"I know you can." He nodded again and then

turned on his heels, striding down the lane. People automatically parted for his big body.

She took her time strolling the grounds. Kellan was correct though, loath as she was to admit it. There was a good amount of boisterous and unruly people, many inebriated, many in colorful masks, embracing the spirit of revelry. The crowd seemed to grow, and the carousers did not always move for her to pass. She recalled now that her father and uncle had always tucked her into bed at the inn before sunset, never exposing her to the nighttime merriments.

She spotted a narrow alley between stalls and decided to take it and cut around the grounds to reach the inn. She'd had enough. Wandering the fair at night was not conducive to peace of mind.

The area surrounding the fair was wooded. She skirted the edges, pausing when a masked couple burst out between stalls into the cover of trees several yards before her. They did not notice her where she stood, frozen, near a tree.

The masked couple was so very lost in each other, they were oblivious to the sounds they made—or anyone that might hear or see them. It was mortifying, and yet she could not move. Her feet were rooted to the spot.

She should avert her eyes and rush away as was proper and leave them to their impropriety.

She *should*.

Heat rushed through her in prickles that she acknowledged were not merely embarrassment. It was the hot pulse of arousal.

She knew the sensation. She had felt it before . . . when Kellan kissed her. *Each* time he had kissed her. When he had groaned and worked his hips against her this morning—was that only this morning? It felt a lifetime ago. Her body had burned and erupted, and yet she still felt bereft and aching. There was more. She knew there was more. An answer to the hollow ache.

She moistened her lips and observed the pair of lovers in silence. Well, mostly in silence. Her breaths fell in hard rasps and her heart pounded loudly in her ears. She leaned her shoulder heavily into the tree beside her.

Her hand moved of its own volition, grasping a handful of her blouse at her throat. She clutched the fabric, clinging to it reflexively, as though she were that female, caught up in the throes of passion.

Her breasts tingled, pushing against her blouse. The friction of her chemise against the pebbled peaks of her nipples was too much to bear.

She bit her lip to silence any sound as the masked man suddenly freed the woman's breasts from her gown and undergarments. The globes sprang out into the open. Gwen had a view of dark-tipped nipples in the moonlit night and then the woman's partner came over her, seizing them in his mouth like a starving man.

"They look as though they are enjoying themselves," a voice murmured near her ear.

She gave a little jump and a gasp escaped her.

She started to turn around, getting only a glimpse of Kellan behind her before he closed his big hands on her shoulders and guided her back around to continue watching the trysting couple.

"I w-was just—"

"Don't move," he chided, cutting her off. "Watch." His hands flexed on her shoulders and that simple touch radiated through her, sending waves of sensation eddying over her skin that seemed to shoot to the most sensitive parts of her: her lips, breasts, belly . . . that clenching ache between her thighs.

She swallowed back a moan and resisted the impulse to twist around and fling herself against him like an animal in heat. "What are you—"

"Don't let my arrival stop you from enjoying the show." He lowered his chin, practically resting it on her shoulder.

She tried again for denial. "I was just leaving—"

"Liar. No, you weren't." He chuckled lightly, low and deep, the sound rumbling along her skin. "You were watching and enjoying it. And you still are."

He was correct, of course, and she no longer

had the will to move away. Even as she trembled before him, her eyes tracked the movements of the fornicating couple.

"We should not be watching them," she whispered in a feeble attempt to deny what she was doing . . . and feeling. "It is an invasion of their privacy."

"Privacy?" He chuckled softly in her ear and her skin turned to gooseflesh. "They're shagging in public. There can be no expectation of privacy. In fact, I would wager they would find it titillating that a beautiful woman was admiring their exploits."

Beautiful? Her?

She swallowed thickly. He was the only man to say such things to her—and she both loved and hated it. Loved how special and cherished he made her feel. Hated how special and cherished he made her feel.

It was a dangerous thing to feel. She could quite easily come to crave it. She could *need* to hear such things from this man. *To need him.* Always. Beyond their one year together.

She started to look at him again, but he turned her chin so that she remained looking forward. Watching the young lovers.

The young man continued his worship of his lady's breasts, his hands feverishly delving beneath her skirts, skating over her stocking-clad legs. The woman's throat arched, her mouth parted on a moan beneath the scarlet of her domino.

This was how it was done. How one surrendered to passion.

And that was acceptable, she realized. She was no child. No weak-willed woman to be led or directed. She could do as she wished, and that meant she could satisfy her truest desires.

Gwen's core pulsed and throbbed as she watched them, her own heart beating faster with the increasing anxiousness of their movements.

She leaned back against the solid length of Kellan, needing his support just then. Wanting it, but also needing it for she no longer trusted her feet to hold her upright. She felt as though she could slide down to the earth and melt into a boneless puddle.

When Kellan's hands slid around her rib cage to cover her breasts through her blouse, she did not even jerk with surprise. Her entire body shuddered with a great wave of relief. *Finally.*

He flexed his hands over her, exerting more pressure, grasping and massaging her aching breasts.

As she watched the lovers strain and groan and peel off each other's clothes, it felt the most natural thing in the world to have the man behind her fondling her breasts.

She arched into his palms, reveling in the hands molding and squeezing the aching mounds.

She did not even object as his fingers quickly plucked free each and every button of her blouse. Cool air rushed over her exposed flesh.

Kellan's hands roughly yanked down her chemise and wrestled her corset lower until her breasts spilled over the top.

Then his fingers were on her again, rubbing and rolling and pinching her nipples until she was crying out, shuddering as desire so bright and sharp burst like stars behind her eyes.

Through her blurred vision, she continued watching the young lovers. The man pushed down his breeches and wedged his hips between his lover's legs. The female cried out as he rocked his body into her. They were wild and loud and indifferent to discovery as he pumped into her over and over again.

"You like that?" Kellan rasped against her ear, biting down hard on her lobe and sending a rush of moisture between her thighs. "You don't know how long I've wanted to play with these plump nipples."

"Ohhh." She whimpered and arched her spine, pushing out her chest, letting his fingers work their magic on her.

"Would you like me to do that to you?" His hot breath fanned over her ear. "Slide my cock deep inside your wet cunny?"

His words only made her lady parts twist

tighter and the ache deepen. Her breathing was a jagged thing now, part whimper, part sob, a storm crashing from her lips.

He seized her hand and brought it around behind her, placing her fingers against his cock. She didn't pull away or recoil like she should. Indeed not. She stroked her fingers over him, learning the shape of him through his trousers. He was big all over.

"Have you ever done that, Gwen?" His head brushed the side of her face as he nodded to the couple.

Whether he meant shagging in public or just shagging at all the answer was the same.

She made an incomprehensible sound that he took for the no she meant it to be.

"Ah, then I would take my time with you and make sure you were nice and wet and ready for it. There would be no pain when I bury my cock deep inside you. Only pleasure. Would you like that?"

She nodded jerkily. "Yes," she choked, so overcome, so hungry for it. He could take her now. Throw her down on the ground and have his way with her right here. She would revel in every moment of it.

She let go of his cock and rubbed her backside into the hard length of him nudging insistently behind her.

He groaned. "Ah, you are a natural, Gwen."

His arm wrapped around her waist, hauling her even closer. He cupped her sex over her trousers, molding his big hand there, curving it along her pulsing mound. He rubbed and squeezed her sex as she watched the couple work against each other wildly.

Gwen bucked against his hand, needing more. More pressure. More friction. An end to the aching hollowness, to the throbbing urge for him to do all the things he described.

She surged and bucked against his touch, hungry and desperate. As desperate as those lovers whose bodies worked and strained in tandem.

"I can feel your heat through your trousers," he growled. "Are you wet, too? Let's see, shall we?"

And then he was opening her trousers, pushing his hand down, burrowing between her quivering thighs. He found her bare flesh, cupped her, skin to skin, his naked palm holding her swollen sex. His fingers played over her folds.

The sensation of him against her slick flesh had her shuddering and choking on a cry.

"Oh, you are soaking," he murmured in satisfaction.

"Ahh." She strangled on a gasp as he stroked a finger along her seam and dipped it deep inside her body.

She swallowed back a cry and lifted up on her tiptoes at the shockingly delicious invasion.

He pushed deeper and curled that finger, rubbing at some deep hidden spot, hitting a patch of nerves she never knew existed. Tremors racked her and her eyes watered.

He brought his other hand to her shoulder and pushed her back down to the ground, urging her off her tiptoes so he penetrated her deeper.

She lost it.

Fell over a precipice.

Her climax exploded and she cried out, standing there, quivering with his hand buried in her trousers.

She came down from her euphoric cloud, her gaze refocusing, finding that in her unfettered release, she'd gained an audience of her own.

The lovers had turned their heads and were now watching *her* through the eyeholes of their masks.

"Oh!" she cried out with mortification and stumbled away, grabbing at her clothing, closing up her trousers and yanking up her chemise and corset.

Panting, she locked gazes with Kellan, and the dark desire she saw there stopped her in her tracks. She pushed back a lock of fallen hair from her face, not giving so much as a blink as she stood trapped, pinned in the fiery maelstrom of his gaze.

"Gwen," he growled.

No man had ever said her name like that.

No man had ever looked at her like that.

No man ever made her feel like she was so feminine, so beautiful and wanted that he would hunt the earth for her and destroy anything that got in his way.

"Gwen." His voice was hoarse now, a whispered plea. He extended a hand toward her, as though inviting her to finish out this experience with him.

She leaned forward, tempted, compelled . . .

Until the young lovers reminded her of their presence. The woman released a keening wail and Gwen started. Their movements grew frenzied. They were still coupling, perhaps heightened in their desire, as Kellan suggested, because they had an audience.

With a strangled cry, Gwen whirled around and fled the scene.

She skirted the fairgrounds, circling back around the vendors' booths until she was almost to the inn. The revelry had not abated. The city's High Street was still crowded, buzzing with voices and laughter and music and sloshing drinks. She shoved her way wildly through the crowd, eager to escape to the sanctuary of her room. Although he shared the room with her, at least she would no longer be out in the open like this, feeling so exposed.

She burst through the doors of the inn, thankfully finding it less crowded with most everyone carousing outside. The desk clerk had dozed off in his chair behind the desk and did not even look up as she rushed up the stairs to her chamber.

Once in the room, she debated pushing a piece of furniture up against the door and keeping Kellan out, but that was childish and irrational. She fought for her air along with her composure. Both were equally elusive to her now. There was no keeping him out. He was in her life. She had done that. Made all the choices that brought them together.

Her heart raced, her breaths coming in hard crashes from her lips—and not just from exertion. No, it had more to do with the wicked depravity she had just experienced than her recent run through the village.

She paced the small space of her room, back and forth, back and forth, her mind racing to match her overexcited heart.

Perhaps he would not come. Perhaps he would simply sleep in the wagon or stall. It would be the least awkward thing. Better for the both of them. A night away. Not in the same room or the same bed. They both knew how awkward that could be. How would she survive it and keep their agreement?

Is that so very important to keep?

What would it hurt if they enjoyed each other

over the course of the next year? Took their pleasure with each other until time ran out?

Even as she asked herself the question she knew.

If they became lovers his leaving would not be an easy or gentle parting for her. She would not wave him off and return to her life remotely the same person. When he left he would take a part of her with him. She would be a broken woman.

No.

The word whipped through her harshly, a bitter wind slamming doors forever shut. She would not be some pale version of herself, left to live out her days not simply alone—but lonely. Indeed not. She would survive. She would *thrive*—just her with her smithy. No matter the outcome, she would not be broken.

Steps sounded outside her door. She stiffened and backed up several paces, stopping when she bumped the bed. She held herself as tightly as a wound coil whilst the key to the room turned in the lock.

Kellan entered the room and closed the door behind him while keeping his stare fixed on her. He turned the lock and she felt that click like a loud bolt reverberating in her ears.

He advanced on her and she felt stalked. He moved like a silent predator, his eyes dark and deep. This was the time to do something. To speak

out or to move away. To remind him that he had
offered to sleep on a pallet on the floor yesterday
and now she felt like that would be for the best.

No words emerged from her mouth.

He stopped before her. His nearness did not
help. Nor the fact that they were alone now and
in proximity to a bed. Her willpower was dangerously thin, a thread ready to snap.

He did not reach for her, however.

His gaze flitted over her face and then moved
down her body, taking in her rumpled garments.
Her arousal still burned hot, simmering in her
veins. She tingled everywhere he had touched her.

His hands lifted and he started on his own
garments. He watched her as he undressed himself, giving her ample time to object.

She could not.

She could only watch. Stare back at him, eyeing
the impressive expanse of his chest, those wide
shoulders. He bent and removed his boots and
tossed them aside. His hands went to his breeches.
Her gaze followed, widening as he shoved them
down his legs.

Then he was naked, his cock springing between them at full mast.

He gave her a moment, waiting.

The choice was hers.

Before he entered this room, she had thought
she knew her mind.

But her body felt something different. It was telling her to take off her clothes. Her hands went to the buttons of her blouse. For however much she did not need him, she wanted him.

He held motionless and watched her undress just as she had watched him. He watched and didn't move until she was solidly naked in front of him. This time when their bodies connected there would be no garments, nothing in their way.

Moments ticked by and they stood assessing each other with hot eyes, scanning each other in a hasty, thorough inspection.

"On the bed," he finally said in a voice as jagged as broken glass.

The dark command sent ripples over her skin and she moved to obey, her heart racing with excitement as she sank down on the bed and scooted back, her bare bottom dragging across the coverlet as she crawled on her elbows, making room for him.

He slanted his head to one side and then the other, examining her at different angles.

She should have felt vulnerable or self-conscious, but she knew he liked what he saw from the way his lids fell heavy over his dark eyes.

Still standing over her, his hand seized hold of his turgid cock, stroking it in long pulls as he slowly followed her down onto the bed. She could not take her eyes off him. He was warrior-big—

all of him, his member included. The head of his manhood looked almost painfully swollen, the tip purpling and glistening with moisture. He rubbed a thumb over it, making the skin gleam.

She wanted to reach out a hand and touch him there but there was no time for that. The bed dipped from his weight.

Everything moved quickly then.

He came between her splayed legs, bumping her thighs wider for him. His hands grasped her hips and he slid her closer down the bed to him. She gave a little squeak, excited at his forcefulness . . . strangely wanting him to be even more forceful, to show her just what that big body of his could do.

He came over her.

She quivered, already primed.

She had been primed since the woods. Her body had not unwound itself. He propped an elbow beside her head to keep the heavy weight of him from crushing her. His chest brushed her nipples and she whimpered.

His dark eyes prowled over her face and suddenly he reached for one of the plaits at the side of her head. Wrapping the hair around his fist, he gave it a sharp tug that she felt directly in her belly. "Ready?"

In response, she kissed him.

He kissed her back, hard, pushing her head back down on the bed.

She couldn't breathe, but she didn't need air. She only needed him. This.

His free hand squeezed between their bodies, finding her sex, his fingers stroking, testing her. "You are still deliciously wet," he panted into her mouth, his relief audible. "I can't wait."

"Thank God," she moaned. "Do it."

He lifted away slightly and then came back down, his cock pulsing at her opening, pressing . . . pushing inside her. She widened her thighs and lifted up to meet his driving manhood. He slid home through her slick heat.

There was no pain as he had promised.

Only sweet relief. Burning fullness.

He groaned and she tilted her hips, taking him in deeper.

He rolled his hips and gave her another little thrust that made her yelp.

He stilled and looked down at her, beads of perspiration dotting his brow. "I'm sorry. Did I—"

"Don't stop!" Her channel clenched around him snugly and she arched under him, needing him to keep going, desperate for him to get her to that place again.

He obliged. As though he had been cut free from a leash, he moved then.

Wrapping an arm around her waist, he held her closer and drove into her, again and again. Her vision blurred and she saw stars each time he pushed into her, creating a delicious burning friction inside her. Her hands wrapped around his thick shoulders, holding on as he rode her hard.

"Gwen," he gasped. "I'm almost there."

"Not yet," she pleaded, a sob strangling in her throat.

His hand shoved between them, where they were joined. He found and rubbed the little bud at the top of her sex in a hard, fast circle. She ground down against him, needing it harder, faster. She released a sharp exhale as fresh moisture rushed between her legs. That combined with another fierce thrust and she was done. Splintering. Flying apart.

He followed her over the edge, crying out and pushing in deep one final time, shoving her higher on the bed as his own release came over him.

He came down over her, heedless of his weight this time, but she delighted in the crush of him over her. It was a comfort. A solace. She had never felt so fulfilled. Her hands stroked his back, reveling in the dampness of his skin, knowing *she* had exerted him. *She* had untethered him.

He remained inside her and she felt him twitch. Her body instinctively tightened around him.

He groaned and flipped over, taking her with him and tucking her into his side. "I think you and I . . . are just getting started tonight?"

She looked up at him. "Really? This can happen more than once?"

He looked down at her and stroked the line of her nose. "I'm hoping it's going to last us a full year."

A full year.

His words both delighted her and triggered a little niggle of discontent. Already, she worried about when the year would come to an end. When he left and this ended. When he took himself from her and this wondrous little bubble burst.

His finger left her nose to trace her mouth. "Why are these beautiful lips frowning?"

She shook her head and turned her face to lightly bite his chest. "I'm not frowning," she spoke into his skin.

"Good." He kissed her long and slow. When he finally came up for air, he murmured into her mouth. "Because I have plans to make you smile all night long."

Chapter Twenty-Four ❧

Five days until the wedding . . .

*K*ellan waited belowstairs for Gwen. He had already seen to the wagon this morning. Everything was packed for the return home, and he was glad they were bringing a much lighter load back with them. He was glad because Gwen was glad. More than glad. She was thrilled. They'd sold out of nearly everything. By all accounts, it had been a successful venture. The profits for the last four days weighed heavily inside his jacket.

He'd paid Adam for his help and the co-ordinator of the fair for the use of the stall. A brown paper–wrapped package sat beside him. He'd been unable to resist the dress he spotted in a shop window this morning. The cobalt blue would look striking on Gwen. He'd only ever seen her in modest dresses of plain wool. She donned them in the evening after working all day, but a woman deserved a new dress for her wedding day. Something special and beautiful. He couldn't wait to give it to her. He felt nervous and excited at the same time, hoping she approved of it.

He sat in the taproom, nursing a cup of tea and eating from a plate of eggs, toast and sausages, in no hurry to hasten Gwen. He had left her sleeping peacefully, a thing of beauty, this morning to tend to their departure.

There had not been a great deal of sleep between them over the last few nights and he hated to disturb her. She needed her rest as he was certain they would be up late again tonight.

He smiled. He could not get enough of her.

The sight of her this morning, asleep naked, the bedding twisted around her tasty curves, was a view he could grow accustomed to. He felt warm inside knowing he would have this for a year. That warmth quickly faded though, when he considered a year might not be long enough. He had never felt this way for another woman. Three nights together might not be a long time, but it was longer than he had ever spent in the bed of any woman.

She was the first. The only.

From where he sat he had a clear view into the reception area. A clerk was greeting people at the front desk, either waving them into the taproom or escorting them to one of the smaller parlors.

A finely attired gentleman stepped into sight, presenting Kellan a view of his back—and a head full of lush gray hair. He used a brass-handled walking cane. It seemed more for show. The man had no difficulty walking. In fact, he moved in such a familiar way that the tiny hairs on Kellan's neck prickled. He lowered his fork to his plate, sitting up straighter, more alert, more wary.

Then the gentleman turned, granting Kellan a glimpse of his profile.

He pushed away from the table, grabbed Gwen's package, and was moving, striding across the taproom toward the man. "Da."

His father turned, his still handsome face lighting up at the sight of Kellan, as though they had not parted ways under perilous circumstances weeks ago.

"Kellan! My lad!" Da clapped him on the shoulder and embraced him, seemingly oblivious to the fact that Kellan did not embrace him back.

"What are you doing here?" Kellan asked the question with a great deal more calm than he felt.

He'd never lost his temper with his father. He knew boys and their fathers often went through their spells of discontent with bouts of aggression toward each other, but that never happened between them. Not only was Kellan not an angry person, but there was that deathbed promise his mother had extracted from him. He had vowed to look after his father, to care for him. That meant getting along.

That said, coming face-to-face with his father now—who appeared to be merry and carefree—rubbed him raw. Despite what he had told Gwen, that he wasn't angry with his father and he understood his actions, he did not feel particularly warm or kindly toward him.

Kellan had come close to death, and his father had been nowhere around. Did his father not even care? Had he not worried about Kellan's fate whilst he escaped town and went about his life, scheming and cheating as usual? Whatever he had been doing this whole time it was certainly not agonizing over Kellan's fate.

"Kellan!" he exclaimed. "My good lad!" His father clapped him on the shoulder again. "It's wonderful to see you, my son!"

The two of them were of similar height, which was to say extraordinarily tall. Kellan could look him directly in the eyes. "Da," he said evenly. "You are looking well."

He looked his father up and down in his fancy togs. He did not recognize the garments as anything he wore at Penning Hall, so that only meant Da had landed on his feet and found himself in another plush situation. As always.

"Oh, I am! I am well! Fit indeed!"

"Mr. Lambert," the desk clerk interrupted, speaking to his father. "This way, if you will."

Lambert. So that was his current alias. Kellan

wondered where he had plucked that name. If he was not adopting another's identity—as he had done with the Duke of Penning—he liked to choose names from favorite books. His father was an avid reader. Kellan could not recall a character by the name of Lambert, however.

"Oh, come. Join me." Da waved him to follow, and Kellan did . . . accompanying him right into a private parlor, where apparently he was dining this morning in luxury.

Kellan hovered on the threshold as his father made himself comfortable in the room, removing his ornate purple jacket and revealing an equally luxurious brocade vest. "Come inside. Don't stand out there lurking in the corridor."

"Anna will be with you shortly to take your order," the desk clerk said, offering a slight bow before departing the room.

Da moved to the door and shut it. "Ah, some privacy so we may speak freely." His father rubbed his hands together. "Wait until I tell you about the juicy fish I have on the hook. She's a lonely widow with more blunt than she knows what to do with. Her husband made his money in coal." His father chortled and rubbed his palms together in avid glee. "It's so easy it should be a crime."

"It *is* a crime," Kellan said dryly.

Da ignored him and kept talking excitedly. "There's room for you in it, of course. I can say you're a business associate I bumped into. She thinks I'm a wealthy silk merchant." He tapped his chin thoughtfully. "She has a daughter with an inheritance of her own, and let me tell you, she has a face like the back end of a mule. She is *ripe* for the picking, lad. Starved for attention. A handsome man like you." He made a tsking sound. "It would take the likes of you very little to charm the lass."

"I can't do that."

"What?" Da looked perplexed, and glanced Kellan up and down. "Well, not as you are perhaps. Where did you get those clothes?" He wrinkled his nose and waved a hand over Kellan's modest attire, encompassing his wool coat, simple jacket and vest and trousers. Clearly they were not up to his father's standards. "If you hope to attract plump pigeons, you know you must dress accordingly. I've taught you that. These garments will get you little better than a quick tumble with a taproom wench—and that's only because of that handsome mien of yours."

"I'm not here to work a deceit with you." He motioned to his father and shook his head. "Any rate, how did you afford these clothes and convince your widow that you are wealthy?"

"I sold some jewels I filched from Penning. I had them on me when I escaped, and I managed to sneak a few other valuables into a knapsack before I got away. It was more than enough blunt to outfit me properly."

Of course. His father would not have left Penning Hall empty-handed. He would leave Kellan, certainly . . . but his pockets would not have been empty. He was too clever to end up with nothing.

His father waved a hand impatiently and moved toward the jacket he had discarded on a nearby settee. "Never mind. It's of no matter. I'll give you some money so that you may properly attire yourself. Something in green. You look particularly dashing in that color."

"No, thank you."

It took Da a moment to stop talking, to realize that Kellan had said no.

"No?" He blinked. "What do you mean, 'no'? I can purchase some—"

"Da, I don't need any money. I don't need any clothes." He shook his head in frustration. "Have you even given me any thought? You abandoned me. You ran off without me. How did you know if I was even alive? Were you worried at all?"

His father scowled. "Of course I knew you were alive. Why would you not be? You're too clever to get caught, and even if you were I knew you could talk your way out of it. And you are alive! You're here!"

"Only after a close brush with death."

"Oh!" His father waved a thick hand in dismissal. "Pfft. You are fine."

A single knock preceded the door opening. The serving girl walked in and asked brightly, "Good morning, Mr. Lambert. What can I get for you?"

"I'll take my usual, Anna."

His usual?

The girl nodded. Clearly she had grown accustomed to his father—Mr. Lambert. She turned her attention to Kellan. "Can I fetch you anything, sir?"

"I am fine. Thank you."

She departed the room, leaving them alone again.

Kellan took a breath and resumed what he was saying before the serving girl arrived. "They were on the verge of hanging me, Da. They actually began the process. I was dangling off the ground, a rope around my neck, choking for breath." He shook his head and took a bracing breath. "Where were you?"

Da blinked at him, looking slightly discomfited. "But . . . you are fine now."

"Because of a woman. She persuaded the town not to kill me. She is the reason I'm alive."

Da punched him lightheartedly in the arm. "See there. You can charm your way out of anything. That handsome face of yours is always breaking hearts."

Kellan blew out an exasperated breath and shook his head again. "You don't understand."

"What then?" His father finally started to look annoyed, the lines in his forehead deepening. "Explain it to me, Kellan."

"I can't do this anymore."

"Do what?"

"The frauds, the scheming . . . the lies. I'm tired of it. Not knowing what is coming from one day to the next." He closed his eyes in a long, weary blink.

"What are you talking about? You're spouting nonsense." He shrugged. "So we got caught. It happens from time to time. In our line of work, how can it not?"

"No. *I* got caught. *You* escaped."

"There was no time to warn you."

Kellan shook his head. "I'm eight and twenty and I'd like to reach thirty. On this path, with you, I doubt I will."

His father leaned back. "You're scared."

"It's more than that." He did not wish to live his life this way anymore—the way his father lived, the way Kellan had always lived.

These last weeks with Gwen had made him realize how he wanted to live his life now. He wanted to do *something* with his days. Build something. Have something real. He wanted to fall into bed every night feeling fulfilled, certain that he had accomplished something even if it was as simple as mucking out a barn stall.

He wanted all that. He wanted that life for himself. And he wanted to live it with Gwen.

"You're angry at me. Very well." Da waved Kellan to come forth. "Vent your spleen on me. Get it off your chest. I will abide it all, and then you will feel much better afterward and we can continue on as we were before, now that we've been reunited."

"I don't want to continue as before. I want . . ." His father stared at him expectantly, waiting. "I want Gwen."

"Who?"

"The woman who saved me."

"Ah." Da's eyes twinkled. "Let me guess. She is rich? Widowed. Hopefully not married. Always told you to avoid that. Too messy when there is another man about. You'll find yourself facing the end of a pistol."

"She is not rich. She is not married . . . yet. But she will be. If she will have me."

Da looked perplexed. "So . . . who is she, this lass?"

"She is a blacksmith."

"A blacksmith!"

"Yes."

"A female blacksmith?"

"Yes." He grinned. "She is very talented. And strong and beautiful."

"And not rich," Da reminded drolly.

"And not rich," he agreed.

"But you love her," Da finished, a resigned tone to his voice.

"Yes. I do. I am in love with her."

"Then that is all that matters." His father stepped forward and embraced him in a warm hug. "I'm happy for you, son." He stepped back. "I'll write. Don't think it's wise to visit you in Shropshire though."

"Likely not. At least not for a while." He imagined after he was married to Gwen the villagers would ease in their thirst for vengeance. Many of them were already friendly with him and seemed to accept him. Fredericks always had a kind word for him. Mrs. Dove. Mrs. Butler seemed to dislike him less after he attacked Meyer. The duke himself was amenable and did not seem concerned with seeking retribution. His father could probably visit them at some point in the future.

"Perhaps you and your wife, and the children I suspect will be in your future, can visit me when I get settled."

Kellan did not bother pointing out that his father had never settled before. Never put down roots. Anywhere. It would be unlikely that he would start now. Instead he said, "I am sure we would like that."

Kellen was floating. He was in love with Gwen and going to marry her. Their marriage would be a real one.

Suddenly, he was eager to be free of his father's company. He had to see her again. He had to tell her how he felt.

"I must be off." He started for the door, pointing a finger to his father. "Keep your promise and write!"

His father nodded jovially and called after him, "I will!"

He hastened upstairs, unlocked the door and burst into the room he shared with Gwen. She was up and dressed and closing her valise. An easy smile curved her lips when she saw him and it stole his breath. He loved this woman. He dropped the parcel on the bed and strode a hard line for her.

"There you are," she said. "I was beginning to—"

He swept her into his arms and kissed her, silencing the rest of her words.

After a moment, she broke away enough from his lips to say breathlessly, "Well, good morning to you, too. Are we ready to go?"

He took her hand and placed it over his ever-ready cock. "I'm always ready to go with you."

Her eyes darkened. "You are wicked," she said thickly.

"You make me so."

"If we don't leave now we won't reach the next town by nightfall."

"As long as we're back in time for the wedding . . . that's all I care about."

Her cheeks turned pink. "The things you say . . ."

"I mean it."

She stared at him for a long moment, her expression curious . . . and a little hopeful. At least he thought that was what he read in her eyes. He *hoped* it was hope. "We could perhaps afford to stay one more night here . . ." She shook her head. "Oh, we really shouldn't. There is so much to do waiting at home for us."

"We can treat ourselves. You deserve it. One day won't make a very big difference. Call it an early honeymoon. We sold out of almost everything."

"Oh, did you pay Adam and Mr. Sawyer?"

He nodded and reached inside his jacket for the money. "Yes. I . . ." Not finding it in his interior pocket, he tried the other side of his coat, even though he did not believe there to be an inside pocket on that side.

And there wasn't.

He stepped back and urgently checked his pocket again. Nothing.

There was no envelope of money.

Gwen watched him warily, the smile on her face turning into a loose, fragile thing.

Panic swelled in his chest. He patted his body fiercely as though it were somehow hidden, tucked away on his person.

Gwen's eyes flared wide. "What is it?"

His heart lodged in his throat. "It's . . . gone."

"What do you mean gone?" She looked him up and down desperately.

"It was there earlier. I paid the lad and Mr. Sawyer and then . . ." He stopped hard, bitter cold washing over him.

"And then what?"

"I . . . saw my father."

"Your father?" she demanded shrilly. "The consummate swindler and thief? What was he doing here?" Her gaze narrowed sharply on him. "Did you tell him to meet you here?"

"No! It was just happenstance." He reached for her arms and she recoiled, stepping back from him as though he were poison. "Gwen, I—"

"You gave him my money." Her eyes scanned his face, gleaming brightly with a pain he had inadvertently inflicted. "You *took* my money. Stole it," she whispered, her voice trembling.

"No. He hugged me. He must have lifted it from me." His father. The most skilled knuckle he knew.

Of course, he had. Kellan should have known. He should have seen it coming. All Gwen's hard-earned money. Gone.

He had only been thinking of Gwen then . . . overcome with the realization that he loved her and wanted their marriage to be real and forever. He had simply been eager to return to her.

He had dropped his guard with his father. He should have known better. He closed his eyes in a hard, pained blink. He knew his father. He should have known.

He shook his head miserably. Kellan could rush downstairs, but it would be pointless. His father would not be there. The man knew better than to linger after the act. He was gone.

"I'm so sorry, Gwen."

"I trusted you." A sob choked her. Her lovely eyes were suddenly bloodshot and red rimmed, gleaming with hot emotion. "I'm a fool."

"No, you're not. You can trust me. I swear it to you. I care about you."

"No!" Her eyes snapped fire and she held up a hand as though warding him off. "Don't say that. Don't you dare lie to me about that. You've lied enough."

"I've never lied to you," he insisted.

He had always been his true self with her. Only her. He could not say that about anyone else. In the years since he lost his mother, he had never had that. Never had a person with whom he could drop his guard and be himself.

And now he was losing her.

"Of course, you have lied to me. Of course, you did this horrible thing. It's what you do. Who you are." She waved around them. "All of this has been a lie. You tricked me. And now I'm ruined. Destitute." Her expression became a little wild then, panicked. She pressed a hand to her chest as though she couldn't breathe. He reached for her again and she twisted away from him. "No. Don't. Leave me alone."

Stopping, he stared at her, dread pooling in his stomach. "I will give you a moment and wait down—"

"No. We are done. I mean *leave*. This room. This inn. *Me*."

He absorbed each word like a blow.

"We can't be done. The banns . . . our agreement. We are to marry," he reminded her.

She laughed then. It was harsh and brutal and felt like a knife twisting in his chest. "I've made enough mistakes. I won't be making another one—especially not that mistake."

"I promise you, Gwen. I have not lied to you. I want *you*. I am sorry about the money . . . I'll make it up to you."

She lifted her gaze and her eyes were clear. Calm. "But I don't want you."

He flinched. The knife in his chest turned and pushed deeper. She meant that. Staring into her face, he saw whatever future he had hoped for with her vanish like smoke in the air. It was gone just as her money was gone.

He strode past her and gathered his valise.

She drifted to the window, and looked out, avoiding the sight of him as though it sickened her.

He paused in the doorway, staring at her rigid back. He inhaled. "I love you, Gwen."

He waited a beat, hoping, futilely it would seem. Then he walked out into the hall, down the stairs and out of her life.

Chapter Twenty-Five ⟨⟩

The day that was supposed to be the wedding . . .

Gwen Cully stared down the congregation with her chin held high as she entered the church. She knew what today was and so did they.

Everyone in town knew she had gone to Woodcastle with Kellan and returned without him. Gossip was rife. She would not be married today, but instead of hiding in shame in her smithy, she had decided to face the world and attend church on this, the day she was to have married, suffering the stares and whispers.

She had been home not even a week, but business was bleak. Everyone thought her a liar and a woman of loose morals. She had kissed a criminal, after all, bold as you please in public. She had lied about being in love with him. Lied about marrying him—at least as far as everyone else was concerned.

Ironically, the part about loving him wasn't a lie anymore. She loved him. She had fallen in love with him and lost him and the wound she bore went deep.

None of it mattered now though. He wasn't here. That was all anyone cared about.

Meyer had paid her a visit upon her return and reasserted his desire for her to wed his son. This time his eldest son had joined him. Apparently the brothers had drawn straws for her and settled the matter of who would have her. Her wishes were not taken into account.

It was outrageous and insulting, but she had not even been offended. Her heart ached too much to take offense. Gwen had simply refused, but she knew she might not be able to do that for much longer.

She might have to sell the smithy, after all. She would hold out for as long as she could, hoping she had enough funds to get through the month, hoping her debtors would not demand payment. Hoping for a miracle.

She had made a mistake. A colossal mistake.

She realized it soon after Kellan had left.

I love you.

She had heard those words so rarely. From her father and uncle and Odette. He had said them though and they reverberated in her heart still, echoing over and over in her head, and she knew.

She had found the beautiful dress on the bed, and she knew.

Why would he have taken her money and

returned to her? And he did return. With the dress. He had intended to marry her.

It didn't make sense that he would give the money to his father and then return to her empty-handed. How did that serve him?

She had been too hurt to reach this logical conclusion in Woodcastle.

He meant what he had said. He loved her.

But now he was gone. At her behest, he had left.

He was gone and it was too late and she couldn't bring him back. She wouldn't even know where to find him.

He would not have stolen her money. She knew it now. Both logic and emotion told her this. She felt it so strongly in her bones that she didn't know how she could have ever doubted him. The man who stood up for her in front of those mean girls, who struck Meyer to protect her, who tended to her with such care after her smithy had been robbed . . . he would not have done such a thing.

The shock and disappointment of losing her hard-earned money had crushed her. Standing in that bedchamber at the inn in Woodcastle, the weight of betrayal had been the only thing she could feel.

Now . . . the loss she felt didn't have anything to do with the money.

She felt only crushing pain to have lost him. To have lost Kellan.

I love you.

And she had let him walk away. So what if she didn't have a penny to her name? They could have been poor together. They could have started over together. A fresh beginning. As long as they had each other it would not have been bad.

It would have been wonderful.

The only people to ever love her had been Papa and Uncle and Odette. She knew the value of love. It was not something to be dismissed so easily. Kellan had loved her and she threw him away. Because she was angry. Because she had not believed him. Because she was scared.

Sitting in the pew, the Meyer men beside her, she battled tears. They had seated themselves right down next to her, their great girths creaking the wood beneath them, and she had not the strength or will to object. Not on this bittersweet day.

She smoothed a hand over the gorgeous blue dress she wore. It was quite certainly the most beautiful thing she owned. Kellan had excellent taste. She surmised he meant for it to be worn today—on their wedding day. There would be no wedding, but she had donned it anyway. Thinking of him, she wore it, her heart aching. She would keep it forever and always think of him when she wore it. She would think of him and what could have been. She would wear it and know she had been loved.

The vicar stood at the front of the church. The sermon, which she could only give half an ear to, was on the subject of fidelity. A fitting topic, she supposed. If she had possessed more faith in Kellan, he would be here alongside her. Her heart would not be broken.

Suddenly the double doors of the church flew open. She heard them dimly, registered the sound of them striking the interior wall, but did not turn to look. Others around her did, rustling in their seats. The vicar froze midspeech, staring at the back of the church.

The skin of her nape prickled. She set her hands on the back of the pew in front of her as though she needed that support. Murmurs broke out all around her and she slowly stood, her white-knuckled hands pushing her up.

Standing, she turned and looked and nearly collapsed. Her knees shook and she quickly grasped the back of the pew again to keep upright.

Kellan's gaze found hers. He marched straight down the middle aisle toward her in long strides. She drank up the sight of him. He looked splendid. Big and handsome. He was dressed as a gentleman, wearing the clothes he wore the first day she met him.

He stopped before her, his dark eyes glittering. "Gwen," he said.

"Kellan," she returned.

His gaze was unwavering, his words resolute, but she saw the insecurity just beneath the surface. He was not confident she would accept him. She had tossed him out, but he had come back anyway even with his fear of rejection.

"He's back! He's come back! Hang him!" Mr. Meyer's son cried out from further down the pew. "Hang him! He defiled and abandoned her. Hang him!" It was most assuredly the first time those words had ever been uttered in this church.

Murmurs rolled though the congregation. People exchanged uncertain looks. Somewhere in the building another voice took up the cry.

Apparently he had not only returned to face possible rejection. Kellen also faced the threat of hanging. Again.

Mrs. Dove, who sat two rows ahead of Gwen, called out to the young Meyer, "Oh, shut up, you big dolt! Don't get that started again."

"Yes," the vicar seconded. "Let us all remain calm and remember that this is the house of the Lord."

Kellen stood his ground, paying no mind to anyone else. Not those crying for his blood. Not Mrs. Dove or the good vicar. His gaze remained pinned to Gwen with an intensity that felt palpable, as firm and real as touch, as sizzling as fire to her skin. "I believe this is our wedding day."

The elder Meyer beside her blustered and attempted to stand.

Gwen shoved him back down with a hand on his shoulder.

"Yes," she answered. "It is."

Elation flashed in Kellan's eyes. He offered her his arm. She took it and stepped out from the pew, joining him in the aisle. Together they approached the smiling vicar arm in arm.

Kellan leaned down and whispered in her ear, "I knew you would look beautiful in that dress."

"If you had shown me the dress first I might not have tossed you out."

He chuckled, his eyes delighted as he gazed at her. "Oh, how I have missed you."

Her chest swelled high on a breath that tightened her chest to the point of discomfort. "And I love you."

As soon as the words were out, the tightness eased and she could breathe again. It was as though her body had been waiting to give voice to those words—to the truth that had been bottled up inside her.

The mirth slipped from his face. He gazed down at her with dark-eyed intensity. "I am going to need to hear that again."

"I love you."

"Again."

"I love you. I love you. I love—" He kissed her. Right there before her friends and neighbors.

"I told you all!" Mrs. Dove shouted from the congregation. "They're the genuine article!"

Epilogue ⚜

*G*wen fell back on her bed with a sigh of repletion, her chest lifting and falling with exerted breaths. It was not uncommon for her to wake up to her husband's most ardent and carnal attentions.

This morning it was his head between her thighs, kissing her awake, his most skilled and clever lips and tongue and teeth sending her flying out of her skin before the sun even broke through the sky, its light pushing around the edges of the curtains in their bedchamber.

A year of marriage had brought forth many changes, but there had been no abatement in his desire for her. Kellan wanted her frequently. At night. In the mornings when they woke. Sometimes he would even take her in the middle of the day, luring her away from the smithy with hungry eyes and seducing hands. Naturally she wanted him back. It was a glorious life living with and loving this man.

"You're a wicked, wanton man, Kellan Fox," Gwen murmured.

With a gratified sigh, her husband fell on his back beside her. "Then we are quite the pair, Gwen Fox, because you are every bit as wicked and wanton."

She grinned and reached out a hand to stroke her husband's bare chest, reveling in the texture, in the soft skin stretched over hard sinew and muscle. He had spent the better part of this year laboring about the place, learning the ways of smithing, and, unbelievably, the process had only made him bigger, harder, stronger. He had been handsome before, but now he was mouthwatering.

"Thank goodness we found each other then."

"I thank fate for gifting me with such an insatiable wife. I am a very fortunate man, indeed."

"Do you know what day it is?" she asked coyly.

He contemplated the question for a moment. "Monday?"

She swatted his large shoulder. "Stop teasing me."

He slid his arm under her waist and pulled her in closer, flush against his side. "As though I would forget what this day is."

"One year," she supplied. "We've been married for a year, and it has been the shortest year of my life."

"Time hurries by when you are having a good time."

"And are you? Having a good time?" She traced a small circle over the center of his chest and tried not to sound insecure. She knew he loved her, but at times she wondered if he wanted a more lavish life instead of their modest living. "Because you know it has been a year . . . and once upon a time we agreed that you could go your way at the end of the year, so if you want to leave—"

He looked at her in astonishment. "Now who is teasing?"

She shrugged. "Well, we *did* say that. I don't want you to feel I am reneging on our agreement—"

"There were many things said when we first met. Once upon a time you also told me that I would not be sharing your bed. That our marriage"—he motioned over them—"would not be as delicious as this."

She snorted. "Well, you definitely made a liar out of me on that score." She cocked her head and teased, "And did I say 'delicious'?"

"The sentiment is wholly accurate." Cupping her face, he came over her, his big naked body wedging between her thighs, spreading her open for him. "Let us put to rest this *leaving* nonsense you are spouting." He gripped his cock and rubbed the swollen tip along her opening, teasing her until she was panting and whimpering and writhing against him, wild pleas spilling from her lips. "I'm not going anywhere." He closed the scant distance between their faces and pressed his mouth to hers in a deep, punishing kiss. "Say it, Gwen," he growled over her lips.

"Oh," she gasped.

"Say you don't want me to ever leave you." He nudged the head of his cock just a fraction inside her, teasing her, tormenting her. "Tell me you want me to stay with you and be with you forever. Say it."

"Yes, yes, yes," she blubbered, crying out as he drove into her. "Stay. Never leave me."

They came together in a wild frenzy, his big body pounding into hers. She turned her face and bit down hard into the bedding, releasing her screech of climax into the many folds of fabric rather than let it fill the house.

They had a guest, after all.

Kellan did not seem to care though.

He was not nearly as mindful of the sounds they were making. His hands locked on her hips, his long fingers digging deeply into her yielding flesh as he drove into her over and over again, tossing back his head and releasing his own shuddering groan of climax as he spent himself inside her.

He dropped over her, his heaviness a familiar and delicious thing. She wrapped her arms around him, her hand stroking the smoothness of his back. "We are both so wicked. I am certain he heard us."

"We are married. This is our home. We are in our bedchamber."

"Still. It *is* shameful. How shall I face him?" She buried her overly warm face into the crook of his neck, relishing the clean male scent of him.

"First of all, my wife, there is no shame between us. Only love."

She lifted her face from his neck to look up at him. "And secondly?"

"Secondly . . . his hearing is not what it used to be. I practically have to shout at him these days. It's doubtful that he heard anything."

She winced. "Yes. I have noticed that about him."

"And you do realize that this is my father you're talking about? An infamous swindler? The last thing you need to feel in the presence of my father, of all people, is shame."

She choked out a little laugh at that. "I suppose so. He's not precisely the most honorable of men."

"Indeed not. But he does adore you. You've won him over completely."

"He is charming," she admitted.

"A condition of his profession."

Her father-in-law was a lovely man. He loved his son. He was happy for him. Happy that he had found love and marriage, even if that meant turning his back on a dishonest life of hopping from one scheme and swindle to the next.

"He has a lot of his mother in him," Mr. Fox was fond of saying.

Shortly after their marriage, Kellan had left her for a few days to track down his rascal of a father. He had found him well entangled in the arms of the rich widow he was currently plying.

The man was incorrigible. He returned most of the money, embarrassed not at all as he offered what Kellan described as a half-hearted apology. He was a thief, a swindler, a charlatan. He would never change. Kellan accepted that, and so did Gwen. But Kellan was also not fool enough to trust him with their valuables or money ever again.

Kellan sighed as he continued, "Yes. He is charming. And he knows it."

"Shall we rouse ourselves and face the day, my love?" Even as she asked the question she was already moving, flipping back the covers and climbing from the warm comfort of their bed.

With a groan, her husband joined her. "I suppose we must." Together they dressed and readied themselves for the day ahead.

"I will go down and start breakfast while you attend to your father," she said as they finished making their bed, a task they did together every morning.

It was as though a tornado had ripped through the bedding. Even if they were not frequent and active lovers, Kellan was a lively sleeper. He moved around and took her with him, always pulling her close as they slept. The end result was a wild tangle of bedding. But he never left her to fix it. They made the bed together as they did everything else. Their marriage was a true partnership, so unlike the marriages she witnessed in life. They were equals in every way.

Kellan moved toward the dresser and lifted a key from the top. Together they departed their bedchamber.

Gwen moved toward the top of the stairs, pausing for a moment and watching as Kellan advanced to the second bedchamber. His father slept on the other side of that door, their houseguest for a week now.

Kellan slid the key in the lock and pushed open the door, calling out a greeting as he did so. "Good morning, Da."

Mr. Fox's cheery response drifted in the air as she descended the stairs and made her way into the kitchen.

Much to her bemusement, Kellan's father was perfectly agreeable to being locked in his bedchamber every night. Kellan had made that a requirement of his visit.

When he first proposed it, Gwen thought him jesting. "You cannot mean to keep your father a prisoner in our home!"

"Only at night," Kellan had replied. "He's free to move about in the day."

It seemed such a ridiculous thing, but then her father-in-law had agreed with total equanimity. "It seems reasonable to me." He had looked at Gwen then. "I am a thief, my dear." Mr. Fox nodded agreeably, nonplussed over the condition his son had set forth.

Still, she had protested. "This seems . . . radical."

"Best to remove the temptation," Kellan had added, his expression easy and mild as the decision was reached between father and son. "He could rob us while we sleep."

She laughed and shook her head as though that were completely implausible and the silliest thing she had ever heard . . . until her father-in-law chimed in, unruffled as he admitted, "I fear he is correct. It is the safest thing to do."

Now, after a week, it no longer felt so absurd. They spent time together in the day, ate tasty dinners—Kellan had become quite skilled in the kitchen—and enjoyed after-dinner conversation and games in the parlor . . . and then Kellan locked his father in his room at bedtime.

She stirred the stove to life and set the kettle to boil. She bent over to gather more wood and yelped as a strong, hard arm came around her waist, pulling her back against an equally strong body.

Her husband pressed his mouth to the side of her ear, "Have I told you I love you yet today?"

She curved her fingers around his arm and smiled, thinking about that . . . about how a day had not passed in the last year where he did not tell her those words. Where *they* did not tell each other those words.

She thought about that and marveled how her life had changed since he burst his way into it. "Hmm. I don't believe you have. Not yet."

"How remiss of me." He tsked. "I love you."

She smiled. "I love you, too . . . *both* of you." She moved his hand then, placing it directly over her stomach.

He stilled for a long moment and then whirled her around, his eyes bright and wild in his face. He looked between her face and her stomach, as though he could already see the life growing there. "Are you . . . Are *we* . . ."

"Yes." She nodded happily and then was swept into her husband's embrace, his happy tears dampening her hair as he choked hoarsely, "I love you. I love you both, too."

If you enjoyed *The Scoundrel Falls Hard*,
don't miss the first two books in
The Duke Hunt series,

The Duke Goes Down

and

The Rake Gets Ravished

by *New York Times* bestselling
author Sophie Jordan.

Available now!

The Duke Goes Down ❧

A garden party, 1838

The day was bright. The weather perfect. The guests attired in brilliant colors that seemed to celebrate the occasion, as though the heavens wished to shine down on the birthday of the privileged and lauded heir to the Duke of Penning.

But it might as well have been a funeral to Imogen Bates.

There was no pleasure to be had for her. She smoothed a trembling hand over her ruffled skirt. It was a new frock. Mama had insisted on the extravagance since it was to be such a special occasion. Mama's words. *Such a special occasion.* Papa went as far as to proclaim it an honor.

Other far more apt descriptors leapt to Imogen's mind. None of them flattering. She would have preferred to stay at home among her books or visit one of her friends in the village—all girls who were never invited up to the duke's grand house on the hill. Lucky them.

Oh, why couldn't I be one of them now instead of stuck here?

Imogen wore a matching blue-and-pink bow in her hair that was ridiculous. A great monstrosity at the back of her head that threatened her very balance. Mama was trapped under the delusion that Imogen, at ten and five, was still three years old. She would not yet permit Imogen to wear her hair up off her neck as most of the girls in attendance this afternoon did. Other than a few thin plaits coiled atop her head, her hair hung loose down her back.

Mama called her lovely. Papa said she looked like a princess.

Imogen knew the truth. She looked more like an enraged peacock in full fan.

There were dozens of people in attendance. All close friends of the duke's family. Blue bloods. Titled. Wealthy. Gentlemen with jeweled signet rings and ladies in tea dresses that far outshone any gown her mother had ever donned—or, for that matter, any gown Imogen would *ever* don. They were modest people rubbing elbows with the crème de la crème of the *ton*.

At least Imogen and her family were not invited to the evening festivities. She would be spared that wretchedness. She did not have to sit down to dinner with any of these people and make conversation with whomever sat beside her. She did not have to feel inadequate in her modest and juvenile attire. She did not have to suffer dancing among them—or even worse. *Not* dancing. Either scenario would be a veritable punishment.

The garden party predominantly consisted of young people. Naturally. As it was a weeklong house party to celebrate the birthday of his lordship, the heir apparent, the guest list was abundant with his friends.

Imogen started across the lawn toward Mama who was chatting with several of the heavily powder-faced dames. Her mother spotted her coming. Of course. She had not taken her gaze off Imogen for very long since they had arrived and Mama thrust her away like the proverbial bird from its nest, forcing her to socialize with those of her own age.

Imogen wasn't normally shy or reticent, but the young people here all touted old and renowned titles after their names. The young gentlemen went to Eton with Penning and the young ladies all took their curtsies at Almack's. Imogen was achingly aware that she was not one of them.

As she advanced, Mama gave a hard and swift shake of her head in a clear warning that Imogen should not join her with the matrons.

Imogen stopped, frowning. She was aware that Mama wanted her fraternizing with the young lordling and his friends, no matter how vast the gap between them.

No matter that Imogen would rather rub shoulders with a pack of rabid hyenas. Hyenas would at least acknowledge her.

Sighing deeply, she turned back and obediently ambled through the garden where a game of croquet was being played out.

She stood to the side watching, trying not to feel obtrusive as a group of young ladies and gentlemen played a lively game, whacking their mallets and laughing merrily. Unfortunately the longer she stood there, watching, being ignored, the more awkward she felt.

After several minutes of that misery, she decided to move along. Clearly not back toward her mother and the old dames where she was not welcome. She felt like a dinghy, cast adrift, lost at sea.

It really was a dreadful day.

She looked around helplessly before settling on the quietly beckoning pond as a potential refuge. She strolled toward its calm waters, stopping when she noticed a group of young men congregating at the edge, initially obscured behind the large oak with bowing branches. They skipped stones, laughing and chatting congenially.

At the center of them stood Penning's unmistakable form. He cut a dashing figure with his dark hair and sharply hewn profile. She recognized only one other person in the group. Amos

Blankenship. Like the young duke-to-be, he was easy to identify, but for different reasons.

Amos Blankenship was blinding in his lime-green-and-gold jacket. Amos's father possessed untold railway shares and his son reveled in his family's wealth, oft tearing through the village in a flashy new phaeton. They might not possess a title, but money like theirs paved the way for them and bought them position. The Blankenship family took pride in leading village society. Mrs. Blankenship was the epicenter of all social activity . . . and the town's biggest gossip.

Imogen studied the group of young gentlemen undetected. The young Lord Penning was no longer boyish. All his softness was gone, replaced by hard edges—a fitting observation on this, the celebration of his eighteenth birthday. He was a man now. She looked down self-consciously at herself, fisting a handful of ruffles in disgust. Whilst she was an overdressed little girl.

He reminded her of one of the chiseled Greek gods at the British Museum she'd visited not very long ago. Except he was attired in clothes, of course. Just last summer she and her cousin Winifred had giggled and gawked at the naked statues longer than they ought to have done. Their mothers would not have approved, which only made them revel in their silliness. There was something to be said of being away from their mothers' gimlet stares that brought out the ridiculous in them.

Deciding she could not stare at the young men forever and remain undetected, Imogen turned in a small circle, renewing her search for a place where she might take refuge. Her choices were limited. She could not return to the house where the older gentlemen assembled over their drinks and cigars. No one wanted to include her in croquet. Mama would not welcome her with the other matrons, and she dared not approach the urbane lads near the pond.

Her gaze arrested on the conservatory in the near distance. She lifted her skirts and walked briskly toward the building.

She sent a quick glance over her shoulder. Satisfied no one was observing her, she unlatched the door and slipped inside. Instantly the loamy smell of plants and vegetation assailed her. She inhaled deeply and started down a row, colorful flora on each side of her. She felt pleased with her resourcefulness. If she only had a book, she could spend out the remainder of the afternoon quite contentedly here.

She stopped before a pair of potted lemon trees, relishing the scent of citrus on the air. She reached out to stroke a well-nourished leaf. She was debating whether or not plucking one of the fruits would constitute stealing when she heard the creak of the conservatory door.

She whirled around, seeing *them* before they spotted her. Penning and his friends. Apparently they'd departed the pond and decided to invade her sanctuary. *Monsters.* Could she find no peace today?

With a muffled whimper, she dropped down before they could spot her and scurried under a table. It was undignified, but then so was she in this dress.

Imogen squeezed herself into the smallest ball possible, wishing she had the power of invisibility.

The voices grew louder, more raucous.

She slunk lower and buried her hot face in her knees. What had she done? She should have revealed herself once they entered the building and then pardoned herself from the conservatory. As simple as that.

Now she was trapped. Crouched beneath a table, cowering without a shred of dignity, praying the young gentlemen soon took their leave so that she might emerge.

Alas the muffled thud and shuffle of their footsteps came closer.

She hugged herself tighter.

There was the scratch of a match being struck.

Ah. So that's what they were about. Evidently

they did not wish to join their papas indoors for cigars, but would indulge among themselves.

"Is your father still keeping that opera singer?" one of them asked.

Imogen had a fairly good notion of what he meant by "keeping." She might be a vicar's daughter, but she was not wholly ignorant on such matters. She read. She read a great deal. She devoured books her parents would not approve should they know of their content. And then there was Winifred in her life.

Imogen spent a few weeks with her London cousin every year. Winifred was very worldly and knew a great many things. Things Imogen's parents would not deem proper—or Winnie's parents for that matter—but Winnie knew of them nonetheless, and she imparted such knowledge to Imogen.

The reply came: "No, he's moved on to an actress."

"Indeed? I might pay the opera singer a call then. I'm a man about Town now. I've got an interest in setting up an attachment for myself. Something regular to see to my needs."

"You've just finished your schooling and you want to take on the responsibility of a mistress?" another voice inquired with a snort.

"She's not a wife," came the quick rejoinder. "A mistress knows how and when to use her mouth . . . and it's not to harangue a man."

This earned several chuckles and remarks of agreements. She thought she recognized Amos Blankenship's braying laugh.

Imogen's face burned.

Penning had yet to comment—she knew his voice well enough—and she was inescapably curious to his thoughts on the matter. Did he, too, plan to take a mistress? Perhaps he already had one now that he was a man of ten and eight. For some reason the notion of this made her cheeks sting. He was a young man of the world now. If he did not have a mistress yet, he likely soon would.

The notion should not offend her. Truly, it should not affect her one way or another.

She shifted her weight and the motion nudged a small stack of planting pots stored beneath the table to her right. She cringed at the slight clanking and hugged herself tighter, holding her breath, waiting for what felt like imminent discovery.

What would they do if they found her? The mortification was almost too much to contemplate. She was hiding under a table like a mischievous toddler.

But then she was dressed like a toddler, so perhaps they would not be overly surprised.

They were still talking and she released her tight little breath. Thankfully they were too caught up with each other and their cigars to take notice of her.

". . . after dinner," one of the gentlemen was saying. "She has promised me a walk in the gardens."

"Now that is a lovely mouth *I* would not mind being used on me."

More chuckles.

More of Amos's bray.

"You best be careful." Penning's familiar voice rang out and she could not help easing her arms around her knees and leaning forward, eager to finally hear him speak. What would he contribute to this wholly inappropriate conversation?

Of course he would be as scandalous as the rest of them. She should expect no less. She recalled him well enough, even if he had spent the bulk of these last years away at school. He'd been an incorrigible boy. She doubted he had changed that much. Mama always said a leopard never changed its spots.

Imogen rather enjoyed this moment of invisibility. No one, especially gentlemen such as these fine toffs, ever spoke their true minds in her presence. She winced. These toffs never even spoke to her at all. She was beneath their consideration.

How different the world would be if people spoke their true thoughts. Chaotic perhaps, but there would be no confusion.

You would know who the monsters were.

Penning continued, "You shall be betrothed by

the end of this house party if you do not exercise some caution."

"Well, married to Lord Delby's daughter would not be such a terrible fate? I can think of far more miserable futures than that," a voice contributed. "The lass is comely. Her papa is well positioned and with deep pockets. It would be a brilliant match for any of us."

"Well, if you don't mind marrying straight out of Eton, then I'm happy for you," Penning said in that all-knowing way of his that had not changed since he was a lad of ten. He always had that air to him. It irked her then and it irked her now. Arrogance must go part and parcel with his noble birthright.

"You expect to do better, Penning?"

"He *is* Penning," another lad chimed in with an incredulous laugh. "He will have his choice of heiresses. Beauty, charm, rank . . . he can take his pick."

"Aye, I'll have my pick," he agreed mildly. *Arrogant prig.* He spoke as though he were shopping for ribbons at the village market and nothing more significant than that. "But nothing would lure me into marriage for another decade at least."

Invisibility, indeed, proved useful. She was correct on that score. He had not changed from that lad who treated her to hard silences, resentful of their parents forcing them to spend time together and vexed when things did not go according to his wishes.

"You mean the vicar's daughter is not your fate then?" a voice trembling with mirth asked.

Imogen stiffened where she crouched. They spoke of *her*?

Masculine laughter broke out.

Hot mortification washed over her, but she strained for Penning's response just the same, curious to hear if he would heighten her humiliation or alleviate it.

If he would be a decent human or not.

"Amusing," he said, "but no." Despite his words there was no amusement in his voice. Only hard denial. Stinging rejection that should not sting because she should not care.

She took a bracing breath.

Of course, he would not agree that their fates were entwined. That would be absurd. A vicar's daughter and a future duke should not even be mentioned in the same sentence, and yet here, among this group of lads, it had somehow happened.

It had happened and she did not like it one little bit.

"Come now, Penning. Once you get beyond all the ruffles and bows, she's a fetching lass."

"I do not see it," he countered.

The heat crept higher in her face.

"Indeed," another voice seconded. "I would not mind exploring beneath all those ruffles and bows."

The burn of humiliation now reached the tips of her ears.

"You lads are debauched. She's a child," Penning blustered. "And a sanctimonious one at that."

She should feel grateful in his defense, except she did not appreciate being called a child. *Or* sanctimonious.

"She's woman enough for me. And I would not be required to put a bag over her head during procreation like the chit my father wishes me to wed."

"No, but you would need to put a bag over her personality," Penning rejoined.

Laughter.

She flinched, feeling their laughter as keenly as the cut of a knife.

She did not know what offended her more: Penning with his clear abhorrence of her or his blue-blooded friends with their lewd comments. It was difficult to decide.

"Come now, Penning. She's a fair lass and there likely isn't much feminine enticement to be had in this little backwater. No brothels here, to be sure."

"Unfortunately," Amos inserted.

The voice continued as though Amos had not spoken. "All your visits home for holiday and she's right down the road. Mightily convenient. You've never been tempted?"

Tempted? Outrage simmered through her. As though she were free for the picking. For *his* picking.

She had never rubbed on well with Penning. He never appreciated being stuck with her on those afternoons Papa visited the duke. He'd made his displeasure abundantly clear, treating all her attempts at conversation with scorn. And now she knew why.

You would need to put a bag over her personality.

His next words only further confirmed his enduring dislike of her. "She might not be hideous to behold, but other things matter."

Might not be hideous to behold? Such a ringing endorsement. That was as much credit as he could grant her? *Wretch.*

"And what would those other things be, Penning? What is more important than a wife who is fair of face and not a chore to bed?"

"I can think of little else that matters more than possessing a lovely wife," another voice seconded.

Possessing? Is that what these lads thought? That a wife was a possession? Papa did not think like that. Is that what Penning thought? She wanted to believe gentlemen did not think this way, but she knew the reality. Men controlled the world and women had to fight and claw their way for a foothold in it. She'd accompanied Papa on many a house call to visit a downtrodden wife, crushed beneath the boot of a domineering husband.

Their neighbor to the east was one such example. Mrs. Henry had five children and a brutal husband who was never satisfied with any of her wifely efforts. She was frequently "falling down." Mama often tended to her after these mishaps—beneath the critical eye of her husband, of course. As though he feared his wife might tell Mama the true cause of her *accidents.*

Imogen held her breath, waiting for Penning's response, her shoulders tightening to the point of discomfort.

Penning chuckled lightly. "One's disposition must be considered. A wife will not stay young forever. Looks fade and then you're left staring across the dining table at someone you can hopefully abide."

"And you cannot abide Miss Bates?"

"Let us just say she has the disposition of a rotten lemon."

Imogen pulled back as though struck.

Everyone laughed. Even Amos, and she had only ever been solicitous to him.

Not just a lemon . . . but a *rotten* one.

"No one is telling you to marry the chit, Penning. Dalliance does not require that level of commitment."

As though dalliance with me is a given? As though I would simply fall into his lap with wild abandon?

"There are any number of females I would rather kiss than a sanctimonious vicar's daughter who finds it diverting to discuss the weather and the latest infestation of wheat mites."

She dropped her hands onto her quaking knees and inhaled a pained breath.

She never knew what to talk about in his exalted presence—and wheat mites *could* ruin a crop. Clearly he could not be bothered with topics so beneath him.

Still holding on to her knees, she rocked slightly. It was one thing to suspect he didn't like her and another thing to hear him say it out loud—another thing to hear him talk about her with all his friends. To hear him laugh and ridicule her to them.

She blinked her suddenly burning eyes. *Rotten lemon.*

The young toffs continued talking and laughing, but she could scarcely hear the rest of their words over the buzzing in her ears.

They moved on to other subjects, but she remained crouched where she was, battling anger and nausea, breathing in the aroma of cigars and wondering how long she had to suffer in silence.

She didn't know how long she waited. It felt like hours, but it could have been minutes. Eventually their voices turned to low rumbles as they moved toward the door of the conservatory. They were leaving at last. Hinges creaked and then silence fell and she assumed they had departed. After a moment, she emerged from beneath the table and rose up into the smoky air.

They were indeed gone.

She turned and grasped the edge of the table as though drawing strength from her ruthless grip. She inhaled and beneath the lingering scent of cigars she caught a whiff of loamy fauna. Imogen looked down at her hands and noticed the small matchbook near her left pinky finger. One of them must have left it.

The door to the conservatory creaked open and she whirled around.

There at the end of the aisle, between stretching foliage, the door drifting shut behind him, loomed Penning.

He'd returned.

He'd returned and now he stared down the length of the walkway where she stood. He regarded her and there was no point in running or hiding. It was too late. She was discovered.

"I forgot my matchbook," he declared.

"Oh." Turning, she plucked it up from the table and faced him again, glad for the stretch of space between them. Hopefully he could not detect the way her hands trembled.

"Were you in here this entire time?" he asked mildly, a tinge of disapproval in his voice.

Disapproval? She would have none of that from him. *She* had done nothing wrong. At least not in comparison to him. "I was."

"You might have announced yourself."

"I did not wish to intrude."

"But you wished to eavesdrop?"

"Not particularly. It was not my intention."

"But you *did* eavesdrop," he said more than asked.

"On your vile conversation?" She lifted her chin. "Yes. I heard it."

He sighed as though afflicted. That was some irony. *He* was the afflicted one? After all the terrible things he had said about her in front of his friends? In front of young Amos Blankenship, no less. No doubt the duke's words would make the rounds in the village. Everyone would look at her and think: *rotten lemon.*

"I suppose I should apologize then." Clearly any apology he issued would not be sincere. He doubtlessly felt compelled as their fathers were friends.

"You should not do or say anything you do not mean. You never have to do that with me. It's no longer necessary." Palming the small packet of matches, she forced herself to stroll forward down the aisle toward the door—toward *him*—

with great composure. She was proud of herself for that. Attired in the most ridiculous frock, still bruised raw from his words, she moved closer to him with a semblance of equanimity.

Upon reaching him, she stopped and held out her hand. "Here you go."

He looked down and turned his hand over. Taking great care that they should not touch, she dropped the matches into his open palm.

"Thank you," he murmured, all the while peering carefully at her face, as though he was searching for evidence that she was not as calm as she appeared—that she was not unaffected. He would be right if he perceived that, but God willing he would not. She did not want him to know how hurt she felt.

He knew the ribald nature of his conversation with his friends. He knew she should be scandalized and offended—and she was. She was actually fine with him knowing those things. As long as he knew she was not crushed. She would not have him know he possessed the power to hurt her.

"Pardon me." She nodded to the door he was blocking, indicating she wanted to pass.

"Of course." He stepped aside, still looking as though he wanted to say something. God spare her whatever lies and platitudes he would offer forth to soothe her. She did not want his sham of an apology. She would not believe him, at any rate, and he could not expect her to—not on the heels of everything she had overheard.

She was well clear of him and out the door when she suddenly stopped and looked back at him.

Bathed in sunlight, he stood in the threshold, one shoulder wedged in the doorjamb, an eyebrow lifted questioningly. And it occurred to her then. He was not sorry. Indeed, not one little bit. There was no regret in that supercilious arched eyebrow of his.

She moistened her lips, outrage bubbling up inside her. "I would just like to say . . ."

"Yes?" he prompted.

"I would have you know . . ." He continued to stare at her in patient expectation, and she blurted, "Wheat mites can be very serious and decimate an entire crop. An entire shire can suffer the ravages of wheat mites."

That said, she turned and left him.

Perhaps she should have said something else. There were a great *many* things she could have said that were more stinging, but that was the one thing that had popped out from her mouth.

She had heard Penning speak unrestrainedly. Now she knew his true mind. There was no confusion. No obscurity. This particular monster no longer hid in the dark.

She'd glimpsed the real Penning, and she

would never forget him or his words . . . even as she managed to avoid him in the days and years to come.

At future gatherings, she kept her distance. Greeted him as required, but said little else. An outsider looking in would think naught of it. One might remark that the vicar's daughter was merely reserved in nature around her betters.

Only young Penning would be able to read more into her reticence. *If* it even occurred to him to do so. If he cared. Perhaps he recalled that long-ago lawn party and the girl in the garish pink dress who stared at him with wounded eyes. Perhaps not.

In the years that followed, young Penning attended her mother's funeral alongside his family. Imogen was aware of him there, a tall, silvery-eyed figure on the periphery, an unwanted presence amid her grief.

Two years later, on the death of his father, Imogen returned the courtesy and did the same, standing among mourners and offering stilted condolences.

Following the demise of the old duke, there was little occasion for them to interact further.

Five years passed with minimal sightings.

She heard of his exploits, of course. The young illustrious Duke of Penning spent most of his time in London, expanding his reputation as a feted nobleman about Town whilst Imogen's life turned to that of caretaker.

She settled into spinsterhood and loyally tended to her father and the vicarage and the people of Shropshire, telling herself it was all she ever wanted. This duty was her calling.

It was enough.

Her life was one of purpose. She harbored no regrets even if, on occasion, the whisper of *rotten lemon* chased through her mind like a slithering snake. Especially every time she came face-to-face with Amos Blankenship in the village. That snake slithered yet.

Her single consolation was the proverb Mama had frequently chirped: *As you sow, so shall you reap.*

The Duke of Penning would have his turn.

She did not know when or how, but when it came for him, she would not pity him.

The Rake Gets Ravished ❧

*H*er corset was killing her.

Mercy Kittinger fidgeted on the well-worn velvet squabs and tried to adjust the boning digging into her ribs. The modiste she had visited upon her arrival to Town insisted the contraption fit her properly and that it did wonderful things for her shape.

Mercy would not know. She was accustomed to the comfort and ease of her own modest garments. She lived on a farm. She never gave a thought to her shape. Nor did anyone else.

Her days were about function, about taking care of her sister and the house and the staff and making certain everyone was fed and everything was running smoothly. That was her life and she liked it very well.

And up until last week everything had been running smoothly.

Then her brother had arrived home. Her feckless, spendthrift wastrel of a brother. Her twin. Not that that bred any special loyalty within him.

Now she was here, doing what she always did—cleaning up Bede's messes.

Mercy paid her fare through the hatch to the cloaked driver and stepped down from the hansom cab. Squaring her shoulders, she faced the building and shivered in the night—a shiver that had naught to do with cold. On the contrary. It was a pleasant evening. Only the task at hand was unpleasant.

She grasped a handful of her silk skirts as she started up the steps to the impressive brick edifice. It was one of the nicer houses in the modest neighborhood. Brightly lit with outside sconces. The three-storied house was no home, however. It happened to be one of London's most notorious gaming hells and where her foolish brother had lost everything. She suspected a great many foolish men lost their fortunes in this place. But as her brother's fortune was *her* fortune, it fell to her to reclaim it.

Nodding once, she entered the building, determination fueling her steps.

The place was busy. She was not the only one entering through its front doors. Nor was she the only woman beneath its roof. There were several ladies, all attired in much the same manner she was.

Just as she had hoped, she did not attract an inordinate amount of notice in her scandalous gown. She was merely another body. Another person getting lost in the revel.

When Mercy had visited the modiste, she requested a gown befitting a woman of looser inhibitions. It had hurt to part with the precious coin, but she had no choice. She knew she could not wear anything from her modest life. She would be playing a role, and it was not a game she could lose. Too much depended upon it.

The dressmaker had not even blinked at the request. The lady had obliged, attiring her in the requested level of bawdiness. She had plumped Mercy's breasts that were on indecent display, the areolas of her nipples very nearly peeking above the edge of stiff black lace, and proclaimed, "*Magnifique!*"

More indecent than the front of her gown was perhaps the lack of sleeves. The whisper of wind over her bare shoulders and arms felt wicked and wholly unfamiliar as she wove through the crowd of tables and bodies. It was as though an entire swath of fabric were missing from her gown.

She felt virtually naked.

One thing was certain. Women of looser inhibitions did not dress for comfort.

Mercy longed to finish this evening's unsavory business and return to her life.

She assessed her lively surroundings. After emerging from the darkness of the night, her eyes did not need much time to adjust to the indoors because the gaming hell was kept in dim lighting, the lanterns and sconces burning low.

Dozens of tables occupied the main room, which might have acted as a ballroom were this a traditional home. But there was nothing traditional about this scene.

Various card games were being played out. The players ranged in age and gender. Some of the faces were tense; others loose and jovial, flushed from an excess of spirits. Liveried servers wove through the rooms, quick to indulge, keeping glasses full to the brim. A small dais at one end boasted a string quartet.

Idly, Mercy wondered where her brother had sat when he was here. Which table had he occupied whilst he gambled away their lives?

Was the man who owned her family lands here even now? Sitting at one of these tables, taking the livelihood from another wretched soul as easily as he had taken it from her brother?

She'd known it had been an easy task. She knew that because she knew her brother. Many an evening had she played whist with Bede after dinner. Always *she* won. She won and she had no special training at cards. She had only ever played with family or, infrequently, with

Imogen. What made the fool think he could win against the seasoned players of a gaming den? With the *owner* of this gaming hell, no less? She might be the best card player in her family, but she had no such illusion that she could stroll in here and handle herself against this veteran crowd.

She would reclaim her home, but not in a traditional game of cards.

No, her methods would be more questionable than that.

Mercy reached out to touch the arm of a woman who had just finished topping off champagne to the occupants at a table.

"Pardon me? Is Mr. Masters in the house this evening?"

The server looked her over from head to toe in a slow perusal. "He is here most every evening," she answered as though that was widely known information. "And day."

That information matched what she had been able to learn about Silas Masters. He kept no other address. This place was his sole residence. He worked and dwelled here.

Mercy nodded slowly and glanced over the room, pretending that she felt no real sense of urgency and was not on the verge of breaking any laws tonight. "Ah, and might you point out the gentleman to me?"

"You don't know him by sight?" The woman looked amused as she asked the question.

"Um, no."

"Interesting." Again with that almost smile.

"What is?"

"It is just that most women who are looking for Silas Masters know what he looks like." Her lips curled in a full-fledged smile now. "That is why they're looking for him."

Mercy shifted on her feet nervously. "Well, I don't know . . ." Her voice faded as the woman raised her hand and pointed.

Mercy followed her direction to a second-floor balcony and the small group sitting there looking down upon the ground floor as though it was their small kingdom.

Mercy's gaze skipped over the gray-haired gentleman and the lady, settling on the man at the center of the trio. He acted as a magnet, sucking in everything—especially her awareness.

"That's him, there. Nice, hmm?"

Yes. That was him. Silas Masters. She had deduced as much. "Oh," she breathed.

"Oh, indeed," the server chuckled.

Mercy nodded, understanding at once why women might wish to seek the company of Silas Masters.

Aside from his apparent fortune, he was quite something to behold. He possessed the kind of dangerously good looks one might expect from the owner of a gaming hell . . . or the gatekeeper to an antechamber to hell.

Thick dark hair longer than fashionable fell past his ears, and yet this man made it look good. Enticing. A style all of his own. Other men might attempt to replicate the look but they would only look foolish and unkempt.

It was the whole parcel of him. Hair. Face. The impressive breadth of his shoulders looming above the balcony. A closely trimmed beard dusting his jaw and cheeks. Sensually curving lips that promised sinister delights.

From across the distance the color of his deeply set eyes was indeterminate beneath the dramatic slash of thick eyebrows, but Mercy imagined them to be equally dark. They were certainly intense as they looked down on his domain.

She thought they fixed on her, but in the dimness it was only conjecture and a vague . . . sense. Her imagination was running wild. She was one person in a room full of people. Why would he be looking at her?

"He is a sight to behold, no?" the woman asked as though she could read Mercy's mind.

She nodded once in agreement, aiming for an unaffected air. "An attractive gentleman."

"Shall I inform him you wish for an audience with him?"

"No," she was quick to answer. Perhaps too quickly, but her pulse jumped at the notion of an encounter with Masters. That was to be avoided at all costs. "That's not necessary."

"But I thought you wished to see—"

"Might you direct me to your ladies' retiring room?" She needed only to establish his presence, mark his location so that she could safely go forth on this evening's enterprise, and now that was done. Stealth and strategy were required. He looked quite comfortable up in his perch. The night was still young.

Now was the time to strike.

The woman shrugged and then motioned toward a door on the other side of the large room. "Through there. Second floor."

"Thank you." Turning, Mercy started across the room. She tried not to look his way again. No easy task when she knew he was up there watching. She was hoping to achieve an air of covertness. Gawking at the man would not accomplish that.

She wove through the room, taking her time, forcing a sedate pace, stopping occasionally to observe a game or two as though she was interested in the play. She did this in case she was being watched. Or perhaps so she would not *become* watched.

She had to resist her instinctive urge—which was to dash for the door leading to the second floor and locate Silas Masters's private rooms, where she assumed he kept all his important documents. She hoped she was correct on that score. She *had* to be right about that. Otherwise she did not know what she would do. Fling herself at his feet, pleading for mercy? That did not seem like a promising plan. He had looked hard and uncompromising from her one glimpse of him . . . not the manner of man given to compassion.

She was close now. The door loomed ahead.

She sidled past a table of gentlemen playing a particularly lively game of whist. A combination of shouts and applause erupted. One of the gentlemen tossed down his cards with a fierce exclamation. Groaning in defeat, he leaned back in his chair. As he stretched his arms wide, his hand bumped into her while she attempted to pass the table.

He shot a foul glare over his shoulder. Clearly he was in a bad mood over his poor luck and thought to vent his spleen on the person who dared to step in the path behind him.

Unfortunately, she was that person.

His venomous look shifted as he assessed her, transforming into something speculative and fairly lecherous.

"Hallo there, lass." A meaty paw reached for her and snatched hold of her wrist, stopping her in her tracks.

Reminding herself that she had no wish to call attention to herself, she forced a smile on her face and resisted recoiling in outrage.

"Come here, lovie," he continued. "Cheer a fellow up, won't you?" His thick sausage fingers tightened their pressure around her, digging into her skin.

She felt the forced smile on her face turn as brittle as glass. "As tempting as the invitation is, sir, I must decline."

"Aren't we the lofty one?" He gave a hard tug and she went tumbling. "Never met a female here who wasn't open to a little fun."

"Ooof." She plopped unwillingly into his lap.

His arms came up around her waist and there was no hiding her outrage now. She was not accustomed to being manhandled. Things like this did not happen back home. Back home she was accorded respect.

"What's the matter, lass? My coin isn't good enough? Are you not here to work?"

She sucked in a hot breath. Well. That was rather presumptuous of him. He thought her a courtesan? Certainly not every woman here was plying her trade. And even if she was, a courtesan, undoubtedly, had her standards and did not have to tolerate him.

"Unhand me, sirrah."

Instead of following her command, his beady

little eyes lowered from her face to her daring décolletage.

She rested a hand there, her fingers pressing into her soft flesh. She knew she should not appear so modest, so skittish beneath his insulting regard, but she could not help herself. His gaze felt like a snake slithering across her bare skin.

He tsked and dared to touch her, peeling her hand off her chest, flinging it away as though it were a pesky crumb. "None of that now. Do not hide such a bounty of loveliness from Howie." Presumably he was Howie.

Enough. She ground her teeth and surged up, determined to free herself from his lecherous advances.

"I am certain there is another lady about only too happy to entertain your abundant charms."

His eyes narrowed. Apparently he did not appreciate her forcefulness. Bullies never did appreciate someone with a backbone. She was yanked back down with jarring force and his hand came up to roughly fondle her breast.

She gasped and reacted. All attempts to appear at ease in this wildly strange environment with this awful wretch vanished. Ease did not exist. There was only instinct.

Her hand flew, her palm connecting soundly and very satisfyingly with his cheek. The sound reverberated through the air. All the gentlemen at the table froze. Even the people in the vicinity of them stopped to gawk in their direction.

Blast it. She had created a spectacle.

A stark red handprint began to take shape on Howie's face.

"Oh," she breathed, dread consuming her, but not regret. She could summon none of that sentiment for putting a stop to his groping.

He lightly stroked his wounded cheek. "You little tart!"

She took advantage of his astonishment and vaulted to her feet. Her action revived him from his frozen stupor. Shaken from his astonishment, he clamped down on her arm. He, too, jumped to his feet, overturning his chair with a clatter and only drawing more attention to them. *Splendid.*

Exclamations erupted all around them, but Mercy did not look anywhere save Howie. Her handprint became less visible as angry red suffused the rest of his face from the flare of his temper.

"How dare you? Who do you think you are?" His fingers tightened painfully on her bicep and he gave her a hard shake that rattled her very teeth.

"Unhand me before I—" She did not get the rest of her words out.

"Hold there." A large hand closed around

Howie's shoulder. She followed that big hand up
its arm to the face of the gentleman intervening.

Him.

The one who held her life in his hands.

The one whom she was here to rob.

Howie twisted around with an ugly snarl that
quickly faded to a squeak when he saw who stood
behind him.

Mercy swallowed back her own pitiable squeak
at Silas Masters's sudden appearance.

This was not supposed to happen. She was not
supposed to meet him. She was not supposed to
come face-to-face with him.

In and out. Undetected. That was the plan.

The blood drained from Howie's face. "Masters," he acknowledged in a voice that had lost its
edge and was no more than a whispery tremble.

"You know I have no tolerance for disorder in
my club, Bassett," Masters said, and the sound of
his growly voice made her knees go weak. Made
him all the more real.

"Y-yes. Of course," the man stammered, releasing her as though the touch of her now burned
him. "P'raps you should have a word with your
girl here then."

"I am not anyone's *girl*," she objected.

"You're *here*," Bassett said with heavy accusation, "and dressed like a trollop."

"What does the manner of my dress signify?"

she demanded. "That it is acceptable to grope me? That I invite your attentions?"

"Precisely." He spat the word without shame.

"Precisely *not*," Masters intoned in his deep yet soft voice—a voice that nonetheless shouted of authority.

Even if he were not the proprietor of this club, this man commanded deference. She doubted anyone ever challenged him.

He continued, "The women here are not in my employ and even if they were, I would not require them to suffer your or any man's attentions."

Bassett blustered and waved at her with contempt. "I have a right to courtesy and respect from this—"

"There you are wrong. The women who patronize my club are guests here just as you are. They should be able to stroll across the floors of this house free of molestation. Since you cannot afford a lady that modicum of courtesy, you have no right to respect and are no longer welcome here."

Mr. Bassett blanched. *"Ever?"*

"You shall have to find other diversions to amuse yourself. Elsewhere."

A long stretch of silence fell.

"What? Now? I must leave?" Mr. Bassett glanced wildly around him as though any of the many faces staring back at him might offer an alternative solution. His face flushed an even deeper red and his eyes suddenly looked watery.

"Indeed." Mr. Masters nodded his dark head once, decisively. "Do not cause further spectacle, man. Have some dignity and take your leave."

With a baleful glare cast her way, Mr. Bassett gave a grunt, followed by a nod, and stormed off through the room, dodging people and tables with angry movements.

The gentlemen at the table whom he had been playing with resumed their game of whist as though nothing untoward had occurred. Apparently he would not be missed by any of them.

Mercy turned her gaze on Masters to find his attention smoothly trained on her.

"Thank you," she murmured.

"You seemed to have the situation well in hand, but my apologies. You should not have been accosted."

"As you said, it was no doing of yours, sir." She swallowed, but it felt an impossible task. There was no ridding herself of the giant lump in her throat. "You need not apologize."

He inclined his head slightly. "Everything that happens under this roof is my responsibility."

Everything?

It was precisely the reminder she needed to put aside any softening she felt over his display of gallantry.

By his own admission, everything that occurred here was his responsibility, including the ruination of a family. *Her* family. *Here.* Under this roof. Had he no care for that? For *all* the families he had ruined, because there were undoubtedly many more. More reckless brothers. More selfish fathers. More ruthless takers like Silas Masters.

With her heart freshly hardened against him, she closed herself off to his outward courtesy and handsome face. Many a lady would doubtlessly simper when presented with such a darkly pretty man. Mercy, however, was made of sterner stuff.

As a guardian to her younger sister—true, Bede was their sister's legal guardian, but it always fell to Mercy to act as mother and father to Grace—Mercy had to be immune. There was only room enough for one husband-seeking, stars-in-her-eyes dreamer in the Kittinger household.

Grace's arrival had been a surprise to their parents. It had been a surprise to all, in truth. At the time Mama was no young woman set to the task of delivering babies, and the birthing of twins had nearly finished her a decade before.

Unsurprising then, perhaps, that she had never recovered from Grace's birth, sadly languishing . . . withering, really, until her broken body finally surrendered to death's embrace two years later. Even before Mama's demise, it had fallen to Papa to see to his three children—or rather, it had fallen to Mercy.

Only a young girl herself, Mercy had stepped forward and taken the reins as lady of the house. Papa had managed the farm and she managed her baby sister and rascal of a brother. At least until Papa sent Bede off to school. At that point her brother belonged to the world and his own many foibles.

Ever since Grace's birth, Mercy had put family first. She had not approached adulthood with the hopes that other young women harbored. She had a farm to run, a family to oversee and a young sister to bring up whilst her brother followed his own merry pursuits.

It was a relentless and grueling task, ushering a young girl into womanhood. Especially when one did not rely on servants and governesses and ladies' maids for assistance. It all fell to Mercy. Everything fell to Mercy.

Mercy had not the leisure herself for merry pursuits. There were no courtships or dalliances or even flirtations that one might expect for an unattached lady. Those adventures were reserved for other young ladies. Ladies like her young sister—or so Grace hoped.

Grace hoped for a great deal. Dances. Parties. Teas. Catching the eye of a handsome young gentleman. She begged Mercy for a trip to Town where she might enter the marriage mart on a broader scale—as though they were good *ton* and not simple gentry.

Mercy fixed her attention on Silas Masters's face, continuing to tell herself not to be swayed by all of his masculine beauty. Grace would have melted into a puddle at his feet. He was not like the country gentlemen in their sphere. Not in the least.

Bede should have warned her.

When her brother first told her of The Rogue's Den and of the proprietor, Silas Masters, he merely described him as ruthless, intimidating and powerful. A very rich man without mercy.

Without mercy. She remembered that specifically because Bede had used her name. The irony had struck her at the time as her brother continued talking, bemoaning this wretched owner of a gaming hell who would take everything from him so callously. From *him*, Bede. No mention was given of Mercy or Grace and what they stood to lose.

And yet Mercy had vowed that she would go to this club and face the purportedly ruthless man himself if need be. Of course, she had hoped it would not come to that.

She would somehow reclaim their lives. She would succeed and not be deterred by Silas Masters's lack of compassion or, as it would turn out, by his dark good looks.

"If you would pardon me, I was on my way to the ladies' retiring room."

His gaze held hers, perhaps a bit too long. As though he could smell the subterfuge on her person. Perhaps he thought her suspicious or simply up to mischief in his establishment. She certainly felt suspicious standing there in her newly acquired gown that felt like someone else's skin on her.

But that was silly. She took a gulping breath. She was being overly anxious. He had no reason to suspect she was anything other than a lady-about-town, here for diversions just like everyone else.

Even though she was not like everyone else. Far from it.

She was in this lion's den to thieve.

To steal from the lion himself. She would not go home empty-handed.

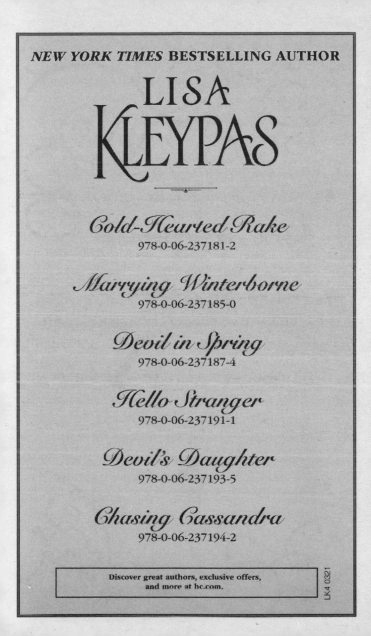